THE COLLIDE

Also by Kimberly McCreight

The Outliers

The Scattering

For Adult Readers

Reconstructing Amelia

Where They Found Her

THE COLLIDE

THE FINAL BOOK IN THE OUTLIERS TRILOGY

KIMBERLY McCREIGHT

HARPER
An Imprint of HarperCollins*Publishers*

This novel is a work of fiction. Any references to real people, events, establishments, organizations, or locales are intended only to give the fiction a sense of reality and authenticity, and are used fictitiously. All other names, characters, and places, and all dialogue and incidents portrayed in this book are the product of the author's imagination.

The Collide

For information address HarperCollins Children's Books, a division of HarperCollins Publishers, 195 Broadway, New York, NY 10007.
www.epicreads.com

Library of Congress Control Number: 2017962472
ISBN 978-0-06-235915-5

Typography by Sarah Nichole Kaufman
18 19 20 21 22 PC/LSCH 10 9 8 7 6 5 4 3 2 1
❖
First Edition

For all of us,

May we rage on against the dying of the light.

#resist

To the wrongs that need resistance,
To the right that needs assistance,
To the future in the distance,
Give yourselves.
—Carrie Chapman Catt (1859–1947),
President, National American Woman Suffrage Association

AUTHOR'S NOTE

This is a work of fiction. The things that you read here did not happen. At least, not yet.

THE COLLIDE

Dear Rachel,

Don't think that I'm not grateful for all you've done. It's probably not possible to be _more_ grateful to another human being. You _saved_ my life. And, up until now, you've been right about me staying hidden. You've been right about everything.

I know you think going to see Wylie at the detention center is a bad idea. When we talked, you did an outstanding job explaining all the really logical, completely rational reasons why it would be dangerous. For her, and for me.

* It's a prison filled with cameras: no more playing dead.
* Ben is _already_ missing. Do I really want to leave my kids orphans?
* I could be putting Wylie even more in harm's way. They could try to use me against her.

See, I _was_ listening, Rachel. And I _do_ trust you.

But I've got to trust my own instincts, too. And for all the risk there is in showing up at that detention center, there's more in staying away. Maybe not a risk of physical harm to me or Wylie. But there are other kinds of pain, Rach. There's other damage that matters.

I was the one person Wylie always counted on. And I lied in the worst possible way. How am I ever going to get her to trust me again? I'm terrified that I may have already lost her forever. So scared that sometimes I think my heart might stop. If I don't start clawing my way back to her right now, I don't think she'll ever forgive me.

And I've already made a difference out here. Those people you suggested I contact, that senator, that friend of yours at the ACLU—they've had such good ideas about what this fight is going to entail. We have to be prepared, there's no doubt about that.

But right now, I need to be Wylie's mom first. That matters most of all. And she needs to <u>know</u> for sure that I'm alive. For that, she'll need to see me with her own eyes. After what she's been through, it's the only option. I can't hurt her for one second more. I won't.

Okay, rant complete. I just wanted to state my case, for the record. And just so we're 100% clear: going to see Wylie is something I'm going to do, with or without your help. Whatever happens, though, know how grateful I am. I'm so glad to have you back, too. I missed you more than you know.

Xx

Hope

WYLIE

I STAND IN FRONT OF THE GRAY DETENTION FACILITY DOOR, WAITING FOR IT TO buzz open. In my hand is a plastic grocery bag stuffed with the mildewed Cape Cod T-shirt and shorts I was wearing when I was arrested.

For the past two weeks, I've been in the standard-issue pajama-like shirt and pants twenty-four hours a day. So stiff, it's like they were designed so you'd never sleep again. My current outfit is the total opposite. Expensive pair of denim shorts, threadbare in just the right places, and an absurdly soft plain gray T-shirt. Without me having to ask, Rachel brought the clothes in for me to wear home. And I'm grateful for that. I've felt grateful to Rachel for a lot of things.

Like starting with getting me out on bail. It wasn't that complicated, Rachel says. Still, they went to so much trouble to get me in there, I didn't think they'd let me go just because Rachel filed a petition for bail review. But I was wrong. Rachel came through for me, once again. According to her, it wasn't just about the papers she filed, though. It was who you called after you filed them, which sounded both totally true and completely shady.

And I do credit Rachel alone, not my mom. *I'm going to get you out of here. I promise. Xoxo.* That's what my mom's note said. And on the other side: *Trust Rachel. She will help you. She saved my life.*

But those were just words. It's easy to make promises and then disappear. It's sticking around to face what you've done that's the hard part.

RACHEL LOOKED SHEEPISH when she came to visit the morning after my mom had appeared like a ghost, pushing that creaky detention facility library cart. She *felt* guilty, too, I could read that loud and clear. We were in one of the small private rooms reserved for meetings with attorneys. The rooms that always smelled like onions and were freezing cold. The ones that Rachel cautioned weren't actually that private at all.

It was Rachel's guilt that erased all doubt. Not only had Rachel known my mom had come to see me in the detention facility, she had known the whole time that my mom was alive.

There was also no excuse for the fact that I'd missed Rachel's deception. But she was usually really hard to read; the guilt today was kind of an exception. Maybe it was so many years of saying whatever it took for her clients. The only real constant was that Rachel always told less than the whole truth. Like it was a reflex. Trying to get a fix on her true feelings was like trying to grab a bolt of lightning in your hands. It probably made her an awesome lawyer. It did not make her an easy person to trust. In my defense, I never fully had. I had just come to accept that I did not.

As I sat down across from Rachel, I wanted so badly for her to be an Outlier, so she could feel the full force of my rage. Rachel had lied to me repeatedly.

Had I felt joyful when I'd looked up and seen my mom—my actual mom, risen from the grave—staring down at me with all that love in her eyes? Sure, I guess. Okay, yes, definitely. But a day later, it was mixed up in a stew of other feelings: anger, sadness, confusion, betrayal.

But my mom wasn't there for me to take that out on her. Rachel was. And so, laying into her would have to do.

"First, I need to remind you, be careful what you discuss in here." Rachel motioned overhead before I could say a word, to the invisible prying eyes in our smelly "private" attorney room. "But I'm sure you're confused."

"Confused?" I snapped. "How about seriously pissed off?"

She nodded, relieved. Glad not to be keeping my mom's secret anymore, maybe. "That's fair, too."

"Explain," I shot back, leaning closer. I pressed a finger into the tabletop. "Right now."

Rachel looked away. "It was a real risk for her to come here, dangerous, you know. But she did it anyway because she wanted to be sure you believed. She knows how much you've been through, and she didn't want you to think I was making it up, or jerking you around or whatever." Worry. For a moment from Rachel. Just a flash. But not a trace of regret. "We are lucky I know the volunteer supervisor here. She did me a solid, letting your special visitor volunteer."

"Right," I said, my anger seeping away despite my grip, like water through cupped fingers. "So. Lucky."

"Listen, if it makes a difference, she didn't know it was going to turn out this way," Rachel said. And this much was true, I was pretty sure. "Your—" She stopped herself, eyes darting around. "*She* turned up out of nowhere at my house the night of the accident. I hadn't talked to her in what, ten years? But she thought someone was following her, and she ended up driving near my house. She was lucky I even lived there after all this time. To be honest, at first I thought she was drunk or having an episode or something. She sounded so paranoid, delusional almost. But she was just *so* freaked out. How could I risk not helping? I don't know, maybe part of it was selfish, too. We didn't end on the best terms, your mom and I. Maybe I thought this was a chance to prove that she was wrong about me."

"Wrong about what?" The question felt weirdly important.

"You know your— She's an avenging angel. And I gave up on noble a long time ago." Rachel shrugged. Another cold, hard truth. Rachel might not have been ashamed, but she wasn't proud of it, either. "Anyway, I didn't think it would be a big deal to ask somebody to drive her car out of there. The girl in the car was the girlfriend of a client of mine. I'd hired her to clean my house, run errands. I knew she needed cash. She'd been sober for two months, trying to get her life straight. So, she needed money, and we needed someone to drive the car away. I thought it would be a win-win."

"Not so much for that girl doing the driving," I said, deciding not to mention the vodka bottle. Maybe the girl wasn't so sober after all, but it felt like just another wrong to expose her now.

"Yeah, not so much," Rachel said. She knew she should feel guilty but wasn't all the way there.

"And after the crash, her disappearing and pretending to be dead was, like, the only logical option?" I sounded pissed, but sadness was closing in fast. "Going to the police or something normal like that was totally out of the question?"

"You know better than anybody that trusting the police isn't always a simple proposition, Wylie. Besides, she was too worried about you guys," Rachel said. "Something about baby dolls? She thought they were meant as a threat to you guys, specifically—her babies."

"They weren't even for her," I said, though my mom wouldn't have known that at the time. "We kept getting them after she was gone. *I* got one in the hospital. Anyway, she pretended like the dolls were nothing to worry about."

"What was she supposed to say? Everybody freak the hell out? Anyway, there were other things, too, apparently," she said. "Emails. Anonymous ones. They mentioned you guys specifically. Warned against the police. After the accident, we were both convinced the only way she could keep you safe was to let the people who were after her think she was dead."

"Great plan," I said, sounding extra snide.

"Well, it's easy to see now that everything had to do with your dad's research. But it wasn't until your dad told her what happened with that assistant of his up at the camp in Maine—"

"Wait, what?" My chest clamped tight. "My dad *knew* she was alive?" Because that conversation could have only taken place in May, long after we believed she was dead.

"Not until *after* the camp." Rachel avoided eye contact. "Once your . . . once she realized that her accident—that the threats—were really about his work, she had to let him know she was alive. Your dad wasn't happy. But he understood, eventually. They decided together it was safer not to tell you and Gideon. That she had a better chance of helping behind the scenes if no one knew she was alive."

Rachel leaned forward eagerly, but it felt forced. "And she's been all over the country, Wylie, working behind the scenes, meeting people, enlisting help from scientists, journalists, politicians. She's been assembling a team to help. Everything has been to protect you."

"Protect me?" I swallowed over the lump in my throat, motioned to the walls of the detention facility. "How is this safe?"

"You're alive, Wylie," Rachel said. "Aren't you?"

"YO, HELLO?" THE tall guard with the long hair shouts at me. I'm still standing at the exit door. Sounds like she's been buzzing it open for a while. "You want to stay in here? Go on, go ahead!"

No, I definitely do not want to stay locked up. I startle forward, gripping my crinkly plastic bag tighter. Besides the mildewed clothes, inside are an envelope with what's left of Rachel's money (a dried and wrinkled eighty dollars) and my mother's wedding ring. Part of me wants to dig the ring out and hold it tight. Part of me wants to toss it down the nearest storm drain. My mom taking her engraved ring off and leaving it behind had been Rachel's idea. Overkill, Rachel acknowledged now. But she had helped people disappear before. Better safe than sorry.

Finally, I step out into the July morning sun, hot already even at seven a.m., the weirdly early release time. I hold up a hand to shield my eyes from the glare as I scan the parking lot. The air is heavy and damp, weighing down my lungs. My anxiety has been relentless since I was arrested. Like a concrete slab strapped to my chest, slowly crushing me. Dr. Shepard said this was to be expected—the stress of the detention facility, the claustrophobia.

Except now that I'm outside, it doesn't seem much better. I need to get going and stay moving. For me, forward momentum always helps; it's the only good thing I learned from the horror of the camp in Maine.

It isn't until I start walking that I finally spot him, leaning against the front of the car at the far edge of the parking lot. Like he didn't want to fully commit to being there. He pushes himself up and waves, smiles way too hard.

Gideon.

Even from this distance, I can feel his guilt. The longer our dad is missing, the more Gideon blames himself. These days, guilt is what Gideon has become.

I've told him that he's holding himself responsible for way too much. The list of Outliers that Gideon gave to Dr. Cornelia might have been a shortcut to a bigger group of Outliers to round up, but I was the one who encouraged our dad to go to DC, where he was grabbed by God knows who. Somebody working for Quentin, I still assume. Though Quentin had seemed genuinely shocked when I told him about my dad the day he'd shown up in his baseball cap at the detention facility. But who else? Senator Russo? Sure, my dad was supposed to meet with him, but Rachel forced the DC police to check him out every which way. There's no record they ever had a meeting scheduled, and there is a mile-deep paper trail proving Russo was in Arizona at the time.

And I may still be convinced Russo has done something really bad, but even I don't think that thing was taking my dad. No one was ever able to find the woman who supposedly had my dad's phone, either. And it's dead now, or destroyed. Regardless, they can't track it down. Leaving the single, solitary clue about what happened to him a security video unearthed of him leaving the airport with someone, then getting into a black sedan. I haven't seen the video, but Rachel has. She says that my dad looks to be walking "normally" in the video, as in voluntarily. But then, he'd been expecting someone from Russo's office to come pick him up. It's not surprising that he would have gone with whoever it was.

The man—we assume a man—is only visible from the back. Shortish, with his hood up. That's all Rachel can say. Basically, he could be anyone. Quentin, even. In my mind, all roads still lead back to him.

I promised Rachel that I'd tell Gideon about our mom. But now that he's here on the other side of the parking lot, I wish I had refused. Because I know just how bad it feels to find out she lied. I've been mad at Gideon a lot lately, but I would never wish that pain on him. I wouldn't wish it on anyone.

Gideon takes a couple steps toward me and waves again. As I start across the parking lot to him, a white van whooshes past in front of me. So close that it sends me rocking back on my heels. I watch as the van pulls to a hard stop at the detention facility gates. A second later, they swing open and it speeds inside. That guard was right, what am I waiting for? Terrible things happen in wasted time.

"Hey," Gideon says when I finally reach him. He motions to my bag. "You need help?"

It's sweet. But sweet Gideon makes the world feel unsteady and upside down.

Even not-sweet Gideon isn't my first choice right now. I would have preferred Jasper. Then I could have finally wrapped my arms around him like I've been wanting to every day for the past two weeks. But getting out happened so fast. They told me only yesterday after Jasper had left the visitors' room that my bail had been posted. And when I tried Jasper's cell today, I got a *the customer you are trying to reach is not available* message. I've tried not to worry. Jasper probably forgot to pay the bill, I tell myself. But each time I believe it a little less.

"I'm good," I say to Gideon as I head around to the far side of our father's car. "But thanks," I add, hoping it will make him stop looking at me like I am the only thing that can keep him from drowning.

"Where to?" Gideon asks once we're in the car, trying to sound cheerful, casual. "Want to grab breakfast or something? The food must be terrible in there."

"Um, maybe later," I say. I should tell Gideon about our mom right now. Get it over with. Instead, I just look away out the window. "Let's get going. As far from here as possible."

I just can't tell him. Not yet.

GIDEON JUST GOT his license. Turns out, he's a terrible driver. Nervous and slow, but then suddenly fast. Not that I should judge. Gideon has gotten himself behind the wheel, which is more than I can say. But when he finally lurches out of the detention facility parking lot, I'm thrown back against the seat, nauseous already.

"Sorry," he says, pumping hard on the brakes. "I'm still getting the hang of it."

I nod and turn again toward the window, watching the worn-out strip malls and boarded-up fast-food restaurants pass. The area around the detention facility is an ugly, desperate place. I should feel better leaving it behind. But instead, my dread is on the rise. Like I already know that what lies ahead is worse than what lies behind. Because this feeling isn't just anxiety. On a good day, I've learned to tell the difference.

Gideon and I drive on for another twenty minutes, exchanging harmless chitchat between long pockets of silence. How was your cellmate? Very nice. What's the food like? Very bad. Did anyone try to beat you up? No. Every time I open my mouth and don't tell him our mom is alive, I feel even more like a liar.

I'm relieved when we're finally pulling into downtown Newton. It looks exactly as it did when I left but feels weirdly unfamiliar. It isn't until we've made the next right that I realize we've turned down Cassie's street. And, up ahead, there it is: Cassie's house, with its gingerbread peaked roof and ivy-covered facade, picture-perfect as ever. I feel the moment Gideon realizes his mistake. He may not be an Outlier, but he's not an idiot.

"Oh, um, I— Crap." He slams on the brakes so hard, I brace myself against the dashboard to avoid bashing my face. "Sorry, I wasn't thinking. I can just turn around if you—"

"No." And even I'm surprised by how forcefully it comes out. I don't really know why. "I haven't, um, been here since her funeral. I don't know . . . I kind of want to see her house."

Want is the wrong word. *Need* would be more accurate. Like obsessively *must.* It feels as though some kind of essential truth is buried in the past—Cassie's past, our past. Like we will only break free of this terrible loop of heartbreak and loss after we force ourselves back to the start.

"Pull over there, just for a minute?" I point toward a nearby curb.

"Seriously?" Gideon asks, gripping the steering wheel even tighter, hunched over it now like an old man. He feels way out of his depth with the driving, not to mention managing me. "Are you sure?"

"Yeah, I'm sure," I lie. Luckily, Gideon has no way of knowing that. "Please, just for a minute."

Finally, Gideon lurches to a stop at the side of the road. The house looks exactly the same. It's only been two months since Cassie's funeral; still I expected more decomposition. Maybe this is why I needed to stop here: to be reminded that the world rages on no matter how many of us are cut down by its wake.

No, it's not that. That sounds good, but that's not why I'm here. It's something else. Something more specific. *Cassie's house. Cassie's house. Why?*

Cassie's journal, maybe? It could be. Jasper and I never did figure out who mailed him those pages.

"WHO CARES WHO sent them?" Jasper asked.

We were sitting across the table from each other in the detention facility visiting room. Day thirteen of my incarceration, day thirteen of Jasper faithfully coming to see me. He sat, as he always did, with his hands tucked under his legs against the hard plastic chair. So he'd remember not to try to hold my hand. He'd forgotten once and had almost been permanently banned. *No touching. No exchanging of objects. Shirt and shoes required.* There weren't many rules. But they were enforced like nobody's business.

"*I* care who sent them," I said. "It makes me nervous not to know. It should make you nervous, too."

"Nervous?" Jasper asked. I looked for an edge in his voice. *Everything always makes you nervous.* But he didn't mean it that way. Jasper wasn't about subtext. It was one of the things I loved about him.

Yeah, loved. I hadn't said it to him yet. It was more like an idea I was trying on for size. But so far it fit. Much better than I would have thought. And I kept waiting for that to make me feel stupid, like I'd been tricked into something. But instead it felt like I'd trusted my way there.

"We should at least investigate," I said.

"It was Maia. We already decided that."

"*You* decided," I said. "*I* want confirmation."

"Wait, you're not jealous, are you?" Jasper teased. I shot him a look, and he held up his hands. "Sorry, bad joke."

And then he blushed, like actual red cheeks, which was kind of old-fashioned. But then our whole two-week-long detention facility courtship had been all chaste conversation and hands to ourselves, in twenty-six-minute, guard-supervised increments. The truth was—despite what we'd been through—Jasper and I didn't know each other *that* well. But as we unfolded slowly in front of each other, we slid more tightly into place.

Turned out, Jasper was goofy. Much more so than I realized. And so brutally, heartbreakingly sensitive underneath. He talked about his dad a lot, what it meant to be afraid you were going to become something you hated. He used that fear to explain how he kind of understood my anxiety. In a way, sort of. And I didn't get the connection. But I loved Jasper for trying to make one.

"I'm going to need to hear Maia say it was her who sent the journal pages before I'll believe it," I said. "Otherwise, it's going to nag at me."

Jasper's face softened. "You want me to go ask Maia?" It was a token offer.

I nodded anyway. "Yes, please."

Jasper took a breath and closed his eyes. "Okay," he said, drawing out the word. "But only because I . . ." The color rushed back into his cheeks. He waited a beat before looking up at me. "For you, I will. But only for you."

BUT SITTING HERE now, staring up at Cassie's house, it occurs to me that it's stupid to bother asking Maia. She'll just deny it. And so maybe that's why I wanted to stop here, to ask Cassie's mom, Karen. She can tell us whether Maia has ever been in Cassie's room alone with the diary. She might even know something more.

"I need to ask Karen one quick thing," I say, unbuckling my seat belt and opening the door. "I'll be right back."

"Seriously?" Gideon asks, but I'm already halfway out the door. "Ugh, then I'm coming with you."

It isn't until I'm on the front walk that I notice the weeds poking up between the stones. The house is disintegrating more than I realized. Karen probably is, too.

"Can I help you?" a woman calls from the neighboring yard before we're even at the door. Her voice is sharp, unwelcoming.

When I turn, there's Mrs. Dominic, Cassie's grumpy, gray-haired neighbor, wearing a lime-green sweat suit, a grocery bag gripped against her right side, even though it seems awfully early to be getting back from shopping. Cassie never liked Mrs. Dominic. And I am pretty sure I'm about to find out why.

"We're here for Karen," Gideon says when I stay silent.

Mrs. Dominic peers closer, looks us up and down. We are up to no good. It's been decided. She takes two steps closer so that she's almost on Cassie's lawn. But not quite.

"Why?" she asks.

My stomach churns icily—my own anxiety this time. But it's followed then by that now-familiar prickly, Outlier heat. *That's* all about Mrs. Dominic. She's too aggravated by us, too interested. All wrong. I don't want to tell her anything. And really, what business are we of hers?

I force a smile. "Thank you," I say firmly. "But we're fine."

As though she had offered her help, not her suspicion.

"Well, Karen's not in there anyway. No one is," Mrs. Dominic says, happy to disappoint us. "She went away."

"Went away where?" I ask, feeling far too devastated, I know.

Mrs. Dominic rocks back on her heels. "I'm afraid I can't say." *Can't* clearly means *won't.* "After what that poor woman went through, it's no surprise she couldn't stay here. Why don't you give me your information? I'll pass it on when she gets back."

This is an excuse to get our names. She has no intention of passing on anything. To her credit, she is pretty convincing. Or she would be for someone who isn't me.

"That's okay." I tug Gideon by the arm. "We were just going."

EndOfDays Blog

November 5

It is critical that we all stand ready when called upon to do what is right. Whatever it might cost each of us personally. Love of the Lord requires sacrifice. That is how we show that we are loyal servants to a higher power.

If we expect to see the benefits of being devout in our own lives, we must be willing to sacrifice so that we can show we are deserving of all that has been sacrificed for us. And one thing we cannot allow is a world intent on racing to the next scientific discovery at the cost of innocent lives.

We must be willing to stand up to such forces. We must be willing to fight righteously for the innocent and the weak. Whatever the cost.

Go in peace, everyone. To the light.

RIEL

RIEL LIES IN LEO'S NARROW BED. EYES WIDE OPEN IN THE DARK. WITH INSOMNIAC Leo's super-shades down, it's pitch-black in his room, even though it's nearly eight a.m. As Leo breathes heavily in his sleep, Riel tries to imagine a night sky above filled with stars. Purple-blue blackness and pinpricks of light. Like glitter. Her sister, Kelsey, loved to do shit like that. To look up at the stars. Pretend they were there, even when they weren't. But all Riel sees is blackness. That's all she's ever seen.

Riel shifts in bed, curls up closer to Leo. Hopes his steady breathing will put her back to sleep. It won't, though. It never does.

Once, after their parents died, Kelsey slept outside in the freezing cold just so she could feel "close to them." To the stars? To their parents? Riel didn't ask. Kelsey's explanations always made things worse.

Kelsey was an old soul, though, a sensitive spirit. An artist, born short a layer of skin. Not just because she was an Outlier, either. Riel's an Outlier, but she's always been hard as nails. She'd survive a goddamn nuclear winter, even when she was trying to die.

Riel had been eighteen and a freshman at Harvard, Kelsey only sixteen, when their parents died last November. Swept away in a flash flood while building temporary housing in Arkansas. Because that was the kind of people they were. Good people. People who died doing the right thing.

Doing good was what Riel had intended with Level99. And maybe that even was what she was doing before Quentin came along in April, only weeks after Kelsey died. Riel was still shredded by her grief, and Quentin made it sound like Kelsey could still be alive if it wasn't for one ambitious asshole: Dr. Ben Lang. Dr. Lang cared only about his new discovery—these Outliers—making him rich. And so, Riel had decided the only thing that mattered was making him pay. She could tell Quentin was an ass from the start, of course. An untrustworthy narcissist. But that had mattered less than seeing to it that Dr. Lang got what was coming to him.

Deep down, she'd also probably known that Kelsey had been doomed from the start, regardless of Dr. Ben Lang. That finding out she was an Outlier wouldn't have changed a damn thing. Maybe being an Outlier didn't make things easier, but it wasn't her whole problem either. Kelsey had started drinking way before their parents died. Riel had heard them talking about getting Kelsey help. But then they were dead. The drugs didn't start until after their funeral. Pot, then pills. Kelsey flew downhill like she was on a damn toboggan.

Riel had reached out to grab her, but she was already gone.

"WAIT, WHO ARE you going with?" Riel asked that last night, as Kelsey raced around her still girlish bedroom—pink walls, boy band posters—getting dressed. It was March, six months since their parents' deaths. For the first time, Kelsey seemed happy, and not because she was high out of her mind.

"My friend," Kelsey said, fussing with her amazing head of dark curls. She was beautiful, but in a soft, graceful way. Riel was beautiful, too, but not that way.

"What friend?"

"You know, the one I met at the museum. Grace-Ann."

"Grace-Ann. Right. Are you sure that's even her name?"

"Why wouldn't that be her name?" Kelsey asked with a laugh.

"I don't know. It sounds made up. Like from *Little House on the Prairie* or something. Anyway, this Grace-Ann's party is out in the middle of nowhere?" Riel had a bad feeling about this party. A really bad one. She'd had a bad feeling about this Grace-Ann girl, too, from the first time Kelsey mentioned her. "You live ten minutes from the middle of Boston. Go out there."

"It's her party and that's where she lives. In a group

home, by the way. Because she lost her parents, too. They took off, they didn't die, but same idea." Kelsey stopped fussing and turned to Riel. Sadness welled up in her, Riel could feel it. "She and I have that in common, and it makes me feel better. Okay? Besides, it sounds fun. The party's in some old research place. Nothing illegal. Just fun. Nothing sounds fun anymore."

Grace-Ann was the same girl Kelsey had spent much of the winter with, trolling the nearby university campuses, looking for boys. One time, they'd ended up stumbling into some psych test and using the twenty-buck stipend to buy beer. Riel was glad it hadn't been Harvard. There was no chance she knew the boys they'd shared those beers with. Still, so many risks. Too many.

"No," Riel said. "You're not going."

"No?" Kelsey laughed.

"No," Riel repeated, crossing her arms. "I have a bad feeling. You can't go."

Kelsey just laughed harder. "Listen, I love you, Rie-Rie," she said. "But seriously, what are you going to do to stop me?" She came over to hug Riel. "Don't worry, I'll be careful. I promise."

Because that was the truth: Riel was in charge without being in charge. All she could do was stand there at the edge of the road, silently screaming *Watch out!* as her sister hurtled headlong into oncoming traffic.

THE NEXT MORNING, Kelsey's bed was empty and unslept in. It wasn't until Riel had searched the entire house and thought over and over, *I could have stopped her, I should have stopped her, I could have stopped her,* that she finally looked out the window. And spotted something. On the driveway.

Riel raced out the front door. Heart thumping. Body shaking. Already dialing 911 on the cell phone gripped in her hand. But when she finally reached Kelsey splayed out there, she could see it was far too late for help. Her sister was stiff and blue. Hours dead. Dumped, by Grace-Ann, no doubt, some girl without parents or a face and maybe a made-up name. Some girl Riel couldn't find to blame.

And so, in the end, Dr. Ben Lang had to do.

ACCORDING TO WYLIE, somebody had written about that psych test in her and Kelsey's copy of *1984*. But that someone hadn't been Kelsey. She'd had no way of knowing at the time that that test she'd taken had anything to do with the Outliers. It had just been about the boys and the twenty bucks and the beer and that terrible bullshit friend. It must have been that "fake Kelsey" Wylie had met.

Leo stirs finally. Without realizing it, Riel has been squeezing him too hard.

"Close your eyes," he whispers. Though she is behind him, he knows. "Try to go back to sleep."

Leo doesn't ask what's wrong. He never does. He doesn't ask questions. Doesn't expect answers. It's why Riel stays. That, and because she loves Leo. Someday, she might even tell him. But then, she has an unfair advantage. She can already feel Leo loves her.

She stares at Leo's back. "I've already been up for too long."

"I could make you tea."

Her dad would have liked Leo and his random cups of tea. Her mom would have approved of his loyalty. *I can't stop thinking about Kelsey.* That's the truth, but Riel doesn't say that. If she does, she might cry. And once she starts, she'll never fucking stop. As it is, her grip is slipping.

"There are people following me," Riel says finally. This isn't what she was thinking about. But maybe it should be. It's definitely a good distraction from Kelsey.

"What?" Leo asks, sounding more alarmed than she was prepared for. He pushes himself up in bed and turns to look at her. Riel wishes she hadn't said anything. "Who's following you?"

"I don't know."

Though she has her suspicions. The agents who had showed up at her grandfather's house, namely.

"IT'S IMPERATIVE THAT we find Wylie Lang," Agent Klute declared once Riel had finally returned to the front door of her grandfather's Cape house. By then, Wylie and Jasper had stroked safely into the darkness.

Klute was super pissed, too. Riel could feel how bad he wanted to slap the smug look off her face. And so she invited him in real sweetly. Just to get under his skin.

"Oh, do come in and look for her yourself," she said, waving a gracious hand. "She's not here. And I've got nothing to hide."

Klute didn't move, though—nothing like someone getting what they want to throw them off.

"Um," Riel said. "Are you coming in or not?"

"Yeah, we're coming in," Klute said finally, waving her to the side and stepping in the door.

"Like I said, Wylie's not here," Riel said when Klute and his partner had finally pounded around the upstairs and downstairs. "Her dad, Dr. Lang, went missing in DC. She probably went there to look for him. Maybe she'll even run into Granddad while she's there?"

Agent Klute didn't look Riel's way, but she felt the split-second tremor when she mentioned Dr. Lang. It was unmistakable. There was a connection between Dr. Lang and her grandfather, no doubt. They might have followed Jasper's phone, but that wasn't the only reason these agents were at her grandfather's house. Not by a long shot.

Hours later, after the agents had thoroughly searched the house and the grounds, once and then again, and they'd asked every possible question in at least three different ways, they finally let Riel and Leo go. Or to be more precise, they kicked them out of Riel's grandfather's house.

Agent Klute got into Riel's face on her way out. "And stay away from Wylie Lang," he growled. "Stay away from this entire situation."

"What situation?" Riel asked snidely. Violence. A wave of it from Agent Klute. So strong, it almost took Riel's breath away. "Maybe if you explain—"

Klute grabbed her arm then and jerked her close, the pain so sharp and unexpected it almost made Riel cry out.

"Stay away. From all of it. Especially Wylie Lang," Agent Klute repeated through clenched teeth. He pointed at Leo then. "If you don't, he'll be the one who pays. I'll personally make sure of it."

"WHERE ARE THEY following you?" Leo asks. "What do you mean?"

Riel didn't mean to freak Leo out. She feels bad now for telling him. "I mean, not all over. There's not like an army of them or something. But every once in a while when I'm out, I'll spot someone watching me. Maybe. I haven't seen that asshole Klute again, luckily. But I think I have seen that white van they were in at my grandfather's house."

"But Wylie's in jail, and you haven't spoken to her," Leo says. "How much farther do they want you to stay away?"

Riel shrugs. "Wylie isn't the whole thing, you know?"

"But you have been staying away from the rest, too, right?" Leo asks.

"I haven't even been to Level99 since my grandfather's house.

You know that," Riel says. "I barely leave your room."

"Good." Leo lies back down. Exhales like he's relieved. He isn't. "They'll lose interest eventually, right?"

"I hope so," Riel says. "Because it kind of feels like I'm running out of places to hide."

WHEN RIEL WAKES again, it's nine a.m. The shades are up and Leo's small dorm room is filled with light, the small slice of bed next to her empty. Riel runs a hand over the cool, crumpled sheets. Leo has Harvard summer program classes and an internship. That's the only reason he even has a dorm room right now. A tiny single—desk, bed, that's it. Long-term visitors, much less roommates, are against the rules. But Leo insisted that Riel stay. Hard to argue when she had no place else to go.

Before, Riel had been sleeping at the Level99 house, ever since Kelsey died in March. But it's not safe for Level99 if she's there now. She doesn't want Agent Klute coming after her and finding them. And also, maybe she just wants a break. From everything. Leo's felt like such a safe place to hide.

Riel picks up her new burner off the nightstand. She's been changing them out weekly. The only people who have the number are Leo and Level99. The phone has one text. Maybe even one that just woke her. A **?**, and nothing more. It's from Brian. It means, *You coming in?* Brian checks in every day. He doesn't actually want Riel to come in, of course. He likes being in charge of Level99. He just likes to confirm that he still is.

Riel reminds Brian all the time that she is coming back when things cool down. That him being in charge is temporary, and only to protect Level99—even if it is more complicated than that for Riel right now. Maybe Brian even knows she's conflicted. Someone has been jumping in and out of Riel's online life. She's noticed. Brian, checking up on her for sure. And fair enough. That's his job now. To protect Level99.

But then what's Riel's job? To protect herself? Wylie? The Outliers? She's not sure anymore, and it makes her feel more lost than she wants to admit.

"My dad is with your grandfather." That was what Wylie said that night right before she dove into the water. And then there was that guilty twitch from Agent Klute when Riel had pursued the lead. Her *grandfather.* He's an asshole, no doubt. But connected to the Outliers and Dr. Ben Lang? How and why? It doesn't make any sense.

And, if so, how the fuck hadn't she seen him coming? What kind of an Outlier was she?

That's the problem, isn't it? Reading's not ESP. It's not a crystal ball. Feelings and instincts are fuzzy things. They change. Shift. Blur. And people will want Outliers to prove they can read minds. Or they won't believe they can do anything. It will be all or nothing. Neither here nor there is the place you get crushed in between.

Senator David Russo was Kelsey and Riel's maternal grandfather, and he'd always hated their dad. According to their grandfather, their dad and his Communist, a.k.a. liberal, ideals had ruined their mother. Making Riel and Kelsey the fruit of his poisonous tree. Their dad was also black, which Riel has always suspected was their grandfather's bigger issue with him, and them.

When their parents died, it was decided that the girls were old enough to take care of themselves. This was true in theory, if not in fact. Riel was three months in at Harvard, studying computer science. The plan was that she would move home and commute to school until Kelsey graduated high school. No problem. They had plenty of money through their mother's trust, too. No problem. Their mother's sister—childless Aunt Susan, a banker from Manhattan—would check in on them occasionally. No problem. They were good kids anyway, responsible.

Of course, just because they *could* take care of themselves didn't mean that they *should.*

They hadn't seen their grandfather in years when he came to their parents' funeral—the cameras were watching, after all. And he didn't speak *to* either one of them at the funeral. He spoke *at* them: a few polite words tossed in their direction like stale candy from a parade float.

It was only after the funeral that Riel had tracked down her grandfather's Cape house and started breaking in on occasion, to mess with him. It wasn't something she was proud of, but it was satisfying.

Riel is about to answer Brian's text—nope, not coming in—when she sees an envelope slide under Leo's door. *Nope.* That's what Riel thinks about that, too. *Don't want that.* But these days ignoring a note under a door is not an option.

Riel pushes herself up out of bed and heads over to pick it up. She lifts it carefully. Inside the envelope is a single sheet of paper, on it a single handwritten sentence: *They know you have them.*

Goddamn it. Fucking enough. Riel jerks open Leo's door and looks up and down the hallway, trembling with rage. She's ready to scream at Klute or whoever left it. But there's no one in sight.

Riel closes the door, heart beating hard as she studies the paper again. The words are still there, unfortunately. Riel was right, there was somebody following her—her grandfather, his people, Klute. They've known all along exactly where she is. Leo's room, that small square of safety: gone. Like so much else.

They know you have them? Have what? It takes Riel a beat. Wylie's pictures? The eight-and-a-half-by-eleven envelope she shoved at Riel before racing out of her grandfather's house.

Riel has only ever taken a quick look just so she knew what she had: pictures of buildings—shitty, blurry pictures. Obviously, they were important to Wylie, but just looking at them it wasn't obvious why. Once, Riel had seen Leo late at night flipping through them in the darkness. He'd told her the next day she should get rid of them. Not because of what was in them. But because they were Wylie's. And he'd been right. Of course he had been.

BREW IS THREE blocks from Leo's dorm. It has long, knotty tables, perpetually packed with nerdy types hunched over laptops. These are Riel's people, even if she doesn't exactly look the part with her fashionable tank top, low-slung jeans, gameboard tattoo, and piercings. But Riel will always be a complete nerd at heart.

As usual in the morning, there is nowhere to sit at Brew. Riel has to hover for ten minutes before a table finally opens up. As she waits, she realizes she can't be sure that it's safer to be in Brew than Leo's room. But at least in Brew, there will be witnesses to any abduction.

After Riel sits down, she pulls out the eight-and-a-half-by-eleven envelope of Wylie's pictures from her bag, sees the name on the envelope: *David Rosenfeld.* She'd forgotten about that.

Riel looks around the café again before she opens the envelope, feels like she's being watched. But she doesn't see anyone looking at her. Then again, these people's whole job is to blend in. Finally, Riel flips through the pictures quickly: a blurry office building, a shelf or rack with what look like big white buckets on it. The buckets have writing on them, but it's impossible to make out. Like she remembered, nothing to go on in the pictures, except how badly shot they are. That and the fact that her grandfather apparently really wants them. *Probably* her grandfather. Riel's real evidence for this is super thin, but the feeling that she is right? Outlier, instinct, whatever you want to call it, it's overwhelming.

David Rosenfeld. He's the next logical step. Riel pulls her laptop out and jumps on the wide-open-to-tracking public Wi-Fi. It's a risk, but there aren't other options. A second later, she has a couple dozen possible Rosenfelds: a lawyer, a dentist, a high school baseball star. And then, there it is, the fourth entry down, a link to an author's website: David Rosenfeld.

Riel clicks through to the site, which drops her onto a glossy home page with a bunch of *New York Times* bestselling books stacked up artfully. The headshot of the author—current reporter, former soldier—on the right-hand side. Rosenfeld. Curly hair, thick black-framed glasses. Cute, even if the picture is a little too much about his biceps. His books are all about Iraq and Afghanistan, except for the most recent, which is called *A*

Private War: How Outsourcing Is Changing the Face of the Military. And there is a related article: "Want Funding, but No Oversight? How the Federal Government Gets Away with Looking at Everyone but Themselves."

This is the right Rosenfeld, no doubt about that. Military financing smells like her grandfather. But what does he have to do with the pictures? It would be a hell of a lot easier just to swing by the detention facility and ask Wylie. But Klute warned Riel specifically to *stay away from her.* It's bad enough that she's ignoring the other part of what Klute said: *stay away from all of it.* Riel is pretty sure the pictures fall into the "all of it" category.

Riel startles when her phone vibrates in her pocket. She pulls it out to read the text. **Be back in fifteen. Forgot something. L.** Shit, Leo will be back way earlier than she expected. And she left out that note: *They know you have them.* She needs to beat Leo back home and get rid of it before he sees it. He will freak out otherwise.

Riel's still looking down at her phone when there's a voice right next to her. "Excuse me?"

She jumps to her feet, clutching the pictures against her body. "What the fuck?" she shouts.

But there's just a skinny, acne-spotted guy who looks about twelve years old, blinking at her. He holds up his nervous hands and moves them around in the air.

"Oh, sorry, no, I'm—" He touches the back of the open chair across from Riel. "I just wanted to borrow this chair."

"Yeah, yes," Riel manages. "Take it."

But as she sits back down, she notices somebody else on the opposite side of the room. Baseball hat and glasses. A take-out coffee in one hand, a braided leather bracelet on his wrist. Sitting at a table. Alone. He was watching her a second ago. She can feel the echo of his stare. Worse yet, Riel has seen him somewhere before. The baseball hat is doing the trick, though—she can't place him.

But she doesn't need to. Between that and Leo about to beat her back to the room, it's time to go. Riel snaps shut her computer and shoves it and the pictures in her bag before heading quickly for the door.

The fresh air is a relief, but Riel still feels jittery out on the sidewalk. She crosses the street quickly and picks up speed, checking over her shoulder a few times. But there's no one behind her. She's at a jog by the time she enters the gates to campus.

On campus, she feels alone, singled out. Scared. Despite all the people—professors, graduate students, summer program students, tourists.

As Riel dives into the flow, someone blows past her, knocking hard into her elbow. Running in the direction of Leo's dorm at the far end of the square. Riel is about to yell at the guy when she notices that he isn't the only one who's hustling that way. Lots of people are. They are all rushing in the direction of Leo's dorm.

No is what Riel thinks as she starts to run, too. *No. No. No.*

She sees the fire trucks first, right there by Leo's building. She blinks hard. But they remain. Lights flashing. And then, only a second later, she sees the flames. Actual freakin' flames. Coming out the windows.

The windows to Leo's dorm room.

TOP SECRET AND CONFIDENTIAL

To: Senator David Russo

From: The Architect

Re: Outlier Identification Modeling

April 3

To summarize today's meeting, they will proceed to run predictive modeling for two potential programs to identify and track subjects demonstrating specified skill set. One model will examine the use of identification cards. The second model will study the possible use of observable bracelets.

Aspects evaluated will include:

—Likelihood of subgroup compliance with protocol

—Cost of protocol

—Ease of enforcement

—Time from initiation to launch

—Likelihood of legal opposition

—Efficacy of protocol in properly alerting nontarget subgroup

Results to follow.

WYLIE

THE MENU AT HOLY COW IS WRITTEN ON A MIRROR BEHIND THE OLD-FASHIONED soda counter in curly white script. It's barely eleven a.m., so we're the only customers, seated at a booth along the wall. We ended up there after we left Cassie's and after we stopped at the drugstore and after we went for breakfast and after we drove around and around. I told Gideon I wanted to go to all those places because I could. Because I wanted to feel free. That's true. It's also true that I'm stalling. Like if we don't go home, I don't have to tell him about our mom. So now, ice cream at Holy Cow.

Nicholas is behind the counter; a gray-haired man with an impressive potbelly, a huge square face, and an intimidating scowl. Cassie always said he was much sweeter than he looked. He would have to be.

Telling Gideon about our mom would be so much easier

if Jasper were here. Not for Gideon, maybe. Gideon still isn't exactly a Jasper fan. But definitely for me. I still haven't been able to reach Jasper, though. Using Gideon's cell, I've tried his phone twice, and both times I've gotten a new recording: *this number is no longer in service.* A definite downgrade from *the customer you are trying to reach is not available*, which I got before. Calling Jasper's mom is my best option now, I know that. But I need to work up my courage first.

"Hello?" When I look down, Gideon is holding out a menu to me.

"Oh, thanks."

The bell on the door chimes as the girl Cassie used to work with and couldn't stand comes in. She used to have bright pink acrylic nails and bows in her long blond hair, but she's cut it pixie-short and dyed it bright white. She has a nose ring, too, and trimmed bare fingernails. I wonder if those things would have made Cassie like her more. Or less. I'm not sure I know anymore. After the funeral and before the hospital, Jasper had once joked about Cassie being a terrible judge of character. And somehow it felt not like an insult, but like an act of love. To remember her fondly, but exactly as she was.

"Are you okay?" Gideon asks.

To say anything now other than the whole truth would feel like an actual betrayal. Still, my mouth feels stuck. I lean forward and imagine punching the words from the base of my gut.

"Mom is . . . ," I begin, but nothing more will come.

Gideon's eyes snap up from his menu. "Mom is what?"

Afraid, that's how he feels. Afraid of something exactly like what I am about to tell him. Something that will make everything even worse. And what I wish most at this moment is that I could have no idea how he feels.

"She's alive," I say, looking down at the table, bracing myself for the blowback: betrayal, anger, rage, hurt. "She's been alive this whole time. It wasn't her in the car."

But nothing. I feel nothing from him. And when I look up, Gideon is just staring stone-faced at the wall. Totally numb. And it is awful. I'd much rather he'd feel something, anything—anger, rage, sadness. This quiet emptiness? It's like peering into a sucking black hole.

"Gideon?" I ask.

"Yeah," he says finally. But still, he feels nothing. And he looks so pale and stunned.

"Are you okay?"

"Sure," he says, raising his hands helplessly. *Am I?* they ask.

And then suddenly, the floodgates open and Gideon's heartbreak plows into me with such force that without thinking I reach forward and clutch his hands.

"I know, I'm sorry," I say, looking away as tears fill his eyes. I haven't seen Gideon cry since we were little kids. And I do not want to, especially not now. "Rachel says that Mom did it to protect us. Not the accident, that was . . . Someone really did try to run her off the road. It just wasn't her in the car. But the staying away after, I mean. It's been to keep us safe."

"I should have known." Gideon shakes his head.

"How could you have?" I say. "Who would ever have thought that—"

"There's an envelope in your room." He cuts me off sharply. "And if you want to know why I was in your room, looking through your stuff—I don't have a good excuse. I went through everybody's room in the past two weeks—Mom and Dad's, yours. I was lonely."

And this is so heartbreakingly true it makes my breath catch.

"What letter?" I ask.

"On your nightstand," he says. "I didn't open it, I swear. But I saw it there. And I thought, wow, that kind of looks like Mom's handwriting. Of course, because I'm me and not you, I didn't have a 'feeling' about anything. I was like, logic says Mom is dead. So it's old or something . . ."

"I didn't have a feeling either until she was standing right in front of me. I had no idea she was alive." But that's true only technically—I was obsessed about the accident not being an accident. Probably because some part of me knew she wasn't dead.

"Wait." Gideon's eyes are wide. "You saw her? Where?"

Crap.

"Only for a second," I say, wishing I could snatch the words back and stuff them down my throat. "She came to the detention facility just so I would know Rachel was telling me the truth."

"Awesome," he says. "Well, I guess we know for sure who's the favorite child now. Not that there was any doubt before."

"Gideon, come on, that's not—"

"Don't." He looks at me hard. His hurt is already hardening around his heart. "Don't protect her. Where the hell has she been then?"

And so I tell Gideon what I know about Mom and Rachel and what happened that last night. As I say it out loud, I realize just how little I do know.

"Where has all this rallying of the troops gotten her?" Gideon asks. "I seriously hope she has something to show for it."

"I don't know. We should ask Rachel. There is something else, though," I say. And I need to get it all out, all at once. Now. "Dad knew."

"What?" Gideon's hurt has caught fire—it's anger now. "Come on. Seriously?!"

Cassie's ex-coworker has appeared at our table, recoiling from Gideon's shouting. "You want me to come back?" she asks, giving Gideon the side-eye. Her name tag says *Brittany.*

"I just lost my appetite," Gideon mutters.

"A black-and-white milk shake?" I don't want anything, but we need to buy something so we can sit here a little longer.

Brittany narrows her eyes at me. "Hey, you're Cassie's friend, aren't you?"

I nod and try to smile, but I'm not sure I actually do. "Yeah, I am. I was."

"That sucked, what happened to her," Brittany says.

And suddenly this feels like an opportunity. To give Gideon a chance to calm, yes, but maybe Brittany is even the reason I told Gideon I wanted to go to Holy Cow in the first place. "Can I ask you something?"

"Sure," Brittany says, though it feels like *no.* I can even feel her backing away, though her feet haven't moved.

"Were you here when she met the guy she was dating?" I'm

hoping she saw something or heard something about Quentin that might help me find out who he is. Or, better yet, *where* he is.

"You mean Jasper?" Brittany asks. "I saw him at a party once. Cute, you know, in a jock kind of way. But Cassie didn't meet Jasper here. They went to school together. Don't you go to school with him, too?"

I feel a guilty pang. It's amazing how I've turned Cassie and Jasper into a thing that never was. It didn't occur to me she'd think I was talking about Jasper.

"No, not Jasper. A different guy, he had glasses. Older, cute, but in a kind of geeky way," I say. "Cassie told me he came in here one day. That was how she met him."

Brittany shakes her head. "I don't think so. Cassie and I were always on shift together. Besides, Nicholas won't let any guys over the age of thirteen hang out here unless they're somebody's dad. Nicholas thinks everybody is a pedophile. So I can't see how she would have met him here."

"Oh, okay," I say, and I want to feel like she's gotten it wrong. But I feel just the opposite. She's right: Cassie didn't meet Quentin at Holy Cow. But then, where did she meet him? And why did she lie? "Thanks anyway."

Brittany takes a couple steps from the table, but then turns back.

"I really am sorry about what happened, you know," she says. "Cassie was a wild girl, but I liked her."

OUR HOUSE SMELLS exactly the same, good in that weird, old-house way. Like lavender with a hint of maple syrup. And I want to be comforted by something that familiar, but all I feel is sad. Like even the smell is just another lie.

Gideon and I sit next to each other on the couch, staring down at our mom's sealed letter, the milk shake from Holy Cow that I drank too fast sitting heavy in my stomach. Gideon went up to get the letter for me because I still wasn't ready to face my bedroom. Downstairs, I already feel swamped by memories. Even the good ones feel terrible, too. Maybe especially the good ones. And something about telling Gideon about our mom has made me angry all over again. I got kind of lulled into Rachel's explanations, which ring a lot less true now that I've relayed them to Gideon. I mean, our dad is missing, and our mom is building some coalition? That might be noble. It might even make her feel like a hero. But we need her home, right now.

"You want me to open it?" Gideon asks after we have been sitting there a really long time.

"No, I will," I say.

My hands tremble as I finally rip open the seal. There is too much riding on what she has to say. I already know whatever's inside won't be enough. How can it be? My heart sinks even more when I see it's just a single page of notebook paper, just a few short paragraphs. Gideon and I read together.

June 17

Dear Wylie,

Rachel has hopefully explained as much as she can about what happened and why. All I can say is that I'm doing the best

I can to be sure you're safe from here on out. I have already found people to help us, including a senator—I can't wait until you meet her. She's amazing. There's a neuroscientist, too (a woman), who your dad has been working with. Real people. Who are smart and committed and are willing to help.

I am sure you are angry, and I know that nothing I write here will make up for the pain I have caused you. But know that everything I did was to protect you, and because I love you.

In the meantime, Rachel will help you. I am so grateful to her. Thank God for my "old lady yoga," as you like to call it, because if she and I hadn't run into each other, I never would have thought to go to her that night. But she was the perfect person. Anyway, let her help you. She saved my life, literally. She knows what to do. And send my love to Gideon.

It's even harder to read than I expected. To think of her sneaking back into the house to leave it after I saw her. To feel how stupidly desperate I am still to forgive her, to find some decent explanation. It makes me feel like such an idiot.

"Is there anything she could say that would make you forgive her?" I ask. Partly because I want him to tell me how I should.

Gideon considers the question for a minute. "Probably," he says. "People who live in glass houses, you know? You're saying you can't forgive her? I mean, no matter what?"

"I'm not sure," I say, and I realize then that whether or not I can forgive my mom isn't even the thing that's bothering me most. I'm just not sure what is. "I'm going to call Jasper's house, see if I can reach him."

"You think he knows something?" Gideon asks.

"No," I say. "But he knows me."

Jasper's mom answers on the third ring. "Hello?" Mad, already. Like we're in the middle of an argument. And she doesn't even know it's me. Things are only going to go downhill once she figures that out.

"Can I please speak to Jasper?" I ask brightly.

"He's not here," she snaps. On second thought, she knows exactly who I am.

"Oh, I, um, tried his cell phone, and it's not working. . . ."

Dead silence. She also knows that Jasper's phone isn't working. She is maybe even the reason why.

"Could you tell him that Wylie called?" I ask. "And that I'm home?"

"I am not telling him a goddamn thing."

Click.

She's hung up on me. My chest is burning as I grip my phone. I know that I shouldn't take her venom personally. But that's easier said than done.

I still have the phone in my hand when the doorbell rings. I want to feel a happy surge: it's Jasper! But already I know it's not.

"I'll check who it is," Gideon offers as he gets up to peek out the window. He turns back to me. "Rachel."

Gideon opens the door and Rachel steps into the foyer, dressed, as usual, in an elegant, perfectly tailored black suit and expensive-looking four-inch black platform heels. Rachel's thousand-dollar rock-star shoes are her screw-you to lawyerly convention. Somehow, she makes this seem brave.

"Glad to see you made it home," she says, and there goes a bolt of lightning. Her feeling, gone before it's even really there. And right now I am definitely too worn out to chase it. "I just wanted to check in and make sure everything was okay."

I stare at her. "I was just sitting here reading the note my not-dead mom left me. So define 'okay.'"

"Oh, right," she says, looking past me. Perplexed. (Maybe.) Flash. Crackle. Gone. "Well, I came by to remind you of the bail conditions: greater Newton area. They can use it against you at trial if you violate, even by accident, not to mention that they will revoke your bail, instantly. It's not worth it."

"I'm not going anywhere," I say. Though I am already pretty sure this is yet another of my lies.

"Good. Also, we got the first set of discovery disclosures from the prosecutor's office today," Rachel goes on, glad to change the subject. Now her feelings are steady, loud and clear: calm, confident, focused. Whenever we talk about my case is the only time they are ever like that. "They're, let's just say, interesting."

"Interesting how?" Gideon asks when I am too slow on the uptake.

"They're thin," she says, pleased with herself now. "Like remember those matches they supposedly had in the first interview?"

"What about them?" I feel a flutter in my chest. The matches really bothered me, right from the start. If they did find matches under my bed, I worried that maybe I did do something awful to Teresa and just don't remember. Because in some small, dark corner of my mind, I still don't trust myself, not completely.

"They've disappeared, apparently." Rachel shakes her head in disbelief. "Now, I don't know if they lost them or if they never had them or what. But they're gone."

"That's great news, right?" Gideon asks, looking over at me. I'm afraid there's a catch. "Does that mean they'll drop their case?"

Rachel shakes her head again. "I wouldn't get ahead of ourselves. They still have proof that the fire at the hospital was intentional. It was 'constructed from combustible materials.' Meaning, apparently, whoever set it didn't need a match."

"Maybe Teresa?" I ask. I've thought a lot about that excitement I sensed from Teresa at the weirdest times. Like she knew something big was coming.

"Pretty sure they still have you in mind."

"Combustible materials? They grabbed me off the bridge," I say. "Not to mention, they took everything off me. How would I even have—whatever that is—to set a fire?"

Rachel takes a breath and looks down, like she's reluctant to say the rest. To spare my feelings. No, like she knows she *should* feel that way. No flash. No crackle. I don't think she feels anything. "Jasper is their theory. They have him on tape, remember, sneaking in to see you."

For a split second I feel betrayed by Jasper. Even though I know he wasn't involved. That's the true danger of the most outrageous lies. Somehow they take on the possibility of truth.

"But he didn't—"

"It doesn't matter what actually happened, obviously," Rachel says. "It matters what they can get a jury to believe."

"Then make sure that doesn't happen!" Gideon snaps, and he's pissed. Probably more about our mom for him. "Isn't that your job?"

Anger. (Maybe.) Flash. Crackle. Gone. That's fair: she saved my mom's life, got me out of jail. How much more is she really expected to do?

"There's a limit to my control over this situation," she says carefully and calmly, and this much is definitely true. "I will do the best I can, but there will be regular people with their own imperfect opinions involved—juries, prosecutors. These people make random, stupid choices."

"Did the police ever find Quentin?" I ask, partly to change the subject, partly because I do feel way more bothered about his whereabouts now that I'm out.

Rachel frowns and shakes her head. But I feel a twinge of something. Flash, then gone. I am pretty sure it could have been guilt, though.

"You did ask them to find him, right? You told them he was at the jail, that he was alive?"

"I made a judgment call, Wylie."

"What? You told me you were looking into it!" I shout. And—stupidly—I feel like I'm going to cry. "He could be anywhere!"

Scared. That's how I really feel. Quentin being alive and out here makes me scared. I don't want to give him that power. But it's a fact.

"In my *judgment*, admitting that Quentin visited you in jail could make you look like his accomplice, Wylie. It could even end up linking you to Cassie's death, which, you know, was another theory they have—that you've killed a girl with fire before." Rachel stares me straight in the eye. Calm. Steady. Controlled. "They probably never would have found Quentin anyway. It's not like they have sophisticated resources. I'm sorry that I lied to you. But I truly thought it was in your best interest."

I wonder for a second whether she thinks I imagined Quentin or made up that he came. I never told Jasper about Quentin coming to see me, that I knew for sure he was alive. And that's the real reason, I think. I was afraid that maybe it never happened.

"But what if Quentin has our dad?" I ask.

"He doesn't have your dad," Rachel says. Guilt. (Maybe.) Flash. Crackle. Gone. She feels absolutely 100 percent sure of this fact, though. But then again, people who are totally sure can also be totally wrong. Being an Outlier has taught me that much. "And if he does, I swear to you, Wylie, I will make it my mission in life to track him down myself and make sure he pays."

Impatience. (Maybe.)

Flash. Crackle. Gone.

"Doesn't somebody at least have to explain the whole thing

in the hospital? Like the NIH or that doctor involved, Cornelia," Gideon says, forcing himself to ask despite—or maybe because of—his shame about anything where Cornelia is concerned. "Doesn't he have to answer for something?"

Rachel shrugs. "The federal government has said all they are going to say about the incident at the hospital, apparently. That's what an NIH assistant general counsel and a US attorney have told me."

"They can't do that, can they?" Gideon asks.

"When the government shouts 'in the name of safety and security,' they can pretty much do whatever they want. Besides, if we want to fight that battle we can, but later on. Right now, I have to focus on keeping Wylie out of jail."

"And finding our dad," I add firmly.

"Of course," Rachel says. Flash. Gone. Too fast for me to even guess. I wonder if she's already given up on my dad. Rachel stands and checks her Cartier watch. "Unfortunately, I've got a meeting I was supposed to be at fifteen minutes ago. We should catch up more later, Wylie. Oh, I almost forgot." She pauses before reaching our door, starts digging in her bag and pulls out some pages. "Your mom sent some emails for me to pass on to you. I printed them out. I'll leave them for you to read." She puts the pages down on the side table near the door. "Oh, and she needs those pictures you took from my house."

Crap. My mom's pictures. I never should have taken them. But I am annoyed my mom cares about them now. We've got so many other things—like where my dad is—that matter so much more.

"I don't have the pictures anymore," I say. "I had to swim to get away from those agents."

"So you just . . ."

"I had to leave them," I say. And that is the truth. It's also all I'm going to say. Even if Riel still has the pictures—which is doubtful under the circumstances—she's underground now. There is no way I could find her. Or maybe I just don't want to. Not just to give my mom what she wants.

"Oh, okay," Rachel says, trying to sound nonchalant. "Don't worry. It's no big deal. The pictures aren't that important."

But when she smiles back at me one last time from the doorway, I can feel one thing absolutely loud and clear: nothing could be further from the truth.

THE WASHINGTON NATIONAL

IN WIDE-OPEN FIELD, IT COULD COME DOWN TO A BATTLE BETWEEN EXPERIENCE AND INNOVATION, FEAR AND OPTIMISM

May 20

It's early days. This presidential race can't even officially be called a race yet, but the potential contenders thus far are a wildly divergent pack.

On the one hand, there are possible candidates like Lana Harrison, the senator from California, who rose to prominence in the recent fight to reform health care and expand civil rights. On the other end of the spectrum is Senator David Russo, who, after a distinguished military career, joined the Senate Armed Services Committee, where he has had a stern eye fixed on national security. Lately, though, his focus has shifted to privacy, which has thrown even some in his own party for a loop.

Lana Harrison says that—rhetoric notwithstanding—Russo's end goal is just the opposite. That Russo seeks to limit individual freedom, not protect it. The real question now is: Who will voters believe?

JASPER

JASPER REACHES FOR HIS PHONE TO SILENCE THE ALARM. HE'S IN SUCH A DEAD sleep, it takes a minute to remember where he is: the dorm, BC. Right. Jasper and his roommate, Chance, have gotten into the habit of taking naps after early-morning hockey practice. When you're eighteen and up before five thirty a.m., then on the ice for three hours, that's what you do.

With his phone in his hand finally, Jasper taps off the alarm.

"I am not going to let that girl drive your whole life off into a ditch," his mom had snapped at him the day after Wylie was hauled off to the detention facility. When she was blaming Wylie for him not going to BC. "She's damaged goods. Please tell me I raised you well enough to see that."

The anger balloons in his chest, being reminded of how much his mom cares about hockey camp, because she's after some NHL pie in the sky and the money that might go along with it. Wait. No. That's not how his mom really feels. Wylie has told him more than once: his mom's worry and love just look like anger. The actual truth is that she cares about *him*, not hockey. Or so Wylie says. Jasper's still working on believing her.

If only his mom knew that Wylie is her biggest defender. But to do that he'd have to tell her that he's been hanging out with Wylie in the detention facility. And it's better not to go there. His mom would panic, angry panic. She's chilled out a lot thinking Wylie is out of the picture. And, yeah, going to hockey camp like both Wylie and his mom wanted was a good call. It's where he is supposed to be. Jasper believes that now. At least, most days.

Jasper puts his brand-new iPhone down gently on the desk that's jammed up against the head of his bed in the small double room he and Chance share. The new phone was a gift from his mom before he headed off for BC. A gift she definitely couldn't afford, one that was supposed to be a reward for him "doing the right thing." It made him feel extra guilty every time he talked to Wylie.

Jasper's bed squeaks loudly as he sits up, and Chance makes the same sick, wet noise he does whenever he wakes up: surprised Scooby-Doo. Most of what Chance says and does is some shade of Scooby-Doo.

"Shut that thing off," Chance mumbles into his pillow, same as he does each day. Like the alarm's not already off. Like Jasper's a pain in his ass. But Chance counts on Jasper to get them both up in the morning and again in the afternoon. Otherwise,

Chance would sleep all day. No surprise, Jasper likes being the guy who can be counted on. And that's the great thing about college: you can decide to be only the best parts of who you are.

Apart from the noises, Chance is a decent guy, too. Straight-up. He's from Terre Haute, Indiana, not exactly known for ice hockey, but it's there according to Chance. He says it's mostly corn and nice people, and once upon a time that might have sounded boring to Jasper. But these days, boring doesn't sound half bad.

"Your problem, Jasper, is that you think too much," Chance likes to say. "More time living and less time thinking, my man."

And it seems to work for Chance. He's at Boston College to play hockey, get drunk, and find girls. In that order. Anything outside those three buckets he tosses like a wrong-shaped peg. Chance believes life is simple. And so it is. Meanwhile, Jasper isn't sure about anything. Except Wylie. Each day he is more sure about her.

Wylie is the reason he finally decided to go to BC preseason, and not just to keep his mind off her being gone. Wylie told Jasper he needed to go to BC back when she barely knew him. And she never wavered.

By the time everything with the hospital had happened, Jasper joined preseason late. It wasn't easy convincing the BC hockey coach to give him a chance. Jasper decided to go with the truth—Cassie and Wylie and the camp and the bridge and then the hospital. All of it out in a rush. Coach had sat there listening with his scraggly, scrunched-up eyebrows. When Jasper was finally done with his wild story, the coach stayed quiet for a crazy long time. Like he was about to drop some serious knowledge.

"Okay" was all he finally said, looking Jasper square in the eye. "But you miss a game or a practice from here on out, you screw up at all, you're gone. You're lucky as hell Samuels is out with a concussion. I got no choice but to take you on, despite the fact that you sound like you could be delusional. Consider yourself already out of strikes."

Strikes. There it was finally. Like father, like son. The judge had said basically the same thing when he'd sentenced Jasper's dad to fifteen years for aggravated assault. "I'm sorry, Mr. Salt, but you are out of strikes."

And fair enough. Jasper's dad had already been arrested more times than Jasper could count. And what he'd done that night was so much worse than anything that had come before. It wasn't just evil. It was animal.

The guy in front of them was driving like a dumb-ass, weaving all over the place, slowing way down, then jerking to a stop. They could see that he was on his cell phone. Stupid, no doubt. But it wasn't until Jasper's dad had to jerk so hard to stop that he dropped his cigarette in his lap that he became a train cut loose on the tracks.

"No, Dad!" Jasper had called after him.

But he was already out of the car.

"Don't," Jasper had whispered inside the empty car as he watched his dad through the windshield, up ahead on the slick road, shouting through the window at the driver of the other car. But watch was all Jasper did. Because he was only twelve at the time. And there was only so much that twelve could do.

Jasper had actually been relieved when the other man got

out and was much bigger than his dad. Big enough, he figured, to easily knock Jasper's dad back in his place. But rage, Jasper learned that night, can make a man many times his natural size.

By the time Jasper was outside the car screaming, "Stop! Stop! Dad, stop it!" his dad's fists were covered in blood, and the man was on the ground, motionless.

All these years later, Jasper tries not to picture the way the guy's face had looked after—lumpy and wet and bright red. It's his dad's face that haunts him more late at night. The way it looks far too much like his own.

"IN A WAY, I am like him," Jasper said during one of his many visits to Wylie at the detention facility.

It wouldn't have been Jasper's first pick for a date locale, but he was getting used to it. On the upside, they had no choice but to really get to know each other. And Jasper was cool sitting anywhere with Wylie. Had he felt that way about other girls? Maybe. Jasper fell hard and he fell often—his mom was right about that. But that didn't mean this time with Wylie couldn't be different. That it wasn't special.

"You're nothing like your dad," Wylie said.

"Come on, that kid that I choked in that Level99 place, the kid I punched in school. I snap, like, a lot of the time," Jasper said, staring at Wylie so hard his eyes had begun to burn. "I may not be the same as my dad, but I'm not sure I'm all that different."

And it mattered to Jasper that she didn't pretend otherwise. He wanted her to know the worst of him (the parts even he hated) and to care about him anyway.

"So, whatever. Even if that is true. You still get to decide what to make of who you are," Wylie said finally. "Dr. Shepard said that to me, about being an Outlier and being anxious and everything. There's a lot of gray in the world, Jasper. Wanting to hit someone isn't the same thing as hitting them. And hitting someone once, or even twice, doesn't mean you have to be someone who hits forever. Not everything is black and white."

Jasper looked up at Wylie then. He wasn't sure if she believed what she was saying. But he was sure that he was falling for her different than ever before. For real. In love. That maybe he was already all the way there.

INSTEAD OF WORKING out with Chance today, Jasper heads home. His mom has been asking him to come every day since he started at camp, and he's been avoiding her. Partly to get back at her. Even though, to Wylie's point, his mom is doing her best. And he should know better than anyone that your best isn't always as good as you'd hoped it would be.

"Oh, you're here!" his mom calls out as she swings open the door, like she was just sitting there, waiting for him. She's so happy that she's pumping up and down on her toes. Jasper feels like an ass. He should have come sooner.

"Yep," he says, stepping inside. "Here I am."

"Well, let me see what I have to feed you." His mom hustles toward the kitchen like she didn't just get home from a double shift at the hospital. Like she isn't probably so beat she can barely stand. "I think there's a lasagna. But that could take a while to heat up. Oh, I wish you'd told me you'd be coming today. I'd have made something special. How about grilled cheese?"

Jasper nods. "Sounds good." He hates grilled cheese. It's something his mom has always refused to know. It's right that he should be forced to eat it now as punishment.

A FEW MINUTES later, Jasper sits staring down at the sandwich that he doesn't want. But his mom is watching him, and the whole point of coming here is to make her feel better. The least Jasper can do is eat the damn sandwich. He takes a huge bite and chugs a bunch of water to wash it down.

"How was practice this morning?" his mom asks. She sounds nervous. Probably afraid of giving Jasper a reason not to come back. "The other boys on the team still okay?"

Jasper nods. And they *are* okay. Everything is okay. Sometimes he still has to remind himself. "Preseason is good, really good. You were right about it," he says. "Chance, my roommate, is a nice guy. Coach is great. A hard-ass. But great."

His mom nods and forces something of a smile. "That's wonderful," she says, but her voice catches.

"Mom, what's wrong?"

Suddenly, she grasps Jasper's hand, making him startle back. Her fingers are icy, bony. So old, all of a sudden. "I just don't want you getting distracted, that's all. Especially not after all the work you've put in getting your life back on track."

"Distracted by what?" he asks. "I was just telling you it was all good."

"By whatever." His mom's eyes dart away. Jasper can't read shit, but she is a terrible liar. "I'm just saying. You're doing well. It's a good thing. We should keep it that way."

Jasper raises an eyebrow. "Mom, what is up?"

"Nothing's 'up'!" she shouts, twisting a napkin so tight it begins to tear. Then she jerks to her feet and starts clearing the dishes. "I just worry about you. That's what a mother is supposed to do."

This is her loving me. This is her loving me, he tells himself. But it's just so hard to believe.

"Mom, I know you only want what's best for me," he says. "And you were definitely right about me needing to go to hockey camp and BC. I totally admit that. It's been really good for me to be there. So thank you for encouraging me to go."

She takes a loud breath, then smiles up at him. Her eyes are glassy. "I'm so glad."

"And I'm being straight with you now. So you be straight with me. Why are you all wound up?" he asks. "What's going on?"

His mom takes another deep breath, looks down at the table, and crosses her arms. "She's out," she says finally.

"Who's out?" Jasper's heart has begun to pound.

His mom looks up at him and shakes her head, eyes brimming with tears now. "That girl," she says, the tears finally making their way onto her cheeks. "*The* girl."

"Wylie?" Jasper almost shouts. "She's out of jail?"

His mom nods. "She called here," she says reluctantly.

"What? When?" Jasper snatches his phone and taps hard through the call log. "She didn't call me."

"Not long ago. Couple hours. She doesn't have your new number."

"You gave it to her, right?"

"I did not," his mom says firmly.

"Why not?" Jasper shouts.

"To protect you," she exclaims, like this should be the most obvious thing. "And I know it's not going to be easy to stay away. But it's already been weeks since you've seen her. You're already out of the habit. A clean break. That's all you need. Don't get yourself tied into knots again. You got out, Jasper. Keep it that way."

But Jasper is already on his feet. *She's out. She's out.* That's all he can think. "I have to go." He's moving quickly toward the door.

"Jasper!" his mom shouts after him. "You have a real chance now. Don't throw your life away for another girl."

Jasper forces himself to stay calm as he turns back at the door. He can do this. He can say no but stay kind. Respectful.

"I'll be careful, Mom," he says, opening the door behind him and backing toward it. "But I need to go see Wylie, right now."

His mom's face is slick with tears.

"Jasper!" she shouts one last time as he steps through the door. "Why do you need them all so much?"

JASPER TRIES TO steady himself as he drives toward Wylie's house in his old red Jeep—officially *his* since he paid his brother five hundred dollars for it. *Why do you need them all so much?* It's ringing in his head. Because his mom isn't wrong, in general. She's just wrong in particular about Wylie.

Jasper pauses at a stop sign as he approaches downtown Newton, meets eyes with a cop parked there, waiting for people to blow through. A reminder: be careful. But Jasper can do this. He can have Wylie in his life and keep himself on the straight and narrow. It doesn't have to be either-or.

Though it is eating at him that Wylie didn't even mention she might be getting out. He just saw her and not a word? Jasper wants not to be hurt. Wants not to feel suspicious. But he is. And he does.

Another five minutes of driving, and Jasper stops again—this time at a red light, ready to turn right toward Wylie's part of town. The so-much-nicer-than-where-Jasper-lives part. Those differences between him and Wylie don't matter. At least so far they haven't. But then Jasper and Wylie have been *together* together in a bubble. What if things are different between them in the real world? What if that's why Wylie didn't tell Jasper she was getting out? Does she have doubts?

A horn blasts behind Jasper. The light has turned green, and he's been sitting there, lost in the tangle of *Wylie loves me. She loves me not.* He startles, punches down hard on the gas, and lifts the clutch. The old Jeep hesitates before finally lurching forward.

Almost instantly, there's a vicious crunch. And then a yelp. Jasper's eyes shoot up as the horn behind him sounds again.

"Shit," he gasps, jamming the Jeep into park. He claws at his door. "Oh, shit."

He jumps out, hands shaking, heart pumping as he races around to the front of the Jeep.

"Oh God, did he hit somebody?" a man shouts from somewhere behind. "Holy crap."

Jasper sees the bike first. The wheel bent, but otherwise in one piece. And then the girl, sitting on the ground, gripping her knee. Her eyes are open. She's breathing.

He finally exhales.

"Are you okay, honey?" An old woman rushes past Jasper and kneels down next to the girl. "Don't get up. You need to take your time. Did you hit your head? You could have a concussion." The woman has short, gray hair and a frumpy tent dress. She turns and gives Jasper the most hateful stink-eye. "Were you on your phone? You were, weren't you? You could have killed somebody! You could have killed her!"

"I'm sorry. Are you okay?" Jasper asks the girl.

She looks down at herself. "Yeah, I think—"

"So stupid!" the old man piles on as he rushes up from behind.

"You honked at me," Jasper says quietly, though he knows that getting into it with them is stupid, pointless.

"I'm calling an ambulance. And the cops!" the woman barks, pulling out her phone. She looks him up and down, disgusted. "What kind of person are you?"

"It was an accident!" Jasper shouts back, his face hot. "A mistake. People make them!"

"Stupid, that's what you are." The man steps closer, spitting and red-faced. "Are you stupid?"

"Stop saying that, man," Jasper growls, his fists clenched. He swallows down the urge to use them. *Don't hit him, he's old. Don't hit him, he's old,* Jasper chants to himself. But he's not sure it is working. He can feel the punch already, the impact.

"Stop yelling! Please!" the girl shouts, startling the old couple. She waves her hands. "It was my fault. I ran the light." She pushes herself unsteadily to her feet. She is pretty and fit in her high-tech, expensive-looking bicycle clothes, even those old-school sweatbands on her wrists and, luckily, a helmet. When she takes it off, her long, dark hair falls over her shoulders. "Please don't call the police. My parents will be mad at me for not paying attention. They're always on me for that. And I'm fine anyway."

Jasper feels a guilty wave of relief. He'd be much happier, all things considered, if they didn't call the police. His mom would say this proved her point about Wylie being a bad distraction. Coach might consider it his last strike.

"I really am sorry," Jasper manages, meeting eyes with the girl for the first time. They shimmer between hazel and gold, like two small kaleidoscopes. Jasper's never seen eyes like that. For a second, he forgets what he was saying. "Um, I didn't see you."

"Well, of course you didn't see her," the woman snorts.

"You kids and your damn cell phones," her husband adds.

"I wasn't on my phone," Jasper says, and pretty mildly, considering how far up in his face they are. "I was distracted for a second and then you blew your horn—I don't know what happened. She said she went through the light."

"It was totally my fault," the girl confirms as she moves her bike off to the shoulder. The wheel is so bent. There is no way she is riding it anywhere. "I'm not used to so many traffic lights."

"I'll drive you home," Jasper offers. "We can throw your bike in the back."

He hates the idea of not going straight to Wylie's right this second. But what choice does he have? He hit this girl with his *car.*

"If anyone is going to drive her, it should be us," the woman says. "You should go get yourself some driving lessons."

The girl looks the woman right in the eye. "Thank you for stopping," she says, calm but fierce. "But if you could stop yelling, that would be great. I know it's making you feel good, but it's not helping me. I already have a headache. And maybe you should worry less about me and more about why your husband is so jacked up that he was laying on the horn like that in the first place."

"Ugh." The woman recoils, disgusted. She waves at her husband to come along. "Let's go. They deserve each other."

And with that, the two march back toward their Buick sedan.

"THANK YOU," JASPER says when the couple is finally pulling away.

The girl shrugs. "The biggest jerks always spend the most time pointing fingers."

Jasper smiles. She's right about that. "Anyway, sorry again. I'm really glad you're okay. I should have been paying more attention."

She tilts her head. "You seem really invested in jamming yourself under the nearest bus. I said I ran the light."

Jasper feels himself blush. He wants to put his hands up to his face to cover it. "Let me give you a ride home," he says. "It'll help me get out from under the bus."

She looks down at her bike, taking in how damaged it really is. Finally, she nods. "Okay."

IT ISN'T UNTIL Jasper has her bike loaded into his Jeep and is finally pulling into traffic that he thinks about Wylie again. But maybe the delay is a good thing. To calm him down. He does wish he could call Wylie to let her know he is on his way. But, conveniently, he doesn't have her number programmed into his brand-new iPhone. God, his mom is good.

"They couldn't roll over your contacts, for some reason," she had said when she gave it to him.

But he hadn't cared at the time. Wylie didn't like to talk on the phone from the detention facility. She said it was too awkward, people waiting in line, listening to your conversation. Not that he could have called her there anyway. Wylie's cell number was the only one he really cared about, and with Wylie locked away that hadn't mattered either until now.

But that's okay. He'll drop this girl wherever she wants to go, then he'll calmly and slowly drive back to Wylie's house. And he'll focus. Because even if he doesn't want it to be, hitting this girl was a reminder: bad things can happen when you're distracted. Even by somebody you love.

"I'm Lethe, by the way," the girl says, bringing Jasper back. He's been inching down Newton's main street, so totally distracted *again.*

"I'm Jasper," he says. "Where to, Lethe?"

"I'm at BC. The campus is just—"

"I know where it is," Jasper says, and too forcefully. "I mean, I just started there, too, preseason hockey camp."

Lethe smiles tentatively, motions to herself. "Lacrosse."

And Jasper feels that familiar tug—it's fate. He knows that's stupid, that *he* is stupid for feeling some kind of connection—even for a second—with some random girl he hit with his car *on the way* to see Wylie. But old habits die hard. And no one's perfect. Not Jasper. Not Wylie. Right now all he can do is be polite and responsible and get this girl *who he hit with his car* home. As fast as he can.

"Lacrosse?" he asks as he focuses again on the road. "That's cool. I would have taken you for a cyclist."

"I'd rather be a cyclist for sure," Lethe says. "But there aren't any cycling scholarships for girls. And I happen to be really good at lacrosse. So my parents are just like, 'do that,' because who I am and what I want don't even matter."

Jasper turns to look at her after he stops squarely at a red light. She seems embarrassed.

"Sorry. I probably sound like a spoiled brat," she says. "I'm grateful, don't get me wrong. I'm just also really annoyed. Does that make sense?"

"Completely," Jasper says. Lethe is describing exactly the way he feels now. "My mom works her ass off to give me, like, everything. But I still wish I had, I don't know, more options or something."

Lethe turns and looks at Jasper for a long time. "Exactly,"

she says. "You know, not that many people are willing to admit it, though. Whenever I say something like that, I always end up feeling like a monster."

Jasper smiles, shrugs. "I have low standards."

She nods. "So if you're at BC, what were you doing all the way over here?"

"I was going to see a friend," he says.

"Oh, I don't want to hold you up," she says. "If she's expecting you."

Did Lethe nail the *she* in a way that was supposed to be a flag or something, or did Jasper just imagine that?

"She's not," he says. "I was going to surprise her."

"Oh," Lethe says—and like she wants to ask something more but doesn't.

THE TWO OF them are quiet then as Jasper drives the rest of the way to campus. Finally, Lethe points toward a gate up ahead. "I'm in Mavis Hall. You can drop me on the corner. It's faster to cut through from here."

Jasper double-parks at the curb. "I'll get your bike."

It isn't until Jasper pulls the bike out of the back that he sees just how messed up it is, totally unusable, actually. When Lethe gets out, they stare down at it together.

"Let me get it fixed," he says, turning to look at her. In the sun, her eyes shimmer. "It would make me feel better."

"No, I can just . . ." But then she frowns. "Can I just say okay?"

Jasper smiles. "I hit you with my *car.* You can say whatever you want."

"Let's start with fixing the bike."

And when Lethe smiles this time, her whole face glows. She pushes her hair out of her eyes and looks down. She has a leather cuff on one wrist. It's the kind of thing that Cassie would have worn. Cassie. Wylie. Lethe? *Why do you need them all so much?* But his mom is wrong. He's just being polite with this girl. It's not an actual situation they're having. Jasper wants to be with Wylie. He cares about her, a lot.

After Jasper puts the bike back in his Jeep, he and Lethe exchange numbers. Then there is a long, strange silence in which Jasper almost tells Lethe that she should know that he is actually in love with Wylie and he is just being nice, fixing her bike. Luckily, he manages to keep his mouth shut.

"I'll call you as soon as the bike is done," he says instead. "Good luck with lacrosse."

"Thanks." Lethe smiles as she turns for the gate. "Good luck with hockey."

WYLIE

"THE HOSPITAL SENT YOUR PHONE BACK," GIDEON SAYS WHEN I FINALLY GET back downstairs from the longest shower I have ever taken. He puts the phone down in front of me on the coffee table. "I charged it for you, too. I mean, it probably has like nine kinds of tracing crap embedded on it. You should take a look at your missed messages or whatever. Then we should burn it."

Gideon thinking to charge my phone feels like the nicest thing anyone has ever done for me. I stare down at it and try not to cry.

"Thanks," I manage.

When I turn it on, one hundred and thirty-six texts flood in. Jasper accounts for 90 percent of the messages, all sent in the twenty-four hours between when he saw me grabbed on the bridge and when he finally snuck his way into the hospital and found me, all some version of "Where are you?" or "Are you okay?"

None of the messages are from today. It's already two thirty p.m. now, and I still haven't heard from him. Jasper's mom might not have told him that I called, except I have a hard time believing that—I *feel* like he knows I'm out. And yet he hasn't called, hasn't come looking. I want it not to nag at me, but it does.

After tapping onto Jasper's old messages, the number of total unread ones drops to twenty-three. A few of the others are from Gideon. They also came in while I was in the hospital, after he stormed out of the house that morning so angry at Dad and me. Before he knew anything bad had happened.

Gideon sees his messages, too. "Wait, um, I don't think I would—"

"It's okay," I say, knowing as well as he does that whatever he had to say to me then probably wasn't very nice. "I'll delete them."

"Read the one from Dad, though," he says, pointing.

"Oh," I say, surprised to see it there. "That's weird."

Because it was sent the day I was grabbed, but at three p.m., after I talked to my dad from the hospital. By then, he knew I didn't have my phone. Why would he have been bothering to send me messages? I have such a bad feeling as I tap on the message.

It's just a single word: **Cassie**. That's the whole of it. It makes me shudder.

"What does that mean?" Gideon asks. "'Cassie'?"

"I don't know."

Breathe, I remind myself. *Breathe.* But it's not easy with all the facts crowding in. First I'm drawn to Cassie's house, then Holy Cow, and now here's a text from my dad with just Cassie's name? These things have to be related. I'm just afraid to find out how.

Jasper. Now I *really* want him here. He is the only person who would truly understand why this has me so freaked out. He was the one who was with me when Cassie died. He was there with me in the hospital, as we swam away from Russo's house in the dark. But my only option to find him now would be to go to the BC campus to search. And I will if I have to, but I would so much rather he just showed up at my door. But why? What am I afraid I might find? Another girl? I wish I was more sure that wasn't exactly what I was worried about.

I turn back to my unread texts, hoping to keep myself from thinking any more about it. **Wylie, Dr. Shepard checking in. I am always here if you need to talk. Call anytime.** Five days later, while I was still in the detention facility, there is another: **Wylie, Dr. Shepard again. Getting a little concerned now that you've missed two appointments. I haven't been able to reach your dad, either. I'm sure you're fine. Just check in.** And then the last one from her, one week ago—a week into my being locked up: **Spoke to Gideon. I heard what happened. Coming to see you.**

"ARE YOU OKAY?" Dr. Shepard asked as I sat down across from her in the detention facility visiting room. "Sorry, that was a stupid question. I'm sure 'okay' isn't the best word to describe how you are. How are you feeling?"

Dr. Shepard laid her hands on the tabletop. And I so desperately wanted to grab them. I just needed so badly to know that I was going to be okay. I wanted to feel some promise seeping through the surface of her skin. But touching wasn't allowed, and I had never in my life touched Dr. Shepard. Besides, that wasn't a promise she could make.

"I didn't do this," I said.

"Of course you didn't," she said.

And she was so genuinely sure of this fact—like without an ounce of doubt. It made me start to cry. Hard and out of nowhere. I'd been working so hard to keep it together, hadn't cried once since they arrested me. But as soon as the tears started, I could not make them stop. Soon I was sobbing so loud that a guard came over to investigate. Luckily, he just kept walking.

"Sorry," I said when my tears finally slowed and I was able to take a breath.

"You don't need to apologize." Dr. Shepard reached over to give my hand a quick, forbidden squeeze. "I'd cry if I was in here, too."

"My anxiety is out of control," I said. "I can't remember what it's like to take a deep breath."

"That's understandable," Dr. Shepard said. "You've never had less control over your surroundings. How are you coping?"

"I'm not, I guess." I shrugged. "I almost passed out once. A guard told me they'd put me in solitary if I did."

Anger popped Dr. Shepard's eyes wide open.

"No, no, no," she said, with a shake of her head. And wow, was she pissed. She looked around the room, as if searching for someone to attack. "That definitely won't happen again. I'll make sure of it. They're legally obligated to make accommodations for your anxiety. *Certainly* they can't punish you for it." She took a breath, tried to calm herself. "But we should focus on what you can do in the meantime. I know that breathing exercises don't always work for you. But your options in here are limited. How about visualization? We did that once, right? Where you picture a place that makes you happy?"

"My happy place?" I asked, trying to smile.

Dr. Shepard smiled, too. "Yes, your happy place. Believe it or not, it does work."

"I'm just not sure where that is anymore," I said, and Dr. Shepard just nodded. "Can I ask you something?"

"Of course," she said, grateful for the chance to maybe have an answer for something.

"I know you can't tell me details of why you saw her or whatever because of confidentiality, but how did you meet Teresa?"

Dr. Shepard's eyebrows bunched up. "Teresa?"

"I don't know her last name. I was in the hospital with her. She told me she was your patient. She was the girl who died in the fire." Dr. Shepard looked skeptical. "She lived with her grandmother? Small with big glasses. She even talked about your red chair."

"I'm sorry, Wylie. But I've never had a patient named

Teresa. And I would remember. That's my mother's name."

"So you never sent your patients to take my dad's tests?" That's what I'd been assuming.

"My patients?" She looked shocked by the suggestion. "That would be unethical, at least potentially. Not to mention that using a sample of only people already in therapy for a psychological experiment would certainly affect your dad's results."

It wasn't until that moment that I realized how much I had made up. So many false connections, so many blanks filled in based on one wrong assumption. No, not assumption. Teresa had brought up Dr. Shepard. I wasn't inventing that.

"Oh," I said, trying not to let my mind spin out into even more troubling explanations.

"I'm sorry, Wylie," Dr. Shepard went on. "I feel as though I've let you down."

"That's okay," I said. "I was pretty let down already."

WHEN THE DOORBELL rings a second time, Gideon and I both flinch. Rachel coming back so soon doesn't feel like a good thing, not at all.

"It could be Jasper," Gideon offers hopefully.

"I don't think so," I say as I head over to look out the window alongside the door.

I blink once, hard. But unfortunately, when I open my eyes, it is still definitely Jasper's mom standing there on our front porch. Still looking pissed. I take a breath, my hand on the knob. When I finally yank open the door, it's like I'm pulling off a Band-Aid.

I am hit square in the chest by a ball of rage. Her rage.

"I am only going to say this once," Jasper's mom launches in, voice quaking. "Leave him the hell alone."

"What?" I look around for Jasper, irrationally hoping he might somehow be hidden behind her.

"Don't you *dare* play dumb with me. He's going to come here to see you. You know that as well as I do."

Defend yourself, a voice inside me commands. But how? I don't even understand why I am being attacked.

"I haven't spoken to Jasper," I say. "That's why I called you, remember? His number isn't working."

"Stupid of me to think a damn new iPhone would keep you from finding him." She shakes her head in disgust. Then points a finger at me. "Of course you had to go and call me. Because you know I can't lie to my son. You knew I'd have to tell him."

My heart catches. Jasper does know I'm out and he didn't rush straight over? He hasn't even texted. There could maybe be a million good explanations. Maybe. But all I feel is hurt.

"I haven't seen him," I say. "And I haven't spoken to him yet, either."

"*Yet,* exactly," she hisses. "Because you're planning on it. I know. Don't you see that this isn't even about you? Jasper wants to save you girls because that's the only way he feels good about himself. Because one time he couldn't save some stranger his daddy was beating on. He's trying to make up for something he didn't even do. That's the problem with trying to atone for somebody else's sins. You just end up tearing yourself apart."

And all I can do is blink at her, because that does sound *exactly* like Jasper. That is why he was with Cassie: to save her. He admitted as much to me when we were racing off to Maine. And Jasper did feel guilty he did't help that man. Have *I* become the new Cassie? Just another messed-up girl to rescue? How could I not have seen that before?

"I know I'm to blame for the way he is," Jasper's mom presses on. "I was the one who made *the* bad choice that was his father. But I can't change any of that. I can only protect Jasper right now. And that is sure as hell what I'm gonna do." She takes a step closer and puts an outstretched hand flat on the door, so I can't shut it in her face. And there's this thing about the way she's looking at me. An intensity that feels like fingers gripping my ribs, from the inside. It makes me wonder just how far she'd go to protect her son. How far she'd go to get rid of me. "You almost ruined him once. I'll be damned if you'll do it again."

"Okay," I say.

But what do I mean? That I'm actually going to stay away from Jasper because she wants me to? For how long? Forever? Weirdly, for a split second, I feel relieved. Like I've been afraid that our budding romance will run its natural course and break my heart and ducking out now would speed the inevitable along.

"Okay? What's that, 'okay'? You've actually got to do something!" she shouts so loud I flinch. Her love for Jasper is so raw and boundless and so strangely much like rage. It takes my breath away. "Tell him something he's got no choice but to believe. Something that'll make him stay away for good. Like another boy you've fallen for. That'll work."

"You want me to hurt Jasper on purpose?"

"Oh, *please*! A few days' sting to save him from a lifetime of ache? I'd make that trade any day. If you cared about him at all, you would, too. He almost *died* once trying to protect you. Isn't that enough? And before you get all flattered and confused by 'you,' if it wasn't *you*, it would be somebody else. It always is."

That's a lie. Her first one. Jasper's mom *is* worried that I might be special. That this time might be different. That's what's got her so worked up. And that tiny tell the Outlier in me can read so clearly changes everything. It makes my guilt, which is so easy for her to use, vanish instantly. It reminds me to do what my instincts said in the first place: defend myself.

"No," I say as clearly and calmly as I can.

"No?" she shouts. "What do you mean, no? You just said okay."

"I changed my mind," I say, willing myself steady in the face of her rising rage. "I won't do that to Jasper. I care about him, too, and I won't hurt him on purpose just because you want me to. And being with me doesn't mean Jasper's life has to fall apart. We could be a good thing."

Partly I am trying to convince myself. It's almost working.

"A good thing?" Her jaw is set as her eyes slice me up and down. "You know, I was once married to somebody who was out on bail. All the time, in fact. Anybody can report a bail violation—drinking, drugs, curfew, those are standard. All I'd have to do is say I saw you somewhere trying to buy beer and you'd get locked right back up. Problem solved."

My face feels hot. "You wouldn't do that."

She laughs angrily, eyes gleaming. "Try me."

"You should leave," Gideon says, stepping forward protectively. "Wylie hasn't done anything wrong. She doesn't have to do what you tell her to. And she doesn't have to listen to this."

"If she doesn't want to go back to jail, she does," Jasper's mom says, more confident now. This bail threat just occurred to her. But it's gripped now in her fist like a spear. "Make any choice you want, Wylie. But don't say you weren't warned."

She means this, too. She'd make up a lie to make it sound like I'd violated bail. And I can't risk getting sent back to the detention facility. Not with my dad still missing, and no one else very interested in making sure he's found. Jasper would understand that. He will, definitely. Once I explain. And then it will all be okay. I'll say what I have to now. There will be time to fix everything.

Too bad I don't believe any of that.

"What is it exactly that you want me to do?" I ask.

"Just a note," Jasper's mom says, trying to sound casual, but she's desperate to close the deal now that she's got me on the run. "Something real clear. Give you both a clean break, anyway. A fresh start."

"Okay, I could send—"

"No," she says. "Right now. I need you to do it now."

Jasper will understand, that's what I say to myself again. I'll write this note, and as soon as I'm not at risk of getting my bail revoked, I'll explain everything to him. And then it will be fine. Too bad it's not any more convincing this time.

I motion her inside. "Gideon, could you take Jasper's mom to the living room?"

"I'm fine standing right here," she says, excited now.

"I can't write anything with you hovering over me," I say. "Go in the living room with Gideon or go back outside, I don't care. But you can't stand there."

She stomps down the urge to bark at me. Instead, she holds up a hand. "The living room will be fine. Thank you."

I STARE DOWN at the blank page once she and Gideon have gone. No words will come. There is a small part of me, though, that has started to think maybe Jasper's mom has a point. That maybe Jasper really is better off without me. But a larger part of me still feels like the note is a bad idea. That it will set something terrible in motion. Something worse than even the end of Jasper and me.

Outlier Rule #7: Knowing something bad is going to happen isn't the same thing as knowing what it will be.

Still, I am not sure what choice I have. Jasper's mom will follow through on her threat. She will do whatever it takes to protect him. And my dad still needs me out here. I can feel both things so clearly they are like an ache. All I can do is take a deep breath as I begin to write, praying that whatever happens now was meant to be.

Dear Jasper,

Now that I'm out, I can see that my feelings for you aren't real. They were about me needing somebody who'd been there through everything. Somebody who understood the camp and losing Cassie.

Somewhere along the line, I got confused between that and something more.

But I don't have romantic feelings for you. I never did. We aren't right for each other. We have nothing in common but what we lost up in Maine. And I don't want to be with someone who is just trying to save me so they can convince themselves they are a good person.

I'm sorry. But I don't want to lie to you. What we had is over.

Wylie

By the time I am done writing, my chest is burning, and the tears have started. I wipe at my face before heading back out to the living room. I don't want to give Jasper's mom the satisfaction.

Gideon is leaning against the wall on the opposite side of the room, eyes fixed worriedly on my phone as Jasper's mom rises from the couch. She's so hopeful it makes me furious. I haven't even held the letter out as she rushes over and snatches it from my hand.

"You can read it if you wa—" But she already is. "I didn't put anything about another guy in there. Jasper would know that's a lie."

But I do wonder if I should have included a line about him being better off without me, just to soften the blow. It's so awful to think of him being hurt this way. But I also know a line like that would have made him want to convince me I was wrong.

"Okay, thank you," she says, already racing for the door.

I expect her to turn back before she goes. To offer me something in exchange for the slice of my heart I've just given her. But the front door is already slamming closed.

Gideon says something then. Words I can't hear. I'm still staring after Jasper's mom.

He says it again. This time he puts a hand on my arm.

"Hey, do you know this number?" Gideon is holding out my phone. There's a text up on the screen.

Hello? Call me back here, it says, dated two weeks earlier. It's from a Boston area code.

"No, I don't know the number," I say, my finger drawing down the screen. There are six texts in all from that same number, each sent without a response from me.

They start curious: **Hello?** Turn threatening: **What the hell is wrong with you? Don't you care about your dad?**

The last one was sent four days ago.

"Who do you think it is?" Gideon asks, and I do wish he sounded less concerned. That he *felt* less concerned.

"I have no idea," I say. "Wait, there's a voice mail from the same number."

I play the message—this one left three days ago—and put it on speaker.

"I still got his phone," the voice says. "Remembah? Your dad's. I don't know where you went, but his phone's dead now. Call me back on this numbah. And then you got to come get it. Your dad needs you. You should call me. Soon."

My dad's phone, not a dead end after all. My fingers are already tapping the call-back button when Gideon leans close. "Are you sure you should do that?"

"No," I say as the phone begins to ring.

It doesn't matter anyway. A recording starts almost immedately: *The number you have called is out of service.*

EndOfDays Blog NEWS: A New Addition to the Blog!

May 25

Dear Readers of EndOfDays,

Beginning today, in addition to commentary on the blog, we will be featuring links to all the news you need! Citing only the most trusted sources.

"Senator David Russo: A Life of Sacrifice," *McCann Report*

"The Armed Services Committee and the Fight for a Safer Tomorrow," *Daily National*

"Why We Should Care About Privacy," *Daily National*

"Cybersecurity: Get Educated," *Freedom Sentinel*

"Whatever the Cost: Senator Russo and the Cyber-Frontier," *McCann Report*

RIEL

IT'S LATE IN THE AFTERNOON WHEN THE FIREFIGHTERS ARE FINALLY FINISHED. The flames spread quickly out from Leo's room and through the old Harvard dorm. The firefighters managed to put it out in Leo's room right away; it was the rest of the building that raged on. Riel knows because for hours she has been watching, tucked up in an alcove of a nearby building, out of sight.

At first, she had been frantic, desperate to find anyone who could tell her for sure that Leo wasn't inside. By now, all these hours later, at least eight different official people have assured Riel that the building is empty—they've checked, cleared every possible space. There have been no injuries at all. It has calmed her, some.

But Riel isn't going to be completely convinced Leo is safe until she hears from him. As it is, she's texted him at least three dozen times. No response. He was on his way home, too. He should be there by now. He should have been there hours ago.

Leo has to be okay, though. Because this is all Riel's fault. She was warned. Klute told Riel to stay away from the "whole situation." He said that Leo would "pay." And sure enough, she pokes around online about those pictures, and boom: his room goes up in flames. And she just got a damn note about them. So stupid.

It isn't until the last fire truck is pulling away that Riel's phone finally vibrates in her hand. **Everything okay? Got hung up in an endless meeting with a supervisor. What's with all the messages?**

Alive. Leo is alive. Thank God.

Riel feels dizzy with relief as she types a reply. **There's been a fire in your room. I'm okay. But you should come back. Now.** If there is somebody watching, it will look better if Leo is there. And Riel is gone.

Okay. Coming. You sure you're okay?

Yeah, I'm fine. Just want to see you.

And now Riel has a second chance to do the right thing: protect Leo. And to do that, she needs to disappear. Riel comes out of the alcove she's been tucked away in and heads down the steps. There's still a decent crowd lingering in front of the building. She weaves her way through the bodies, toward the nearest campus gate.

"Excuse me!" Riel calls as she pushes forward. She hates how panicked she sounds. She feels it still, too, even though she knows now that Leo is safe. She swallows. Takes a breath. "Excuse me."

Riel is almost through the crowd when she feels something clamp around her forearm. When she looks down, there is a hand wrapped around her; on the wrist is that leather bracelet. Shit. The man from Brew. She knew she recognized him. *Make a scene*, she tells herself. *Make a scene.*

"Get off me!" she screams so loud her throat burns, yanking her arm away. But his grip is too tight. He tugs her closer.

"Where are the pictures?" he whispers harshly in her ear. But not angry, not like Klute. All this man feels is cold, hard focus. He has his hat tipped down, so she still can't get a good look at his face. But what she can see doesn't look all that familiar, vaguely maybe. Riel doesn't recognize his voice, either. And yet she still feels sure she knows him. From somewhere. Somehow.

"Get off me!" Riel shouts again, even louder. As loud as she can.

People have turned. A young woman—wispy blond hair, large glasses—steps forward. She isn't afraid to get involved.

"Hey, you!" she shouts, pointing at Riel and the man. "Let go of her!"

Other people are staring now, too. The man loosens his grip but doesn't let go. It's enough. Riel jerks her arm free and darts into the crowd.

She sprints away toward the nearest Harvard University gate. She doesn't turn back, doesn't slow down until she's run all the way to the far side of the quad. When Riel finally does check behind her, the man from Brew is nowhere in sight. A little flicker of doubt then. Like Riel is leaving the most important thing behind. She scans the crowd again for the man, hopes for a second look. But he is nowhere in sight.

Riel does eventually spot someone, though. Way in the

distance. Agent Klute, standing at the edge of the crowd in front of Leo's dorm, staring right back at her.

Riel grips her bag with her computer and Wylie's photos as she spins in the opposite direction, racing through an alley between two dorms to the nearest gate, and then the street beyond. She'll dive down into the nearest T station. Or disappear into the maze of crooked Cambridge alleys. Riel knows how to get lost if she needs to. She's a genius at not getting found.

Riel checks one last time at the steps of the T. No Agent Klute. No man with a bracelet. Nothing but the smoke rising in the distance from Leo's dorm.

And Riel. Once again, all alone.

DOWN IN THE T station, Riel jumps on the first train. It's headed toward Beacon Hill, it turns out, with its overpriced boutiques and expensive coffee shops, as good a place as any to get lost.

Once she's off the train and up on the crowded sidewalk—bustling with fancy old ladies and moms in yoga pants pushing expensive strollers—Riel checks over her shoulder again. Still no Agent Klute, no man with the bracelet. No one at all. She spots a sign halfway down Newbury Street: *Trident Booksellers & Café.* It feels like that's where Riel was headed all along: free Wi-Fi, a café, thoughtful, bookish people likely to intervene if someone else tries to drag her off.

Inside, the bookstore is a cheerful double-wide townhouse with lots of reclaimed wood and handwritten signs. It smells of pine. There is a girl with a high ponytail and square thick-framed glasses behind the register. She's reading when Riel steps inside: *Animal Farm*. She smiles as Riel slides by, headed for the café.

She needs to check her phone. On the walk from the T to the bookstore, it vibrated three times—three texts from Leo, surely. He's probably at campus now and can't find her. She needs to tell him not to worry, to explain why she left. But she can't bring herself to, not yet. Because she will need to say good-bye, too. For good. Or at least for a while. For Leo's sake.

Once she's upstairs in the café, Riel orders the most expensive coffee on the menu, hoping it will buy her more time to sit there unbothered, then tucks herself into a corner where no one can sneak up on her. She opens her laptop. It's a risk being online again, of course. But it's a risk not to get some answers, too. Like what the hell does her grandfather have to do with any of this? And the first rule of any reconnaissance mission? Cast a wide net. *Senator David Russo*, she types.

The first article that pops up is a feature from *Cigar Aficionado*, posted online only hours earlier. It's a profile of her grandfather and his clock collecting. Riel remembers her mother talking about it once, but in a way that sounded like an insult. More attention to those stupid timepieces than he ever paid to an actual person, something like that. According to the article, her grandfather has recently started collecting compasses, too, after getting one as a gift from a corporation whose board he once sat on years ago, long before he was a senator.

"I love my clocks, but they're always losing time," the article quotes him as saying. "Even in the harshest conditions, compasses always find their true north."

There is a picture of him to go along with the article. Out

in his workshop with his tool belt on, looking like a kindly old grandfather, devoting his time to fixing broken-down things. It has nothing to do with the person he really is, of course. Looking at the picture makes Riel feel ice cold.

She closes out of the article and returns to her original search, scanning for some connection between her grandfather and the Outliers. Something that proves she's right that he's behind Agent Klute, behind all of it. Something that also hints at why he wants those pictures so bad that he's willing to kill to get them. Because even if he'd known that Riel and Leo weren't in the room, the dorm itself was filled with people. A fire was a huge risk.

But combing through everything about her grandfather is not an easy task; there are *a lot* of articles about him in the last year. One stands out, though. It's about a critical military research spending bill that is in front of the Senate Armed Services Committee, research intended to protect against future invasions into citizen privacy. The article itself is so terribly written, which may be why it catches her eye. Just a bunch of words strung together so they sound impressive but don't amount to much. That article links to another about her grandfather being on the Armed Services Committee for years. It's filled with praise and more praise. So totally over-the-top that it doesn't even read like it could be real. When Riel finally clicks through all the layers of both articles, she finds a random blog linked to both—EndOfDays—that looks like it's curating a bunch of news sites, but actually, once Riel does some more digging, seems to be creating all the content. But it isn't until Riel clicks back to her original list of search results that she finally spots the thing that matters most, something from a reputable newspaper: "Senator

Russo Officially Announces Candidacy for President."

Riel holds her breath as she reads the headline again. Only one week old. This was always a possibility, she supposes, her grandfather running for the highest office. But in the way that getting hit by a car is always a possibility. Something so terrible you don't let yourself think too much about it.

Riel's phone vibrates with yet another text.

Riel holds her breath as she finally digs her phone out.

Where are you? Are you okay? Leo's text reads. **Please answer. I'm starting to freak out.**

She quickly types out a response. **I am okay. But you need 2 be REALLY careful. You are not safe. Got to ghost for now. I love you.**

Riel's stomach twists after she hits send. The first time she's told Leo she loves him, just as she's saying good-bye. She shouldn't have wasted so much time. She should have told Leo earlier how she felt—when there was still a chance for it to matter.

Riel opens the back of the phone, plucks out the SIM card, cracking it in half as she walks over to the garbage. She flinches as it strikes the bottom with a hollow sound.

As Riel makes her way back to her table, she tries again to picture the man from Brew, the one with the hat who grabbed her. She couldn't see much of his face either time. But it wasn't actually his face she recognized anyway. It was the shape of his body, the way he held himself. *Where? Who?* And then, suddenly, she knows.

Kendall.

"That's Kendall. The police guy," Brian had said as they watched the live stream of what was happening at the camp. Because by then Riel was already suspicious of Quentin. That was why she'd had Brian plant the cameras before leaving. "Wait, what's he holding?"

"It's a gun," Riel said, feeling sick.

The rest happened so fast: Kendall out of the frame, a popping sound, a wounded old woman stumbling into view. Riel had been the one to send the police to the camp. Anonymously, of course. By then, Level99 had cut the camera feed, couldn't risk it being traced. It wasn't until hours later that they picked up chatter on the police frequencies: everybody at the camp was dead.

Kendall's face wasn't easy to make out in the video. But the way he moved with that huge gun was unforgettable. Smooth, forceful authority. It was him at Brew, and then later outside Leo's dorm with his hand on her. Riel is sure of it. And realizing that the man who grabbed her is the same man who killed all those innocent people should terrify her. But the truth is, she feels relieved. Hopefully that means Kendall is somebody on their side. That Riel can feel it, even if the evidence is thin. Because right now, people on her side feel in really short supply.

RIEL WAS ELEVEN and Kelsey eight when they met their grandfather for the first time.

"You girls remember your granddad," their mom had said with a razor-sharp edge. "Oh, wait, no, of course you don't, because he's never met you. What are you doing here?"

"Can't I stop by and say hello to my daughter?" their grandfather said, smiling hard as he stood in their living room with his coat still on.

Their mom crossed her arms. "Well, I think that depends."

She ended up inviting him for dinner when he wouldn't leave but also wouldn't explain why he had come. It was obviously a token offer meant to get him to go. But he took her up on it anyway. He waved some signal out the door to his driver, who kept his shiny black Mercedes sedan idling at the curb for the full two hours.

The dinner was miserable, endless and awkward—their mother making hostile small talk as their father quietly seethed. The feeling was mutual, too. Their grandfather didn't look once in their dad's direction.

After they were excused from the dinner table, the girls sat on the top step, listening. Waiting for their grandfather's terrible secret to be revealed. Because he was definitely there for a reason, the girls had no doubt about that.

"Does he seem kind of . . . ," Kelsey began in a hushed whisper.

"Evil?" Riel finished her thought. From their grandfather, Riel had felt only cold, dead nothing. Like oozing tar. "Yeah, I'd be careful reading him. Your heart might stop."

"Oh no, I left our book down there," Kelsey said. Riel had driven it into her sister to be cautious with their journal. Even if she didn't know why. Riel felt sure it should be guarded at all times.

"It's okay, I think they're done," she said, knowing

it would do nothing to come down on super-sensitive Kelsey now. "He should be leaving soon."

Except their grandfather didn't leave—like their dumbfounded parents surely both intended as they excused themselves to the kitchen to clean up. Instead, he headed to the living room, where they could hear him walking around. Picking things up and putting them down.

"So, the reason I'm here," their grandfather began finally when their parents had returned. "I wanted to let you know that I'm running for the Senate."

"What?" their dad laughed.

"Yes, senator from Arizona." Their grandfather was deadly serious. And pissed that their dad had laughed. His anger shot up the stairs like a bullet.

"You just moved there," my mom said.

"Ten years nearly," he said. "Long enough for it to be my home."

"A senator?" Their dad's disgust had ripened into anger. It felt hot and sharp, too, even all the way up the steps. "Why?"

"I believe I have a legitimate chance of winning." Their grandfather sounded so smug. "And that I ought to try."

"Because you have a chance of winning?" their dad huffed. "Sounds like a great reason for devoting your life to public service."

"Not just a chance of winning," their grandfather corrected. "A *legitimate* chance. I don't know that I will, of course. But you miss one hundred percent of the shots you don't take."

"So it's a game?" Their mom's voice was sad in a way Riel didn't understand.

"A game implies chance," he said. "This is more of a contest of skill. Spoils to the victor."

They went back and forth like that, taking swipes at each other for what felt like forever. Until all the polite barbs had been used up and only the impolite ones were left.

"It's late," their grandfather said finally, just before they launched into those. "I suppose I should go. I do hope I can count on your support, though. I would imagine there may be questions, requests for interviews directed your way and such. There are only you and your sister now as my family." Dead silence followed. Riel could picture her mom staring hard at their grandfather in disbelief. "Well, I'll see myself out then."

Their grandfather looked up the steps on his way out the door. Met eyes with Riel. That heavy tar filling her lungs.

"Ignorance is strength," he said with a smile. And then he raised a fist in the air.

Just three words that made no sense. But they felt nasty, icy. Brutal. They made the hairs on Riel's arms stand right on end.

IGNORANCE IS STRENGTH, Riel Googles now. After all her searching about her grandfather, this is where her mind has stuck. That has got to mean something. And it will be her last search, she promises herself. It has to be. She is running out of time. She will not risk Leo more by poking around in places online that she shouldn't. Places that could be easily traced on the bookstore's wide-open public Wi-Fi. Riel will have to find out whatever else she needs another way. But then before she can think any more about what next, there it is. Right there at the top of the search results: *Top ten quotes from the novel* 1984.

Riel closes her eyes. Fuck. The book. *Their* book. That's what their grandfather had been doing while he was all alone in the living room that night. He'd been reading their damn book. That's how her grandfather, Senator Russo, knows about the Outliers: from Riel. Or not about the Outliers. No, but the idea. The seed had been planted in his mind. The possibility. Way back then.

Riel is on her feet now, staring down at her computer. Hand gripping her stomach. She doesn't remember standing. But she is. Riel looks around the bookstore café—no Kendall or Klute, no other threat. There is just a mother and her kids now on the opposite side of it. Nothing else has changed.

And yet, everything has. Riel can see it now. Time is moving in reverse. The beginning where Riel thought the end had been.

That moment with her grandfather so long ago was way before any of Dr. Lang's studies. What had the charming Senator Russo done with the innocent ramblings of two little girls? Something terrible, Riel knows that much. Now she has to figure out what—but in a way that keeps Leo safe.

She slides her laptop into its case, and when the woman is distracted by her younger child, drops that, too, into the garbage can before heading downstairs from the café.

"YOU FIND EVERYTHING you're looking for?" the girl behind the register at the front of the store calls as Riel passes on her way toward the door.

There's something about the way the girl does it, too. Calling after Riel when she is already almost gone. Like it's about way more than even she realizes.

Riel pauses, turns back. What does she need that this girl could give her? Why did this girl feel compelled to offer? A bookstore. A book. An author. That's it, no doubt.

"Could you look up something for me?" Riel asks.

"Sure," the girl says, stepping over to her computer.

"Rosenfeld," Riel says, spelling it out for her. "He's the author. The book was something about the military."

"Sure, no problem," the girl says, but keeps her eyes on Riel, narrows them, concerned. "Are you okay?"

The girl's an Outlier for sure.

"I don't know," Riel says because that's the goddamn truth.

"Yeah." The girl nods finally like she understands completely. She turns back to the computer. "Rosenfeld. Here it is." She turns the screen around so Riel can see for herself. "*A Private War: How Outsourcing Is Changing the Face of the Military*. It's on the recent nonfiction paperback shelf. Come on, let me help you find it."

WYLIE

DETECTIVE OSHIRO SITS IN OUR LIVING ROOM, EYEING GIDEON AND ME nervously. It's just past four thirty p.m., and he's been looking at us that way for the entire fifteen minutes he's been here. He came fast when I called, but now he mostly wants to dart for the door. I can feel that much loud and clear.

I've tried to explain enough about what's going on to get his help tracking down my dad's phone, but not so much that he gets completely freaked out. It's easier said than done. In the story Oshiro knows about me, I am the grieving daughter of a dead mother. Which is kind of still true, at least the grieving part. So I have no plans to tell him that my mom is actually alive. That I was right—in the end—about the vodka bottle. Oshiro feeling sorry for me is probably the biggest thing I have going for me.

"But, to clarify, you *are* out on bail?" he asks hesitantly. "Legally?"

He won't be in the room if I'm a fugitive. Oshiro has already decided that. But this is exactly why I trust him. Because he has his limits. Oshiro was willing to refuse to show me the accident file until he had permission, even when yes was all I wanted to hear. He cares about what is right most of all. I believe, in the end, that will work in our favor.

"Yes, I am officially out on bail," I say, glancing in Gideon's direction. He nods dutifully. "Also, I didn't have anything to do with the fire. You don't have to believe me on that part, but it is true."

Oshiro nods noncommittally. "And you say that everything that has happened, including your mother's accident, is somehow related to this research your father does?" He's not trying to hide how skeptical he is. I respect that, too.

"I don't have proof yet, but yes," I say. "My dad is an official missing person, though. You can ask the DC police."

"I already did," he says. "That's the reason I'm here. Your story checked out. Some of it at least. Listen, Wylie, I'll help you in any way I can. *Legally.* But jurisdictionally, your dad's case belongs to the DC police. I can't take over." And, boy, is he relieved, that's the truth.

"Oh," I say, and my throat seizes so sharply I let out a sad little hiccup. It's pitiful.

Oshiro exhales. "Listen, why don't you tell me what you need help with exactly," he says. "And then we'll see."

"Would it be possible to trace a phone number?" I hold out my cell to him and point toward the call log. "We tried calling the number back, but it's out of service now. She's the person who found my dad's phone right after he disappeared, in some market in DC. Or at least that's what she said when I called his phone and she answered. She called and texted a bunch more times while I was in the detention facility from this number. One of her messages said that my dad needs me."

"Who is she?"

"I don't know. When we spoke the first time, she gave me a name and a PO box. I wrote it down and we passed it on to the police. But that was weeks ago. When you call my dad's phone now it just goes to voicemail, and mailbox is full. Her name was something with a J—or maybe an L or a K. I'm sorry. Sorry, I don't remember anymore. A lot has happened. But I know the police never found her. Or my dad's phone. I really need to, though. There could be—who knows what's on it? Texts, notes—there could be some real evidence that helps find him."

Detective Oshiro rubs a hand across his face. "Have you reached out to the officers in DC on your dad's case?" he asks. "Following up on something as basic as this would be protocol."

"I've called them," I say. And I did. True, it was only moments ago, and I was glad when I didn't reach them. But still not a lie, technically. "I'm sure they're doing the best they can, but I kind of feel like they've written my dad off. They have this surveillance video of him getting into some guy's car 'willingly.' My lawyer has talked to them. It's like they've decided he just ran off. But he wouldn't do that. Not to us. And not after what happened to our mom."

Now I feel officially sick. Because that is me actually pushing the lie about my mom being dead. It's also a reminder about what my mom has actually done: run off totally, voluntarily. I still can't believe it. Or maybe I just don't want to. I'm not sure right now that I can tell the difference.

Oshiro stares at me. "I've met your dad and I agree. I don't think he would do that." He holds out a hand. "Okay."

"Okay?" It takes me a moment to realize he's motioning for the phone. "You mean you'll trace the calls?"

"I can't make any promises. The tech department has a list of priority cases, and given that your dad's isn't even in our jurisdiction . . . It could take a couple of days, at least."

"A couple days?" My heart sinks. "I'm just—I'm worried that he's running out of time."

It isn't until I've said it that I realize just how afraid of that I am. It's like there's a giant clock ticking down in my head. Oshiro sighs again, then rubs at his forehead some more. He isn't a wait-it-out kind of person, either. He is meticulous and relentless.

"There is one other option," he says, already filled with second thoughts. "It wouldn't be official. And I'm not promising I'll be able to arrange it. . . ."

"Please, yes, anything," I say. There is a desperate burn at the back of my throat. "Whatever it is."

"I'll try. Again, no promises." Oshiro stands and nods. I feel him consider saying one comforting thing and then another—none of which I can get a fix on—before he decides to say nothing. I'm grateful. "I'll be in touch, Wylie. In the meantime, be careful, okay? Don't violate your bail conditions. They won't care how good you think your excuse is."

• • •

"NOW WHAT?" GIDEON asks once Oshiro has left and taken my phone.

"Find Quentin," I say, but halfheartedly. My mind keeps going back to him, but how would we even begin?

"I thought we didn't even know his real name," Gideon says.

"We don't. We know absolutely nothing."

"Oh," Gideon says, a little let down. He still thinks being an Outlier means I have so many more answers than I do. "Maybe it's for the best."

"But," I say hesitantly. "I do have one idea."

I just wish I felt more convinced it was a good one.

A BLOCK AWAY from the Level99 house I see the sign: *D & G Construction.* It's stuck into the lawn on top of a fresh pile of dirt. But aside from the sign and the dirt—which definitely screams remodel—the house looks exactly the same. Sloped steps, faded blue-gray paint, the buzzer with all its code-ready numbers.

I take a deep breath and try to remember the sequence as we head up the steps. On purpose, I didn't practice in the car. I was too worried that overthinking would make me forget. Instead, I press the numbers as they come to me. And then we wait. One minute, then two. Nothing.

"This happened the last time," I say, trying not to feel discouraged. I'd been so intent on not bringing Riel back into this by mentioning her to Rachel. But for some reason—maybe not a good one—I've given myself a pass suddenly. I'm still trying to figure out why.

I punch the numbers a second time. But still the door stays closed. Now my stomach is officially tight. I'd been getting my hopes up about Riel and Level99. I hadn't realized how high until this moment, as they free-fall to the floor.

Gideon leans closer to peer through the front bay window. The paper that had been covering the inside of the windows on the ground floor is gone. You can see clear inside. "Was it empty before?" Gideon asks, his voice muffled against the glass. "Because it looks like they moved out. There's nothing in there."

I come to lean over and look myself. The furniture was old and run-down when I was there with Jasper. But there was furniture. Now there's nothing but dust balls gathered on the floor.

"It does look like they're gone," I say.

Riel said that Level99 might have to move, now that Kendall knew where they were. Still, I don't really feel like they're gone. It doesn't matter, though, if they refuse to come to the door.

"Okay," Gideon says. "What next?"

WHEN WE ARRIVE at Delaney's it's only six p.m., early for a college bar. The place is empty, except for one nondescript old white guy—smallish, khakis, white head of hair—sitting at the bar near the door. Definitely not a student.

Delaney's looks way more run-down in the fading daylight than it seemed late at night when Jasper and I were there. The red paint is chipped, the wallpaper peeling. It smells ever so slightly, too, of something that could be vomit. On the upside, there's no bouncer in sight.

Gideon's phone alerts him to a text right after we've stepped in the door. He pulls it out and looks down.

"Rachel," he says, and then reads it aloud. "'I hope you guys will be right home? In the meantime, got the attached from your mom.'" He taps on the screen. "It's an email. Addressed just to you and not both you and me, which is totally a nice touch." But Gideon is way more hurt than annoyed. "Do you want to read it?"

"Yeah, but after we're done here." Though the truth is, I'm not sure I do. Every one of my mom's explanations just makes me feel worse.

I spot Leo at the far end of the bar, drying glasses and stacking them on a high shelf. He doesn't look in our direction as we approach, though he must have seen us come in. And as we get close, I can feel his hostility. High and sharp, like a barbed-wire fence.

"I just need to talk to her," I say quietly when he still does not look our way.

Leo shakes his head, keeps his eyes down. And for a split second, I feel his contempt overtaken by heartbreak. Something has happened to Riel? I pray it has nothing to do with Quentin. It was one thing not to tell Jasper about Quentin being alive—but Riel? Maybe I should have had Gideon warn her right away, while I was still in detention.

"You know, you're not the only person who's had some hard shit in their life," Leo spits out, finally looking my way. "Riel was actually doing okay for like five seconds. Living her life. Surviving. And then you showed up, acting like she owed you."

I would expect to feel shamed or guilty, but suddenly, all I am is mad.

"She *did* owe me." I am trying to keep my anger in check. But it's expanding out like foam. "She almost got me killed at the camp? Remember? Because I do."

Leo hesitates with his hand on a glass, a vicious reply lashing through his mind. But instead of saying it out loud, he looks over at Gideon, suspicious suddenly. It's not worth trying to get Leo to trust Gideon, too. He doesn't even trust me.

"Can you give us a minute?" I ask Gideon.

Gideon eyes Leo in return. "Sure thing," he says finally, heading to the front of the bar to sit next to the old man.

"Quentin's alive," I say, once Gideon is gone. "I thought Riel should know. He could be anywhere."

"Can't you just leave her alone?" Leo asks.

"Did you hear me? Quentin's alive, and I don't know where he is. Riel could be in danger."

Of course, that's not the only reason I'm there. It's not even the main one. The ugly truth is that I want Riel's help, Level99's help tracking Quentin down. And yes, maybe then my dad's phone or that girl who had it if Oshiro has no luck. But then how guilty am I really supposed to feel? Riel is an Outlier. This is her situation, too.

"I'm not telling you shit," Leo says, glaring at me so hard now I feel pressure on my face. "Anyway, I couldn't even if I wanted to."

"What do you mean?"

"Riel ghosted," he says, and I can feel his chest catch. He misses her that much. "There was a fire in my room. And she freaked. Probably trying to protect me, is my guess."

"A fire?"

"Yep. Ruined most of my shit. We weren't there when it happened."

There is a loud burst of laughter then from the front of the bar. It sets my teeth on edge. Both Leo and I look over. It's Gideon and the old man, deep in best-buds conversation, apparently.

"You should go," Leo says. "You've already caused enough trouble."

He goes back to work behind the bar, resting something down at his feet so that he is out of view for a minute. It's while he's out of sight that I feel his nervous twitch, a guilty pang. There is something else he thinks he should be telling me. But he's torn about it.

"If you hear from her, could you—"

"No," Leo says when he stands, and I don't know whether I'm getting used to his anger or if he feels less angry. But the blowback's not as intense anymore. "I won't tell her anything for you."

"Not even about Quentin?"

I wait for him to say okay, to at least acknowledge Quentin on the loose is troubling. But he just keeps on with his work behind the bar, ignoring me. I stand there for one long, awkward moment more.

"Okay, then," I say, before turning for the door.

"Hey!" Leo calls after me once I'm a few steps away. "Take this around back if you're headed out."

Leo has set a milk crate full of empties on the bar. And for a second, I think he must be joking. But the look on his face is deadly serious.

"What?" I ask.

"Take it out," he repeats like it's the most normal thing in the world to be asking me to do. Like I work there.

But it's so weird, the whole thing, that I do the only thing I can think of. I say, "Okay."

The crate is lighter than I expect when I lift it off the bar, but it smells so strongly of rancid beer that I have to hold my breath to carry it, hoping that it doesn't drain onto my shoes.

"Put them in the recycling," Leo says. "All of them. You can leave the crate out back. Just make sure it's empty."

I raise my eyebrows but bite my tongue. Mostly because next to Leo's contempt I sense something else: intent. This request isn't an accident. My gut says just to do what he wants, even if I don't understand. "Yeah, um, sure."

"Tell that guy you're with that he shouldn't be so chatty," Leo says, locking eyes with me. *Get out. Get out.* That's what he's feeling. "It's not good for anybody."

GIDEON LOOKS AT me and my milk crate full of beer bottles when I've finally made my way over to him. He makes a face. "What the hell?"

I shrug helplessly as I hold the crate awkwardly away from my body. The old man glances in my direction but doesn't meet my eyes. Still, I feel the most awful chill. From him, because of what Leo told me about the fire, because I hate finding yet another dead end. At this point, who knows.

"We should go," I say quietly.

"Sure thing." Gideon turns back to the man—casual, friendly. Totally clueless, of course. "It was nice to meet you." He raises a fist. "Stay strong."

• • •

"WHAT WAS THAT?" I ask when we're outside.

Gideon shrugs. "We were just talking about some story that came on the news about how credit card companies know everything about us. Like the FBI. They were saying they could predict who's likely to commit a crime, get divorced, all sorts of crazy stuff, based on your shopping habits."

"And 'stay strong'?"

"Oh, he was all fire and brimstone about how this was the kind of thing that was going to ruin civilization as we know it." Gideon laughs. "Crazy conspiracy dude. But fun to talk to."

"Sounds hilarious."

Gideon takes the crate of bottles from me.

"So, what's with the garbage duty?"

"Leo asked me to throw them out," I say, and now that we're out the door it feels even weirder.

"That's kind of random, isn't it?" Gideon asks.

"It's something, for sure."

GIDEON AND I walk on in silence the rest of the way back down the alley alongside Delaney's. We pass through where Jasper and I sat waiting weeks ago. *Jasper. The note.* Every time I think of what I wrote to Jasper, my chest aches. I can't say for sure it was the wrong thing to do under the circumstances. But nothing about it was right.

Once we get to the recycling bins, Gideon crouches down and starts pulling the bottles out and tossing them. He feels sorry for me now. Like actual pity—so sudden and out of nowhere—that it's all I can do not to cry.

"Maybe that old guy was onto something," Gideon says, trying to sound cheerful.

"What do you mean?"

"Sometimes the more you try to figure things out, the harder they are to understand."

"He said that?"

"Not exactly. Some quote: 'Ignorance is strength.'"

"Ignorance is strength," I repeat. And there it is, lodged in my heart like a dart. "What does that even mean?"

Gideon shrugs. "Less is more, maybe. I think. I don't really—" He's frozen, hand in the box as he stares down.

I lean closer, afraid to see what's there. "What is it?"

Gideon reaches in and lifts out a plastic folder, closed with a flap and an elastic tie. "I don't know." He holds it out to me. "But it's got your name on it."

To: Wylie
From: SwimTeacher
Re: July 2

Dear Wylie,

I know Rachel will explain everything she can, but I wanted to tell you a little more about why I'm not there. I've been trying to find people who would agree to stand behind your dad's research, who will help get the word out. Because you know they are going to try to make it go away. And I don't think they care who gets hurt.

I already saw Dr. Oduwole once, she's the neuroscientist from UCLA your dad has been working with. I need to see her again. Now. Together she and I are going to figure out how to get your dad's research out, right now. That's why I need to be out here right now.

Rachel knows what she's doing, though. She saved my life. And then she kept me alive. She will do the same for you.

I love you so much. More soon.

XX,
Mom

JASPER

JASPER SITS IN THE LITTLE WAITING ROOM—FOUR CHAIRS, ONE PLANT, AND A huge bottle of hand sanitizer next to a basket of pens and some clipboards.

He didn't remember his appointment with Jason until after he dropped off Lethe. And he would have taken a pass and gone straight to Wylie's if he hadn't also gotten a text from his coach at almost the exact same time: **Mandatory team meeting 7:30 p.m.** No way can Jasper miss that meeting. That's the kind of strike that would finish him. And he can't exactly claim that he's juggling Wylie and life if he lets that happen.

There's not enough time to go over to Wylie's and back before the team meeting. But there is still enough time to make his appointment. And so, maybe it's fate. Jasper'll keep his session with Jason, go to his meeting, and *then* go get the girl. Because despite what his mom thinks, Jasper can do this—he can be with Wylie and still keep his life on track.

Besides, Wylie is actually good for him. Jasper went to therapy at the free campus counseling center in the first place because she suggested it. And not just to work out his guilt about Cassie and what happened on the bridge—though that was a decent reason in and of itself. Wylie thought he should deal with all the baggage he was still dragging around about his dad. And he knew she was right.

After one session with his therapist—a chill dude with a beard and a plaid shirt who looked like he should be brewing beer in his basement—Jasper wondered what took him so long. In two weeks, he has seen Jason four times. And he feels four times better. It's not like Jason necessarily has answers. But he is seriously good at helping Jasper figure out the questions.

"Biology isn't destiny, Jasper," Jason said at their first appointment. "There's life experience and, you know, free will. Even if you have a tendency to get too angry too fast, you are not doomed to end up like your dad."

Jasper had tried telling himself that before, lots of times, but Jason was an actual trained professional. Hearing it from him made a difference.

"Hey, Jasper." Jason appears now in the door to his little office. "Come on in."

Jasper makes himself comfortable on Jason's couch, or as comfortable as he can be. Because therapy is helping him, but that doesn't mean it's super enjoyable.

"Wylie is out," Jasper begins before Jason even has his

notepad in hand. Jason knows the whole story—what happened at the camp with Cassie, and then on the bridge, and then later at the hospital. And he has done a good job of not seeming shocked or skeptical or whatever, no matter how he might really feel.

"That's what you've been hoping for, right?" Jason's face stays still, like he's got no personal opinion on the matter whatsoever. "Have you seen her?"

"Not yet. I was on my way to her house earlier, but I ended up hitting this girl with my car," Jasper says. Out loud it sounds way worse. But it's still a relief to admit what happened. "She's okay and everything, luckily. She even said it was her fault. That she pulled out in front of me. But I also wasn't paying attention."

"So, you still feel responsible?"

"I hit her with *my* car," Jasper says. "So, yeah. I mean, I *am* responsible."

"Even if the one person in a position to truly let you off the hook—the person you hit—says you aren't?" This isn't a judgment, even though Jasper feels like it is. It's an actual question.

Jasper shrugs. "She was just trying to be nice."

"Or you're keeping yourself on the hook," he says.

"Why would I do that?" Jasper asks. Not *no way!* Or *that can't be!* Because it feels like Jason might be right.

"I don't know. Why do you think?"

This is a therapist thing. You don't have to be a genius or go to therapy for very long to pick up on it. They ask you questions that they definitely already know the answer to. It's stupid. But, man, does it totally work.

"I don't know why," Jasper says.

"Well." Jason considers. "Any guesses?"

Jasper shrugs. Then he says the only thing he can think of. "I guess it feels like I'm beating other people to the punch."

Holy crap. That is *exactly* why Jasper does it. How has he never realized it before?

"That makes sense," Jason says.

"Shouldn't it make me feel better?" Jasper asks. "I mean, to realize it now. Like relieved or something?"

"I don't know," Jason says. "How does it make you feel?"

Jasper's throat starts to burn. "Sad."

"Sad can be an okay starting place, you know. It can get you someplace good eventually."

Maybe, but right now Jasper needs to change the subject from him being sad. Because he is actually a little worried he might cry. And therapy is one thing. Bawling in therapy is another. Also, he needs to get to talking about Wylie. Jasper's relationship with her is the bigger issue right now.

"Do you think it's wrong to need people?" Jasper asks. "My mom says that I need girls too much."

Jason tilts his head to the side, considering again. "I guess it depends on what it is you need them for."

"To make me feel better." Jasper knows this, though he would deny it to his mom until his last breath.

"Most people enjoy other people's company. There's nothing wrong with that."

"What if I need them to make me feel like I'm a good person?"

"Then I'd say we should work on you feeling like a good person regardless," Jason says. "Because you deserve to feel that way. But you needing Wylie doesn't mean you two can't also have a good relationship. The two aren't mutually exclusive."

And as soon as Jason says it, Jasper realizes it's true: Wylie is the perfect girl *for him.* And, yeah, maybe they are still working stuff out. But Wylie is different. What they have is.

JASPER IS ON a high as he leaves Jason's office. He's really ready to go see Wylie now. He checks his watch. Just enough time to stop back at his room before meeting with his coach at seven thirty p.m., then he'll head right to her. One of his teammates must have screwed up—got drunk, got into a fight. If it was hockey-related, the meeting would be at the rink after practice. But the coach said a quick meeting. Jasper will be where he's supposed to be and then he'll be on his way to Wylie's.

And, yeah, he is a little nervous. Getting to know each other with no table in between, no guards hovering nearby will be different for Jasper and Wylie. But they're ready for what they can be.

As soon as Jasper is upstairs in his dorm hall, he spots something taped to his door. He picks up the pace, but it isn't until he's standing right in front of his room that he can see it's an envelope held up by a torn strip of masking tape. Jasper's name is written in big awkward letters on it.

He peels the envelope off the door and rolls the tape between his fingers, takes a deep breath as he tears it open. Weird notes never mean good things. These days, they are definitely bad.

Dear Jasper . . . His eyes jump to the signature at the bottom of the note: *Wylie.*

For a second, Jasper's dumb-ass heart leaps, but then he starts to read. The note is definitely in Wylie's handwriting. Jasper reads it once, then blinks and stares hard at the terrible words. Reads it a second time. It doesn't sound like Wylie. Except it *is* her. There's no denying it's her handwriting.

Jasper is still staring down at the letter—the shitty, shitty letter—trying to understand it. *We aren't right for each other.* No, he's not trying to understand it. He's just trying to make it go away.

There's a loud sound then at the far end of the hall. Jasper's eyes shoot up and catch a glimpse of someone—Wylie, maybe—moving fast out the door to the stairs.

"Wait!" he shouts after her. His voice sounds so desperate echoing down the empty hall.

Jasper feels desperate, too, as he runs toward the door. But he and Wylie can still work things out. She's just having doubts. That's totally cool. He has them too. But Jasper can see so clearly what he and Wylie could be.

The door to the stairs at the far end of the hall is easing shut when Jasper finally reaches it. But he can hear footsteps on the stairs.

"Wylie!" he calls down.

Silence.

"Wylie!" he calls again. But the only answer is the sound of the door at the bottom, slamming shut.

TOP SECRET AND CONFIDENTIAL

To: Senator David Russo

From: The Architect

Re: Opposition Research

April 14

Awareness and identification continue to be the areas that need improvement in campaign projections. In layman's terms, the average voter doesn't know enough about you. 64 percent polled have no immediate association between you and any one issue. For comparative purposes, 75 percent recognize Senator Lana Harrison (CA)'s name and 58 percent identify civil liberties as her principal issue.

To be successful in a nationwide contest, you must move aggressively toward a single target issue. Polling indicates that your comments about privacy and security resonate with more than 75 percent of the American public. We recommend that "privacy and security" become the cornerstones of your campaign.

Please review the attached and we can discuss the details and further polling in our next meeting.

RIEL

THERE'S A GIRL WORKING THE DESK AT THE HARVARD UNIVERSITY POOL—PRETTY, with straight brown hair and very pink lips. Perfect makeup aside, though, the girl is a mess. Riel can feel it the second their eyes meet. Somebody has broken her heart. It's only one thing about her, but it's the only thing Riel needs.

"I think my boyfriend is here to see a girl he's been cheating on me with." Riel leans over the desk like the two are on the same team. "She's a swimmer. I don't have my ID, but I really need to bust them together."

The girl's eyes are already wide as two boys come in through the door behind Riel, gym bags over their shoulders. Both Riel and the girl turn to glare at them as they flash their IDs. *Men are all such assholes.* Or something like that. That's how the girl feels. And these days, Riel doesn't necessarily disagree. Not *all* men maybe, but too many.

"Go ahead," the girl says. "I hope you catch that fucker."

RIEL DOESN'T KNOW Marly's last name or where she's from, but she does know that she came close to making the Olympic swim team when she was a junior in high school. Kind of makes Riel feel like an asshole now that she didn't bother to get to know Marly more, even though she was Riel's most trusted helper—aside from Leo and Level99.

Leo met Marly in art history, but she was a psych major with plenty of lab work under her belt. She was able to reformat Dr. Ben Lang's Outlier test into a kind of multiple-choice BuzzFeed quiz. Something like: "Are You an Introvert?" or "Which *Game of Thrones* Character Are You?" or "In a Zombie Apocalypse You Would . . . ?"

The quiz Marly designed was "Are You an Outlier?" It gave you a score—Outlier or not. It also explained what being an Outlier was. The quiz laid it all out like the Outliers were an established scientific fact that everyone had been talking about but somehow the person taking the quiz had missed. In the end, more than seventeen thousand people took the test through social media sites and the bare-bones app Riel set up. Way more than they had ever expected.

They posted the Outliers quiz online on May 1, two weeks after Quentin first showed up and pointed Riel at the bull's-eye that was Ben Lang. By then, Kelsey had been dead nearly two months. But the full shitshow of the camp had yet to play out. And Riel didn't know yet that Quentin was way worse than just an ass. Helping him had been one way of Riel getting back at Dr. Ben Lang for what happened to Kelsey. Posting his secret tests online was another. Not that Dr. Lang ever even knew. As soon as the camp happened Riel pulled all the tests down. Who knew whether it had been fast enough. She didn't think about who she might be putting at risk. But deep down she'd known. That's why she never mentioned the quizzes when Wylie showed up asking for help with the girls in the hospital.

That's the thing about that kind of grief: it can eat you alive, but before it does it can make you blind, and reckless.

Riel had said once to Wylie that she'd wanted justice for the Outliers. That that was why she'd gotten mixed up with Quentin. And that was true. But somewhere along the line she decided to settle for personal vengeance.

Riel sits halfway up the bleachers alongside the pool. The air is humid and sharp with chlorine. Trying to pick Marly out from the rows of gliding bodies isn't hard. Marly is always first. Riel knows it before Marly even climbs out of the pool, *M. Pérez* printed on her swim cap.

Marly is an Outlier herself, so once she is out of the water, it doesn't take long for her to feel something, someone out of place. When she finally spots Riel, she freezes, towel in hand, glaring.

And, wow, is she pissed. Riel can feel it all the way up in those stands. Shit. Riel hadn't even thought Marly being angry was a possibility. *That's* how wrapped up Riel has been in her own shit.

As Marly's eyes dig into her, Riel is careful not to block her own feelings. If Riel wants Marly's help, she needs to be like a dog rolling on its back—exposed and vulnerable.

It's not easy. As Marly heads closer, her anger burns Riel's skin.

"What do you want?" Marly shouts up to Riel finally, her voice extra loud on purpose.

There's a man sitting twenty feet to the right. He's watching their conversation now. Listening to every word. A chill runs through Riel. Could he be there *for* Riel? Could he work for her grandfather? But, no, he was there before Riel arrived; he couldn't have followed her. He's staring because Marly is shouting. That's all. Still, Riel really wishes Marly would lower her voice. She'd ask her to if she wasn't convinced this would piss Marly off even more.

But despite her anger, Riel is still sure Marly is the right person. She is honest to a fault, and no one will ever connect them—Riel had started distancing herself from Marly right after the shooting at the camp. Froze her out is probably a better description. After all those people died, Riel had wanted to forget everything. It would have worked, too, if Wylie hadn't shown up, asking for help getting those girls out of the hospital.

Of course Riel could have explained some of that to Marly, who'd never done anything but *everything* Riel asked. The real question now is whether she can get Marly to forgive her. Because she's standing there, still glaring up at Riel, like she's hoping to make her bleed.

"Listen, I get why you'd be—"

"You *get it*?" Marly snaps. "What do you think you get?"

This is a trap. No doubt. Marly's arms are crossed, her weight back on one hip like she can't wait to snap a blade shut the second Riel wades inside. But there's sadness there, too, underneath all Marly's anger. That's one of the hardest parts about being an Outlier: realizing that almost every bad feeling is only one degree removed from heartbreak.

"I don't know," Riel says quietly. She holds up her palms. At least that is the truth. "I don't know anything anymore."

"I did every goddamn thing you asked and then, poof." Marly makes an exploding gesture with her hands. "You were gone. I thought after that girl Wylie showed up looking for you that maybe something would change, that you'd get your shit back together. I thought maybe we'd finally get on with this plan of *yours*, in which I did all the shit to find the Outliers and you did nothing. But nope, you just stayed gone. You never had a plan for what to do after we found them, did you?"

And the answer is no. Riel made it seem like they'd post the tests, Marly would contact the girls with the high scores—the real Outliers—and then they'd all "take action." But really she'd never worked it out beyond the whole ruining-Ben-Lang by posting all his secret research everywhere. Marly is right: there never was a plan. Nothing past phases one and two, especially not after she made the mistake of helping Quentin.

Riel starts down the bleachers, glancing back once at the guy who is definitely not watching them anymore. He never was.

At the bottom, she stands in front of Marly on the pool deck, arms open, unguarded and defeated.

"I'm sorry," she says.

"You're sorry?" Marly asks, with a fresh wave of anger. They are moving in the wrong direction. "You think that's going to be enough?"

"I fucked up. I took advantage or took you for granted or whatever. You have every right to be pissed. And I don't have a good excuse. I just cared more about things other than your feelings." Riel had expected there'd be a certain relief to admitting this. But saying it out loud just makes her feel shittier. She takes a breath, braces herself. "And I know what will definitely make it worse is asking you for something more—"

"But you're going to ask anyway, aren't you?"

"I don't have a choice."

"Unbelievable." Marly shakes her head, disgusted. But there is the faintest glimmer of something else underneath for the first time. Hope. Marly still wants so badly to believe in Riel. To trust her. For this moment right now to rewrite all that has come before. It makes Riel feel like such an asshole. "Come on," Marly says finally. "You're not even supposed to be in here."

With that, she walks off. And Riel can do only one thing: follow.

THE LOCKER ROOM is empty. Marly checks under the bathroom stalls to be sure. At least it no longer seems like she is deliberately trying to throw Riel to the wolves.

"You know, I made contact with at least a hundred of the girls who had self-identified as Outliers with the online quizzes. Do you have any idea how long that took?" Marly asks, but doesn't wait for an answer. "Used an anonymous untraceable Gmail from the library in downtown Boston, just like you told me to. And to actually make contact with that one hundred? I had to write to *thousands* who scored high. Literally. More than one thousand messages. And most of them didn't use real emails when they registered, so there I was, day after day, going to the damn library to write emails that bounced back anyway. But I kept at it, email after email, explaining this crazy thing, all to help your damn cause. Because I thought it was our cause. And then, by the time I got them together and got them all to trust me, sort of, you were long gone. And I was like, *don't worry, hang tight, she'll be back in touch with a plan real soon.* Except guess what?"

Riel takes a breath. "I didn't come back."

"Exactly!" Marly shouts, her eyes bright and wide. "Six weeks and no word. No plan, except that Wylie girl showing up randomly while I was working out. Tell me honestly, did you ever even have a plan?"

All Riel can do is blink at her. Because the answer is no.

"Those girls felt alone, you know," Marly goes on when Riel stays silent. "They didn't all have anxiety or depression or anything, you know, diagnosable. But they were too sensitive, or too emotional, or just wrong—that's what they've been told their whole lives. And I was like, not only are you fine the way you are—it's an actual thing. You're an Outlier. And don't worry because we're here now. But then *we* left them, too."

Marly turns to the lockers behind her, jerks out a new towel and some clothes. She is trying to find her anger again. It's easier than the sadness. But, as an Outlier, Riel can still feel that hope underneath. It's the only reason she will keep trying to win Marly over, even though all the facts suggest she will never succeed.

And that's why it matters, all of this. The Outliers. Even considering what Riel's lost, who and what the Outliers are is still something worth fighting for. Because knowing how people truly feel—getting to the heart of it—can make a difference. It can make the world a better place. A more honest, hopeful one. Even if it's not crystal-clear perfection. Even if it's not a skill anyone will ever be able to line up and dissect.

"We can reach out to those girls again. I'll explain to them that us disappearing before was my fault," Riel says.

"Why would we do that?" Marly asks.

Riel hesitates. Takes a deep breath. "Because they could be in danger. Because I am, maybe." She just needs to get it over with now. There's no more stalling. "There are people following me. My grandfather, I think."

"Your grandfather?" Marly asks. "What the hell does he have to do with anything?"

And so, standing in that empty, humid locker room, Riel explains what she can about how her grandfather is involved and why. It isn't much. But she does know that it started with her and Kelsey's copy of *1984* and that it ends with Wylie's photos. In the middle is her grandfather becoming a senator. And being on the Armed Services Committee. And running for freakin' president. And maybe meeting with Wylie's dad. And the girls in the hospital. And setting Leo's room on fire and not really caring who he killed.

"Leo's room was on fire?" Marly whispers, actually scared

now. And really, really listening. "Is he okay?"

"Yeah," Riel says, though she realizes she can't actually be sure of that anymore. "At least he was. But I still have the pictures. Which means I think they are still after me, and—by extension—Leo. I don't know why the pictures would be worth burning down a dorm full of college students. But I have to figure it out. That's why I need your help."

"My help," Marly huffs. But that hope is taking up more space inside her now, growing steadily. "Doing what?"

"Be a go-between. If I get caught reaching out to Level99 and the other Outliers again, I could be putting Leo in even more danger."

"And why me?" Marly asks. "Because I was stupid enough to trust you before?"

"No," Riel says, careful to hold Marly's stare. "Because *I* trust you."

WHEN THEY'RE BACK at Marly's summer dorm room—Harvard swimming preseason—Riel and Marly spread Wylie's pictures across the bed. There are eleven in all, each the size of a sheet of paper, and exactly as uninteresting as the last time Riel looked at them. Riel counts the photos again. She could have sworn that there were originally twelve. She worries she somehow left one at Brew, but she can't see how.

"Are those buckets?" Marly asks, pointing to the series of roundish white objects on what looks like a metal shelf.

"That's what I thought." Riel peers closer. She tries again to make out the writing on them. "Like for plaster or paint or something? Like in construction."

"Didn't you say Wylie's mom was a professional photographer?" Marly asks, holding up a different photo and frowning at it.

"Yeah," Riel says, fingering another—in it is a row of computer screens and a man in profile pointing across the room like he is giving a tour. He doesn't seem aware of the camera. Beyond the computers is a glass window with more machines, and something like a long table in the center, like for examinations.

"These don't exactly look professional," Marly says skeptically.

"Maybe she was trying to hide that she was taking them," Riel says, which feels true, but also not like the right explanation.

"Okay, so now what?" Marly asks, looking up from the photos.

"You'll help?" Riel asks. So far, Marly agreed to let Riel come back to her room to look at the pictures, but that was it.

Marly looks down and considers the question for a minute more. Finally, she nods.

"Yeah, I'll help," she says. "But to be clear, I'm doing it for the other girls—the Outliers. Because I feel like I owe it to them. As far as I'm concerned, I don't owe you a thing."

TOP SECRET AND CONFIDENTIAL

To: Senator David Russo

From: The Architect

Re: Identification Cards

April 20

To summarize, procedural details for the Outlier identification card program will be outlined as soon as possible after the current research integrity threat is effectively contained. Most effective responses to the anticipated legal, economic, and practical obstacles to the identification card program will be addressed at that time.

JASPER

FOR TWO HOURS AFTER HE GETS WYLIE'S NOTE, JASPER DRIVES AROUND.

He'd like to think of himself as the kind of person who—after getting a note like that—wouldn't go anywhere near the person who sent it. That he's a person with some self-respect. But at the end of all that going nowhere, there Jasper is: driving past Wylie's house, more than once, like some stupid-ass, brokenhearted puppy. Thank God he manages to make himself keep driving.

Jasper would also like to think that he's the type of person who, after a bunch of embarrassing drive-bys, would feel stupid enough that he'd at least go home and try to sort himself out. But apparently, Jasper isn't that dude, either. Because ten minutes later, there he is on his way up to the front door of another girl's house. A girl he *definitely* has no business being near.

•••

"OH, HI." MAIA looks surprised and confused, no doubt, when she opens the door. It doesn't help that it's after nine p.m. Late to show up at anybody's door. "Jasper, what are you doing here? I haven't seen you since—come in, come in."

Maia's hair is blonder and longer, held back in a wide red headband, and she has on a yellow romper that would look stupid on almost anyone else. But there's no denying it looks good on Maia. Jasper's not surprised she's getting prettier. That's what girls like Maia do.

Is that why he's there? Because Maia's pretty? He's convinced himself he's there honoring the thing Wylie wanted—to see who sent the journal—even though she broke his heart. Too bad he didn't figure out the real reason before he rang her bell.

"Well, come in." Maia reaches out and tugs on his bare arm, fingers lingering on his bicep. Maia is good at that, too—doing things and seeming like she didn't.

They stand inside her vaulted marble foyer with its fancy spiral staircase, freezing cold from the blasting air-conditioning. Jasper crosses his arms to stay warm, wonders if all rich people like their houses so cold.

"So, what's up?" Maia says, tilting her head farther to the side.

"I, um, just came by to ask—did you ever send me something?"

Maia laughs, pulls her chin back, then narrows her eyes, which weirdly makes her even cuter. "Send you what?"

There isn't going to be any good way to explain this without the whole thing sounding like the wild accusation it kind of is.

"Some pages from Cassie's journal?" Jasper asks, and then his stupid voice catches, tearing a massive hole open inside him. And for the second time in as many hours, he feels like he is going to cry. But that can't happen. Here, in front of Maia, would be totally humiliating.

"Hey, are you okay?" Maia asks. She guides Jasper over to a bench against that fancy spiral staircase. "Sit. Listen, I didn't send you anything. How would I have Cassie's journal anyway?"

And what can he say to that: that he thinks Maia is so obsessed with him that she somehow snuck into Cassie's house after she was dead and tore out mean, hurtful pages so that Jasper would be extra needy and want to be with Maia?

Jasper shakes his dumb-ass head. "I don't know." He leans forward and puts his elbows against his thighs, resting his head in his hands. "I don't know anything anymore. I'm just trying to figure out who would have sent the pages to me. None of it makes sense."

Maia puts a warm hand on Jasper's back and starts rubbing up and down in a way that feels good. Better than it should. And when Jasper turns to look up at her, Maia holds his stare. He wonders for a minute why he never gave Maia more of a chance. She might be different than he thought. She might even be a cool person. And she's so beautiful right now that Jasper isn't feeling the ache of his heart, hanging by a thread.

"Have you thought about maybe Wylie?" Maia asks. "I mean, no offense, but there has been something seriously messed up about her for a long time. You know she was seeing a shrink in, like, middle school."

And just like that, Jasper is slapped awake. That's why not Maia. He pulls away, jumps to his feet. How could he have even let himself think about her for a minute? Is he really that out of control?

"The only thing that's wrong with Wylie," he says, before he strides for the door, "is that she was ever friends with you."

JASPER JUST ENDS up at Cassie's house. Like he's on autopilot now. He didn't plan on going there any more than he'd planned on going to Maia's. But there he is. And inside there might be answers.

Wylie was right that Karen is the best person to ask about the pages. She hasn't been anything but nice to Jasper since Cassie died, but he still isn't looking forward to seeing her. He doesn't feel like he has a choice anymore, though. Understanding where the journal pages came from would at least give him an excuse to talk to Wylie again. Yeah, he does realize that's a part of all this. It's a part of everything.

Jasper knocks hard on Cassie's front door. Waits. Knocks again. Waits some more. It's almost ten p.m. Maybe Karen's asleep. Jasper's about to give up and head back to his car when the front door finally opens.

It's a man with a salt-and-pepper ponytail and a matching beard. He's wearing shorts and a light gray T-shirt that says *Life's a Beach*. For a second, Jasper thinks he has the wrong house; he even steps back to check the house number.

"Can I help you, son?" Calm, serene.

Vince, Cassie's dad, Jasper realizes as soon as he says "son."

His hair is longer and he didn't have a beard at the funeral. But Vince called Jasper son a few times back then, which Jasper liked more than he wanted to admit. Weird that Vince is here, though. He and Karen have been divorced for years now, and from what Cassie said, it had been pretty far from friendly. Then again, maybe losing your only child changes that.

"Um, have you, maybe, seen Cassie's diary anywhere?" Jasper jumps right in. Immediately, he regrets not giving it some lead-up. He should have at least started by explaining *why* he's looking for the journal: the pages being sent to him. As it is, Jasper wanting Cassie's journal must seem creepy. But if Vince is put off, he doesn't show it.

"Would you like to come in, son?" Vince asks, and nicely, too.

"Yeah," Jasper says. "Thanks."

VINCE MOTIONS JASPER to take a seat on the couch, which is kind of awkward given that it's the exact spot that Jasper and Cassie last had sex. Jasper hates himself for remembering. Especially because Vince is looking right at him. So Jasper starts talking, and too fast.

"Somebody mailed me some pages out of Cassie's journal. And I was kind of hoping that Karen would be able to tell me who might have sent them. The whole thing has been freaking me out for a while."

"Oh, well, Karen might be able to, but she's not back until the end of next week," Vince says. "Two months in Europe. Sounds odd, probably, but she needed the time away."

"Oh, okay," Jasper says.

"That is strange about the journal, though. We could take a look in Cassie's room," Vince says, rising to his feet. "Don't know what we'll find. But sometimes a single step forward lights the rest of the way."

"Yeah, thank you," Jasper says, relieved that Vince isn't bothered by him being there. But then Vince seems pretty weird himself. "That would be good."

IN CASSIE'S ROOM, Vince and Jasper open and close drawers, check in corners and under stacks of paper, looking for her journal. But the more they look and the more they turn up nothing, the hollower Jasper feels. Like he already knows that none of this was the answer to anything to begin with.

"Oh, look here," Vince says finally, turning around with a small black book in his hands. "Here it is. And I had no idea Cassie even kept a journal."

But when Vince holds it out to Jasper, he cannot get himself to take it. He's suddenly too afraid of what he might find inside. What if there are even more pages about how much Cassie loved Quentin? What if there are parts that say she never cared about Jasper at all? He's not sure he'd be able to take that right now. After Wylie's note, he's too fragile.

But Vince is still hanging there with the journal in his hands. Jasper needs to say something. "I really just want to know who sent the pages I already got. I don't want to read any more."

"Oh, well." Vince flips quickly through the journal. "It does look like there are some sections missing. But I'm afraid that doesn't tell me who could have taken them. We will need to wait until Karen gets back to ask, though there's a good chance she won't know, either. So many of Cassie's friends have been in and out. And before then . . . well, we didn't pay the attention we should have."

There's a noise then, some kind of crash followed by a thud downstairs. They both startle and look toward the door.

"Squirrels," Vince says with an exasperated shake of his head. "They get in through the attic. They used to stay in the walls, but lately they've been getting into the basement. I should go downstairs and be sure the door is closed. I'll never hear the end of it from Karen if they get into the house itself." He puts the journal down on a side table. "But I will say that reading the journal is an awfully big risk. The thoughts in someone's head are just that: thoughts. Are you still getting parts of it mailed to you?"

Jasper shakes his head. "No, they stopped."

"Maybe that's the thing that matters then," he says kindly, and Jasper does feel relieved. "That it's over. Maybe what you need to focus on, son, is letting go. Believe me, I know. Sometimes that can be the hardest thing."

BACK ON CAMPUS, Jasper goes straight for a run. Doesn't even stop back at his room. He has to burn some of what he's feeling off or he might explode. There are lots of people out still, but on their way to bars or parties. It's eleven p.m. Way too late for a run. Still, the harder Jasper runs, the better he feels, and the farther he wants to run.

As his feet slap against the pavement, he replays in his head each sentence of Wylie's note over and over, waiting for the words to lose their shape. When they don't, he tries instead not to think about the letter at all. But that doesn't work, either. How could Wylie just decide that he wasn't right for her? That they were too different? Who said they were trying to be the same?

Jasper also hates that Wylie's reasons for breaking up with him sound so much like Cassie's. But Jasper also wonders whether the way he choked that kid at Level99 didn't factor in. Still, Jasper went after that Level99 kid way before Wylie was arrested. And still—in twenty-six-minute increments—they'd fallen for each other in that detention facility visiting room.

Hadn't they? Or had Jasper made that up, too?

ONE KIND OF nice, kind of crappy thing about having to see Wylie at the detention facility? Sex wasn't even on the table. They couldn't even touch hands, let alone something more. Still, Jasper somehow managed to get the conversation there anyway. But it was Wylie who grabbed hold of the bait.

"You know how it is when you accidentally have sex with somebody," Jasper said. He'd been telling a story about a friend of his, not even himself.

"Nope," Wylie responded. "I don't know. I've never had sex. With anyone."

Wylie had never had sex, and Jasper had. Obviously

more than once, including with Cassie. There it was now, out there on the table between them. Wylie was staring at Jasper, too, like there was a right thing to say at that moment. And a wrong thing. But Jasper had no clue which was which. He had never before wanted so badly to be able to feel his way to an answer. As it was, all he could do was stare back at Wylie and hope that she'd be able to feel that his heart was in the right place, even when he totally screwed it up.

"It's okay," Wylie said finally, rescuing him. "You don't have to say anything. I just—I wanted you to know."

"Oh," he said, exhaling hard. And the rest was a guess. "Yeah, I'm, uh, glad you told me."

Wylie smiled. "Me too."

JASPER HAS RUN two more hard laps around campus when he feels a twinge in his knee. He can't risk blowing it out. Now more than ever, he needs the ice. The game. The pain. Otherwise, he might actually end up taking a swing at somebody on dry land.

Jasper takes a hard left at the west gate of BC, looking down at his Runkeeper app as he turns back toward his dorm. His eyes are still down on his phone when he collides with somebody running in the opposite direction.

"Watch where you're going!" A girl's voice. And there she is, knocked to the ground, looking pissed as she yanks her earbuds out. For a second, Jasper wonders whether he's imagining her.

"Seriously? Do you just have a thing about running into people?"

But no, it's her. The girl on the bike. The girl he already ran into once *with his car*. The girl whose bike he destroyed. Crap. The bike. Jasper completely forgot about fixing it. He should have dropped it at a shop while he was out. He hasn't even taken it out of his car. The letter from Wylie made him forget everything.

"Sorry, I didn't see you," he says, hoping that they can somehow breeze past the whole subject of the bike.

"I'm beginning to sense that happens to you a lot," she says. And then she smiles, finally.

"They said your bike would be ready tomorrow, hopefully." The lie popped right out of his mouth. So much for avoiding the subject of the bike. "I can drop it off for you."

The girl narrows her eyes like she doesn't believe him. "Drop it off? What makes you think I'll give you my address?"

Jasper feels his cheeks flush. He knows she's joking, but his skin just feels so raw. "Oh, well then—"

"Um, that was a *joke*." The girl leans in. "You should try to lighten up."

Jasper's chest opens a little, like a bubble crowding out his insides has just burst. He smiles, for real. "Yeah, I probably should. Definitely, actually."

"Why don't you call me when the bike's ready, and I'll come by and get it?" Is she flirting? Maia was one thing, but this girl is less obvious. Wylie's note has made him doubt his ability to read even the most straightforward emotions. "And maybe you can buy me dinner or something, too. You do owe me."

And with that Lethe jogs off. Jasper stands there for a minute, watching her go, her long ponytail swinging back and forth. She glances back once over her shoulder to wave. Like she knew for sure he'd still be standing there, watching her go.

WYLIE

IN THE MORNING, AFTER A TERRIBLE NIGHT OF MOSTLY NO SLEEP, I LIE IN BED thinking about that picture Leo gave me or, rather, hid for me. It's bothering me so much it makes it hard to even enjoy being back in my own room.

The night before, I waited until we were safely back in the car to open the folder Leo left for me. Inside was a grainy and off-kilter eight-by-ten black-and-white photograph of a car. A black sedan, nondescript but for the license plate, which was visible. In the background, there was also a sign that read *For assistance call the main office.* There was a phone number, too. But other than the sign and the license plate, there was just the car and a little bit of flat gray sky.

"What's that?" Gideon had asked.

"One of Mom's pictures, I think," I said. "I found an envelope of them in Rachel's house after I got out of the hospital. Mom must have had them with her when she was followed. I don't remember this one picture specifically, but they were pictures just like this."

"These are the pictures Rachel asked about," Gideon said. "Didn't you say you had to leave them?"

I nodded. "With Riel," I said. "I didn't tell Rachel that part because I guess I didn't want her trying to find Riel. I wonder where the other pictures are. There were a bunch of them."

"Maybe this is the only one that matters?" Gideon offered.

And it seemed like a reasonable suggestion last night. But now as I lie in my bed in the light of day, it no longer does. There's a knock then at my bedroom door.

"Come in!" I call.

Gideon opens the door but stays in the doorway. "We got a text from Oshiro," he says, then reads out loud: "'I've got some information for you. Come to my apartment: 72 Sleeper Street, PH-C. Seaport District. Ten a.m.'" He looks up at me. "What do we do?"

Gideon is right to hesitate. It's a little weird for Oshiro to be asking us to go to his house. But when I search myself for real doubt, for some sense that we might be walking into a trap, I feel nothing but how torn I am between wanting all the answers about my dad and wanting only the good ones.

"We go," I say, getting out of bed. "Definitely."

"WHAT DOES IT feel like?" Gideon asks as he turns on the car and starts driving toward Oshiro's apartment. There is no judgment in his voice. His motives are pure and simple: he just wants to understand. "I mean, the whole being-able-to-read-people thing."

It isn't until I pause to consider how to answer him that I fully realize that I am no longer just reading feelings. *Go to Oshiro's.* That was intuition, unattached to a single person. In a matter of weeks, since finding out I was an Outlier and with no formal training, I've gone from reading people to reading situations. That much better, that fast. No wonder they are trying so hard to contain this. To contain us. Someday who knows what we will become?

"Sometimes I feel it as a physical thing in my own body. Like, right now, you're freaked out, but trying not to be—I can feel that. Like it's my own heart beating fast. I used to get confused, but now I can tell the difference between someone else's feelings and my own. And then there's my own anxiety, too, which I have to separate out. It's getting easier to tell the difference between all three. Also, the more I learn to read people, the more I also have a gut feeling just about things."

"What do you mean 'about things'?"

"Like: yes, go to Oshiro's," I say. "That's not about reading one person."

"Intuition," Gideon says, and like maybe he knew that already. I wonder if in his less angry moments with our dad, they talked about where this Outliers research could be headed.

"But that part—the intuition part—isn't as consistent." As I explain it to Gideon, I'm only fleshing out the details myself. "Sometimes I'll be right, but only sort of. Like Jasper was thinking of hurting himself, I was right about that. But he'd changed his mind before I got to the bridge, and it ended with me caught and in the hospital. That I didn't see coming. So it's not like my intuition always keeps me out of trouble. It's not like my intuition is foolproof."

"Not ESP." Gideon smiles, but sadly.

"No," I say. "And it's kind of a problem. I mean, how do you even prove something is a real thing, that it matters, when you have to admit right away that it's kind of fuzzy? They will use it against us. I know they will."

"There are some people, dudes especially, who will try. But that doesn't mean they'll succeed," Gideon says. "You want to know how it feels *not* to be an Outlier?"

"How?"

"Like nothing." He shrugs. "That's the weird thing. I don't miss it at all. I just walk around the world making my decisions my way, using facts, not feelings. But it doesn't feel like there could be something more because I don't even know what that more feels like. And I swear I can't remember a time when I had some kind of real overwhelming feeling about what I should do. Not even one that I ignored."

"Oh," I say, and the gulf between us suddenly feels infinite. Gideon and I are twins. We have so much in common, almost everything. Except this. And suddenly, it feels like the only thing that matters.

"Do you feel sorry for me?" Gideon asks. And there is no challenge in his head or his heart.

I shrug. "I'd say both situations have a downside. And an upside, too."

"Maybe," Gideon says. "But I do think people will want there to be one winner. One truth. Look at that blog. Hell hath no fury like people who don't like what Dad's research could be saying, even if they make up what that is."

"Yeah, EndOfDays," I say as we pull off the highway into downtown Boston. I hate the way the name pops into my head like one firecracker after another. End. Of. Days. "But that's not . . . they're not regular people."

"No," Gideon says. "He's a fanatic. I'm just worried about the regular people listening who don't realize it."

WE DRIVE ON into Oshiro's neighborhood. It's one of those that's turning over from old factories to new luxury lofts. Empty buildings sprinkled between bright bistros and hip cafés. There's even an art-house movie theater, where they probably bring soy-milk cappuccinos to your seat. And nearby, a pack of strung-out-looking white kids hang on a stoop in front of a boarded-up warehouse like it's a fortress they just claimed.

"Turn right in three hundred feet, and your destination will be on the left," the GPS voice instructs.

It's risky to be using the GPS. Somebody could already be tracking us. But we are heading to Oshiro's at least. If there is someone following, it couldn't hurt for them to know we've got a cop on our side.

Finally, we turn left between two brick pillars into a pristine parking lot. A row of white vans at the back are lined up like service vehicles for a luxury hotel. In front of us is a very fancy converted loft building.

I look around. "Kind of nice for a police officer, isn't it?"

And there it is, a bad, bad feeling. Not my anxiety and not me reading Gideon. This is something else. It's a bad feeling about this disconnect between Oshiro's fancy apartment and his job. I'm not sure why it matters, though. But it does. It's like an echo almost.

"Have you changed your mind about going in?" Gideon asks, seeing the suspicious look on my face, no doubt.

"No." I look up again at the building as I open the car door. "And yes."

THE GRAY-HAIRED, SQUARE-FACED doorman eyes us disapprovingly over his desk in the glamorous lobby, confident as we approach that he can sweep us away with just the one look.

"We're here to see Detective Oshiro?" I shouldn't have said it like it was a question. I hate when I do that.

"Name?" he asks, eyeballing me harder.

"Um, Wylie."

The doorman takes a deep, disgusted breath as he picks up the phone. But he lights up when someone answers, and when he speaks, his voice is suddenly soft and polite. A woman he has a crush on—Oshiro's wife or girlfriend, I'm guessing. "There's a Wylie down here to see *Detective* Oshiro." It's code for *they don't even know his first name.* He looks us up and down again. "Yep, no problem." He hangs up the phone but still wants us to leave.

And this is precisely why being an Outlier is a gift and also definitely a burden: I don't *need* to be in the doorman's head that deep. Don't *need* to know about his unrequited love. It's not useful. But know it I do. To get a read on him at all that comes up first. When you're an Outlier, you don't get to pick and choose.

Finally, the doorman points toward the elevator at the back, still super grumpy. "Penthouse C."

THE DOORS TO the elevator open into a spectacular loft—wood beams and exposed brick and lots of windows.

"Yeah," Gideon says quietly. "We might want to make sure there's an explanation for all this."

A woman comes bounding around the corner, tall and fit-looking in her sleeveless T-shirt and jeans, biceps as defined as a yoga instructor's. Her hair is light brown and shaggy and she has a dazzling smile.

"You must be Wylie," she says, her handshake a vise. She turns to Gideon and shakes his hand, too. "And you're Gideon. I'm Elizabeth, Evan's wife." She says this like it is supposed to mean something to me. I blink at her. "Oh, Detective Oshiro, I mean. Sorry, I forget that he never tells anybody his first name. He probably didn't tell you anything about me, either."

Detective Oshiro himself comes around the corner then, wearing jeans and a well-fitting T-shirt. Seeing him out of his sharp suit is like seeing him standing there in his underwear.

"You didn't tell her about me, did you?" Elizabeth needles him playfully.

"Can we at least go sit down before you start berating me?" Oshiro asks.

"IT'S BEAUTIFUL HERE," I say as they lead us into a vast open living room with even more windows. They wrap around the room, the Boston skyline on one side, the water on the other. "Like the nicest apartment I've ever been in."

"My job isn't nearly as noble as Evan's," Elizabeth says, sitting on one side of the modern sectional couch and crossing her long legs beneath her. Gideon and I take a seat on the shorter end. "But it does pay the bills."

"Elizabeth works for a credit card company in risk and cybersecurity," Oshiro says, and I can feel how in awe of her he is. It's something way past love. "I expected she'd be able to find out what you needed much faster than I could through department channels."

"A credit card company?" I ask. "To trace my dad's phone?"

"Credit card companies could launch a rocket into space." Elizabeth gets up to retrieve some printouts off a sideboard. "I'll admit, it isn't exactly how I pictured spending my career, but someday soon I will retire and help people properly like Evan. So, I can't tell you *who* specifically called you. Not surprising, it was a disposable phone bought with cash, *but* I was able to get into the phone company's database and—"

"She risked a lot doing that, you know," Oshiro scolds. I'm not sure if it's directed at me or Elizabeth. "I told her not to."

"Thank you," I say, looking first at Elizabeth and then at Oshiro, because that seems to be what he wants me to do. To be grateful. No, that's not it. He just wants to feel less worried. What he cares about most is Elizabeth and her well-being.

Elizabeth shoots him a look. "Enough browbeating, Evan. And have a little faith. I am good enough not to get caught." She hands me the papers she picked up. When I look down, it's a list of addresses, as well as carefully collated sets of directions with corresponding maps between each location. "This is a list of where the phone was when each call was placed and each text sent. They started out in DC, then ended up here. That's where the last voicemail was left, three days ago." She points to a spot on the map. "It's about an hour from here, in Framingham."

"But you *shouldn't* go there," Detective Oshiro says, his arms crossed. He stops himself from adding something like: *I won't allow it.* But he'd like to. "You have absolutely no idea what you'll find. It would be extremely dangerous."

Elizabeth keeps her eyes on me as she sits back down, closer this time. "He really does believe that. He didn't even want me to tell you the address." She glances at Oshiro. "But we agreed that the information is not mine to keep. It belongs to you."

"No, I agreed after I called down to DC the second time," he says. "And they told me your dad's case was closed."

"How can it be closed if our dad's still missing?" Gideon asks.

"Exactly. Even more troubling was how fifteen minutes after I got off the phone with DC, my sergeant calls me into his office to tell me there's been a complaint about me interfering in investigations in other jurisdictions. I was told if I did it again, it could cost me my job." Oshiro shakes his head. "Now, I don't know who's covering up for what or why, but I am sure no one's looking for your dad. I'm sorry."

My throat tightens as I look up from the maps. "Thank you for telling me."

"We are going to help, though," Elizabeth says brightly, leaning over to grab my hands. "So screw the DC police."

I hate that I have to ask for something else when they are

already being so generous. But I have no choice.

"You've already done so much, I know, but can I ask—"

"No," Oshiro says with a sharp wave of his hand. "Absolutely not."

"Evan," Elizabeth says, quiet but firm. "Of course you can ask, Wylie. We will do whatever else we can. Tell us everything you need."

"Can you find out who's behind a blog?" I ask. "It's called EndOfDays."

"EndOfDays?" Elizabeth makes a face. "Well, that's cheerful. I should be able to do that, no problem. But before we do anything else, why don't you go open a fresh Gmail account so we have a reasonably safe place to stay in touch?" She motions Gideon over to a computer on the coffee table.

"*And* could you also track down a license plate?" I ask, already bracing myself for Oshiro's response.

"A license plate?" he shouts. Like I just said "cocaine."

Elizabeth holds up a hand to Oshiro. "Evan, calm." She turns to us. "These days, hacking into the DMV isn't what it used to be, that's what he means. They have so many flags, for terrorism mostly." She turns to eye Oshiro. "But Evan, *you* can look up one license plate. On the books, officially. No one will even think twice."

Elizabeth tilts her head to the side and smiles: *Come on, honey.* That's *the* look. Just like the one that Lexi gave Doug, like the one that my mom used to give my dad. The kind of look that makes facts so much less important than feelings. The kind I might have used on Jasper one day, if I hadn't written that— I push the thought away. One day—after I take the note back—I will.

Oshiro exhales, aggravated. But he is no match for Elizabeth's look. "Fine, what license plate?" he asks. I dig the picture out of my bag and hand it to him. Oshiro is alarmed. "This looks like a surveillance photo. Where is this from?"

"I don't know," I say.

Oshiro holds the picture out to me, his finger pointing accusingly at the car. "That is a government license plate. What are you mixed up in, Wylie?"

"I don't know" is all I can think to say. And it's so true that I am afraid I might burst into tears.

"I'll look into this license plate on one condition," Oshiro says, setting the photograph down on the polished coffee table.

"Anything," I say without hesitating.

"I'm coming with you."

"Coming with us where?" I ask.

"Framingham," he says. "Because I know that's where you're headed. And, as much as I'd like to, there is no way in good conscience I can let you go alone."

November 17

Today a true believer was put in my path. She was a newcomer and came up to me after the meeting. She told me that the struggles I had shared with the group had really touched her. That my devotion to finding a cause was noble.

And then she told me a heartbreaking story about some horrific things that had been happening in my own backyard. I knew then that was where I needed to begin. Close to home. Helping girls being exploited by fame-hungry scientists is exactly the kind of cause I've been looking for.

And if I can save these girls from the wrongs a man I once knew is committing, I believe that will keep on saving me—one day at a time.

RIEL

MARLY PARKS A BLOCK DOWN FROM THE LEVEL99 HOUSE IN ONE OF THE FEW shady spots. The house looks empty, but Riel knows it isn't. She had thought about telling Level99 to leave after what happened at her grandfather's house. They all listened for some chatter about Level99 in connection with the camp. But it never came. Actually, there was hardly any chatter about the camp at all. Riel shouldn't be surprised, but still it's amazing how things, people, can just be erased.

And Riel still needs to be careful she doesn't somehow lead somebody to Level99 now. She doesn't think anyone followed her *to* Marly's, much less from Marly's to Level99. But Riel isn't taking any chances with Leo's life. If one of her grandfather's henchmen—yes it is true, she's sure of it, they're his—catches her putting Level99 on the case, that will probably not be considered "staying away from it." It could put Leo in even more danger.

But she needs to show up at least once with Marly so Brian has no choice but to acknowledge her going forward in Riel's place. Riel just needs to do her best to stay out of sight. The plan is for Marly to head to their front door and for Riel to sneak around back.

"What happens after I dial the code?" Marly asks, turning to grab her bag from the backseat. It's caught up on some big hand weights, and she has to tug hard. Having spent the night in Marly's room, Riel can say for sure she's a fitness fanatic. But even for her car weights are overkill.

"Ready to work out at a moment's notice, huh?" Riel asks, motioning to them.

"Yeah, I work out whenever I get stuck in traffic," Marly says with a shrug.

"Really?" Riel asks.

"No, not *really*," Marly huffs. "The weights belong to a friend. I'm returning them. I thought you were an Outlier. Can't you tell when someone's joking?"

Marly is right: Riel is so wound up, she's clouded. And she needs to be sharp as hell. Not only does she need to get to the back entrance of the Level99 house without anyone seeing her, she needs to be ready to deal with Brian's shit once she gets inside. Because with Brian, there is always *a lot* of shit to be dealt with.

He's angling to be Riel's official successor, not just her temporary stand-in, and it's making him even more of an ass than usual. Though what he should really be doing is trying everything to win Riel over. It will be her choice who will lead Level99 after her, whenever she decides to step down: today, tomorrow, ten years from now. There are moments when right now feels like the time, considering everything. But for the moment she can feel she needs to hang on—for the sake of Level99.

Regardless, she already knows for sure that her successor would never be Brian. Brian is an amazing hacker, to be sure. But being a hacker and being a leader are not the same thing. Also, he is just an asshole. It's too scary to think about what might happen if Level99's power fell into the wrong hands.

BENNETT BARA HAD shown up to see Riel shortly after Kelsey's funeral. He had been her father's friend for years, first his professor as an undergraduate, then a neighbor and a running partner for years. Bennett came to Thanksgiving often, the girls had been paid to rake his leaves. He always brought them science-y birthday gifts. Bennett had never had a family of his own, and so he had semi-adopted theirs, but was always careful not to impose.

Riel had known nothing about Bennett's connection to Level99 before the day he turned up at the end of March, asking Riel to run the whole show.

"Your parents knew," he said matter-of-factly.

"Really?" Riel felt vaguely betrayed, even if she knew that was kind of ridiculous.

"Your father was going to take over for me," Bennett said, the effects of his advanced-stage pancreatic cancer visible now as he lowered himself with much effort into a chair. "I began making arrangements as soon as I was diagnosed. When I still had plenty of time."

"Oh," Riel said, not shocked that her dad had agreed to help, though she could not picture him at the helm of a bunch of young hackers. He never had patience for hipsters.

"Yes," Bennett said. "And now I would like you to take his place, Riel."

"Me?" Riel asked, feeling equal parts panicked and thrilled. Actually, no, mostly just panicked. "Why me?"

"Because you are the best person I know for the job. You're a computer science major at Harvard University," he said. "That makes you more than qualified and—"

"I *was* a computer science major. I dropped out, remember? I was only there for three months, and I didn't learn anything useful. Nothing like *hacking*. It was a lot of theory. That's it."

"Technically, you took a leave. I checked. You and I both know you are welcome back anytime. Besides, computer skills matter, but other things matter much more," he went on. "I need to be sure the person in charge will never use Level99 for personal gain or an unethical cause. Good judgment is the most critical skill."

"And how do you know that I have good judgment?" Riel asked, hoping both to wriggle off the hook and get more deeply lodged on it.

There was something about Bennett showing up and saying he needed her. She did plan to go back in the fall when she was ready. Maybe this would make her feel like she was.

"I know your judgment will be sound because you are a piece of your parents," he said. "Good runs deep."

IN THE END, Bennett had been right. And having Level99 to throw herself into after Kelsey died had probably saved Riel's life. Even the change of power had been much easier than Riel had expected. That was the benefit of Level99's strict monarchy: there was no argument about the rules of succession, and the modest stipend that went along with being in charge.

No one bristled that Riel was an outsider—the new leader almost always was. Within days, Riel felt like she'd been born to lead Level99. She was that damn good at it, too. And with Kelsey gone, Level99 and Leo were all that mattered to her.

Now it was Leo and the Outliers. They needed her more than Level99 ever did. It was probably time to move on anyway. She had re-enrolled and was set to start classes at Harvard in September. But she would not leave things to Brian. No way.

"After you push the numbers, tell them Joseph Conrad sent you," Riel says as Marly opens the car door. "Ask for Brian once you're in. Tell him I'll be coming around the back. He needs to unlock the basement door."

RIEL STAYS LOW as she slips between two buildings and into the tightly packed backyards. She's using Level99's emergency escape route. Pretty fast, Riel realizes this "escape route" sucks. It would require scaling fence after fence through the neighboring backyards. Turns out climbing just one fence is really fucking hard, especially in the July humidity. Riel puts *find new escape route* at the top of her mental Level99 list.

She is huffing and puffing by the time she finally makes it to Level99's backyard. Brian is standing at the basement door, arms crossed, looking, as usual, kind of like a hawk—white-blond hair, shadowy eyes, sharp nose, gameboard tattoo that Riel wishes he didn't have. It makes him seem too permanent.

"Finally," he snaps, turning back down the stairs.

It's not the waiting that has pissed him off, though. Brian really hoped Riel was never coming back. He'd been pretty sure that he wasn't temporary after all.

Riel follows Brian down into the Level99 basement, to the familiar long table of hooded, headphoned twentysomethings hunched over laptops, none of whom look up. She feels such a wave of relief seeing all of it. Like she's home.

By contrast, Marly is standing on the opposite side of the room, looking alarmed. Whatever she thought Level99 was going to be like, it wasn't this. And it is true that it kind of looks, and smells, like a dungeon. An unfriendly one. But it grows on you—or it has grown on Riel.

"So, what's up?" Brian asks, sitting aggressively at what has always been Riel's desk. This is on purpose, of course.

"I'm back," Riel says. This isn't true. But Brian is already way too comfortable.

"You're back?" Brian asks, trying to sound casual. But he

does not feel that way. Farthest thing from it. "For good?"

"We'll see, but right now I need something," she says. "Or a few things, actually."

And where to start: Wylie, Kendall, the Outliers, Rosenfeld? Her grandfather? So many questions, so few fucking answers.

Riel feels Brian trying to calculate the best way to play the situation. He knows he shouldn't cave too fast. That he can't be too accommodating or Riel will know he's just trying to butter her up. But being helpful is also a way to get on her good side. He knows that, too. God, he is so goddamn obvious.

"Well, we are kind of busy," Brian says, opting for a compromise: hard to get. "We got the presidential race heating up. Speaking of which, I didn't know that your grandfather was—"

Her eyes shoot up. It's not Brian's words that piss her off, it's his tone: it's just so full-asshole. "Just so we're clear, who my grandfather is has *never* been a secret," she snaps.

Brian lifts his hands. "Whatever, if you say so."

"And these requests aren't optional. I'm still in charge, remember?" Riel says. "I need you to find out who Kendall really is, and I need you to find some girls for me."

"Girls?" Brian asks, like she's asking him to round up goats.

"Girls identified as Outliers."

Brian has heard the term, obviously. He was there helping Quentin, too. Riel did draw a line between Level99 and the Outliers, though. Level99 tracked down Dr. Lang's research and hacked into his data, but that had been under the pretense of stopping some asshole scientist from exploiting people—solidly within their mission. Her work with Marly and the tests—that was all on her own time. She couldn't use Level99 for her own personal vendetta. This now, though, was different. This was about protecting innocent girls.

"And Kendall?" Brian asks. "You mean the guy who killed all those people?"

"Yes, that guy. But before you do any of that, I need you to check on Wylie first," Riel says. "Last I heard, she was still in jail. I need to be sure. Also, I need an address for this guy."

Riel digs out of her pocket some folded pages. She hands one to Brian with the name of the Outliers from the hospital she'd dug up with Wylie; the other has David Rosenfeld's name and the title of his book. The book is better—and scarier—than she expected. Riel didn't read much, just enough to get his main point: the government does even more fucked-up shit than she realized.

"Okay, that's like ten things," Brian says. "What's in it for me?"

"What's in it for you? How about not losing your goddamn job?" Riel snaps. "I wasn't asking. I was telling you."

Riel can feel Brian swallowing back about ten different ways he wants to tell her to go screw herself. Instead, he rubs his jawline and looks around. Some of the younger hackers are listening now. They know the rules: Riel is the boss. They'll throw Brian out on his ass if she says the word.

And Riel feels better being reminded of this. Her power might be limited to this place, this moment. But power is like fire: to spread it's got to start somewhere.

"Fine," Brian says, looking down. "We'll look into it."

"Into what?" Riel asks.

"*All* of it," Brian says. "It could take a while, though. It's *a lot*."

"Start with Wylie and the Outliers then," Riel says, handing Brian a second page. "This is a list of what we have on them. Some are just names, and not all the emails work. We need them to come to the address at the top. Today."

Brian checks his watch. "Today? And go somewhere? They don't even know me."

He has a point. And she can feel Marly eyeing her—*not as easy as it looks, is it?*

"Then just get us contact information for all of them," Riel says. "We'll figure out how to get them there."

BY EARLY AFTERNOON, Riel and Marly sit on the floor of Marly's room, waiting. They'd ended up spending two hours at Level99 sending messages to the Outliers. Marly's email had been pretty vague—she apologized for not being in touch, described a threat to the Outliers, said that volunteers were needed. Oh, and that there was no reason to panic, though. That was it, more would be explained when they came that afternoon.

At least Wylie had been pretty easy to find. Or it was easy to figure out where she wasn't: jail. She'd been released on bail. Where she was now was a mystery. Riel felt proud of that. She'd taught Wylie well. But there was something else Riel felt when she thought of Wylie, something much darker. Something she didn't like at all. Worry.

Brian found David Rosenfeld's address easily, too. Trickier were Kendall and the truth about her grandfather. Those were going to take more time. Brian said he'd keep working and report back. Riel had her doubts, about how hard he would try or how likely he was to succeed. But it was too risky to poke around more from Marly's. Whatever Brian found would be better than nothing.

"How many actually said they would come again?" Riel asks as she checks her watch. She gets up and starts to pace back and forth in front of Marly's door. She's worried that this rounding up of the Outliers has been too easy. Maybe no one will show.

Marly pulls a piece of paper out of her back pocket. "We reached twenty-seven of the sixty-five locals, including the girls on the list from the hospital," she says. "Twenty-one said they wanted to help. That's nearly eighty percent, and only a few hours' notice." Marly is trying hard to look on the bright side, spinning the numbers in the best possible way. When you start with seventeen thousand possibilities, twenty-one definitely sounds like a tiny number. Still, there's comfort in Marly staying an optimist. One of them needs to be. "Not a bad start. Coming here tonight are only eleven. Short notice and all. People have parents. Are you ready with some kind of, like, speech or something?"

"Speech?" Riel asks.

It seriously had not occurred to her, but Marly is right, a good leader would have some kind of kick-ass inspirational words prepared. Riel did that the first day with Level99. She'd been so worried about getting everyone's respect. Somehow, right now, she'd overlooked that she's the de facto leader of this Outlier shitshow. She is, though. Of course she is. And Marly is her trusty lieutenant.

"Yes, a speech about the whole Outliers thing?" Marly feels let down, but she's trying to hide it. "What it is. What it means. What the hell you think your grandfather might be up to."

"But I don't know," Riel says, and suddenly she feels so dumb. "I don't have answers about anything yet."

"You still know *way* more than these people will," Marly says. "Some of them don't know anything. The girls in the hospital don't, and the maybe-Outliers—"

"Maybe-Outliers?" Riel asks.

"Oh, that's what I call the Outliers we identified through our test," Marly says, a little sheepishly. "I mean we don't actually know how good that test was. Self-reporting measures are kind of inherently suspect. You learn that even as an undergrad. Those girls might be Outliers, but it's not the same as them being officially identified in one of Lang's tests. He included biological data like heart rate and all that. Just to be clear, *I'm* a maybe-Outlier," Marly says. "No one has officially tested me."

"You're *definitely* an Outlier," Riel says. "I can feel it."

Marly is embarrassed by how badly she needed Riel to say that. But Riel really has no doubt. The way emotions flow back and forth between them is like a current. Not that, technically, Riel has ever been tested either.

"Anyway," Marly says. "The maybe-Outliers at least got a little description of Outliers when they took our online test. But from those email exchanges I had with the girls from the hospital, I think they still believe what they were told: that there was some terrorist attack."

"So they got sprung from the hospital and just accepted what they'd been told?" Riel asks. "If they were actually Outliers, you'd think they'd be suspicious."

Riel makes another mental note: *tell them not to be so gullible.*

"Come on, you and I both know how easy it is to ignore your gut when the world tells you to," Marly says. "Anyway, explain a little at least. The basics, that's all I'm saying. So we're all on the same page."

"Too bad I can't promise them everything is going to be okay."

Marly shrugs. "If they really are Outliers, they wouldn't believe you anyway."

IT'S NEARLY TWO o'clock when the first girl arrives. She has red curly hair tucked under a red bandanna, and she is so afraid. Afraid to be knocking. Afraid to come in after Riel answers the door. She wants to be there. She just wants to be reassured that Riel and Marly are for real.

"I'm Elise," she says. "I was in the hospital."

Her voice catches on the word "hospital." She may not have known what was going on in there, but at least Elise knew it was wrong. Riel is going to put that down as a mark in her favor.

"You're in the right place," Riel says. She should have some sense that Riel is telling the truth. Beyond that, she'll have to reassure herself. All these girls need to learn to put their own minds at ease.

Riel is ready to step up and be a leader; she'll even figure out the right thing to say. But she's not wasting her time holding hands.

•••

AN HOUR LATER everyone has arrived, eleven girls in all. Some sit on Marly's bed, others stand along the wall, the rest sit cross-legged on the floor. Some narrow their eyes skeptically, others look scared. Together they feel way too much for Riel to get a clear read on how any single one of them feels. And actually, that's okay. Riel isn't sure she wants to know.

Three of them are from the hospital—Elise, Ramona, and Becca. And it comes out quickly that they all took one of Ben Lang's follow-up tests, for fun (Ramona) or money (Becca). Elise was thinking it might help for college—how is totally not clear. The rest of the girls are the maybe-Outliers from the online tests. Together, the group is of every shape and size and skin color. They have different tastes in clothes and different mannerisms—bold, anxious, silly. Some look like they might come from families with money; one girl is almost homeless. Their differences are comforting. If they are not all the same, they will be harder to contain. Impossible to destroy.

"Thanks for coming," Riel says finally, as she stands in front of them. "Some of what I'm about to tell you might sound kind of out there. So listen, really listen. Then ask yourself whether you believe me. If you still think it's bullshit: no hard feelings, seriously. You can take off anytime. What we want is for you to listen to your own gut. About everything. That's why we're here." Riel pauses to look around the room. "I want you to realize how much time you've spent ignoring how you really feel. How much energy you've wasted listening to a world that says you're wrong before you open your mouth. What you need to do now instead is to own it—how you feel, who you care. Own your truth. So if your gut tells you to go right now, go. What I want most is for you to follow your instincts and walk out that door."

Riel lets the silence stretch out long and uncomfortable after that. But nobody moves. Not an inch. Not a single girl.

"Okay then," Riel says when it's obvious no one is going anywhere. "Welcome. You're all Outliers, at least we're pretty sure you are. Now let's talk about what the hell that means."

Riel goes on then, getting into details. She does her best to explain Dr. Lang's research and what "reading" is. She tells the group more than once that if Wylie were there, she could explain the science much better. Riel does the best she can, focusing on the basics: there is research that proves Outliers exist, there is good reason to believe the girls in that room are some of them, and that makes what they can do and who they are special. It also puts a target on their backs.

Maybe.

"Where *is* Wylie, anyway?" the girl named Ramona asks.

"She's been in jail. They think she set some fire in the hospital," Riel says. "They just let her out on bail. I don't know where she is right now."

"Oh." Ramona feels a wave of unmistakable guilt.

"Why?" Riel asks. "What?"

Ramona looks around the room at the other girls. But they just stare back at her blankly. They can feel Ramona's guilt, too. In a room full of Outliers, nothing is secret.

"Don't bother lying," Riel says before Ramona responds, relieved for the example. "And this applies to all of you. You can't lie to other Outliers. You can all read each other. If you stick around, I'll teach you how to block—which honestly might be the most important thing—and then you can keep some things to yourself. But when someone blocks, you'll probably know they're hiding something. Who knows, maybe we'll figure out another, better way of blocking that would be invisible. That would definitely help." Riel turns back to Ramona. "Anyway, you feel super guilty about Wylie. You might as well spill why."

Ramona looks down, sad now more than guilty. "I told the police that I thought Wylie had probably set the fire," she begins, then looks up, eyes wide, desperate. "I mean, Wylie wouldn't explain anything in the hospital, and there was all this weird stuff happening, some doll and all that. She chased after this guy and, like, tackled him. She was all over the place. I wasn't sure about the fire, but she was definitely lying about something."

"She was," Riel says. "You were right about that. You were just seriously wrong about what. Next time maybe get some facts before you toss somebody under the bus."

Ramona looks down, willing herself through the floor. And Riel feels like an ass. She's the last one who should be trying to claim some moral high ground.

"Listen, everyone makes mistakes," Riel goes on, more gently. Or as gently as she is able. Then she looks back over the girls. "But from now on, we've got to have one another's backs. All we have in this particular fucked-up situation is us."

JASPER

IT WAS ALREADY THREE P.M. WHEN JASPER DROPPED OFF LETHE'S BIKE AT THE repair shop. They told him it wouldn't be ready until four p.m., leaving him with a dangerously long hour to kill. Especially dangerous because the only repair shop he knew of was right near Wylie's house. And so there he is, driving closer now, only a few blocks away.

Jasper just wants to look one last time at Wylie's house before he all-the-way closes the door to her, to them. Closure, that's it, that's what he tells himself as he finally turns his Jeep down her block. He doesn't even care if he spots Wylie, actually. This is just about marking a place—her house—to say his final good-bye.

Too bad it's such a pathetic lie that Jasper can't even bring himself to believe it as he spots her house up ahead.

It's also not lost on Jasper that he has already begun fucking everything up like his mom was afraid he would, starting with missing the team meeting the night before.

"Dude, where the hell were you?" Chance had asked when he finally got home from his run at eleven thirty p.m. last night. "Coach was seriously pissed."

"Shit," Jasper had said, closing his eyes and hanging his head as he remembered the team meeting. After all that, coming back specifically to make it, he got Wylie's note and forgot all about it. "What did he say?"

"'Where the hell is Jasper?' That's what he said. I lied and told him your mom was sick," Chance said, pleased with himself. "He seemed to get over it after that, but you might want to have some proof, or whatever, that she was sick. Also, I wouldn't do it again."

"Thanks, man, seriously," Jasper had said.

And he is still grateful. Coach mentioned a doctor's note at practice that morning, and that was after making him stay for an extra hour of drills and then to clean up the locker room. Hopefully, he can talk his mom into getting a note for herself. She does work in a hospital. Of course that means he'll have to come up with a good reason he missed that meeting, one that doesn't involve Wylie.

Except sitting there now, parked in his Jeep a block away from Wylie's house, those reasons feel in kind of short supply. Jasper doesn't see any signs of life up at Wylie's house anyway. Like it's past midnight, instead of past three in the afternoon.

Okay, so that's it. No one there, nothing else to say.

Jasper is about to roll past the house when he catches sight of the front door. It's hanging wide open just like it was the last time, when Wylie was in the hospital and someone trashed the place. *That* he's at least got to check out.

He parks across the street and up a bit, out of sight between two other cars. Jasper watches the house in his rearview, for one minute, then two. Nothing. Just the door still hanging open weirdly. He's just started to think that maybe he should just get out and at least go close the front door, when a huge guy appears in Wylie's doorway, toting a cardboard file box. He pauses on the steps, looking right, then left, before heading down to the curb with the box. He waits as a white van drives down the street and pulls up alongside him. He puts the box in back, then climbs into the passenger seat before the van pulls away.

Holy shit. Who the hell was that? *What* was that? Suspicious as hell, that's what. Jasper finds himself following the van before he's fully decided it's the best idea.

Is there a part of him that's hoping if he follows this huge, maybe dangerous dude, maybe up to no good, he might somehow win Wylie back? Definitely. Does he know that's stupid? Yep. Too bad that's not going to stop him.

THE GUY—OR whoever is driving the guy—drives for a long time, an hour nearly, much longer than Jasper was prepared for. Soon they have left Newton behind, and also any sign of life. All around are just trees and more trees.

Eventually, the van pulls off the main road onto a long, unpaved driveway that disappears between the trees. Jasper passes the driveway and finds a place to park his Jeep out of sight. Only choice is to head back on foot.

Jasper is about a hundred yards down the potholed driveway when he finally makes out a couple of warehouses up ahead in the distance through the trees. They are long and beige, one behind the other. But it's so quiet and totally deserted out there in the woods. It's seriously a weird place for warehouses, at least ones where anything good is going on inside.

Jasper makes his way carefully onward, staying along the edge of the driveway, reassuring himself the whole way that he can turn back any time, dive into the trees if he needs to. There is a good distance still between him and the warehouses. And whatever is in that van.

Jasper stops when he finally hears the voices. No, not *voices.* One voice. A man's. He is pretty sure he knows it, too—one of the agents who followed them to the house on Cape Cod. He never saw the guy's face. But he'll never forget that voice coming from Riel's grandfather's front door as he and Leo and Wylie hid in the office. "Klute," Wylie had said after. He'd come by her house before, too, apparently.

When Jasper leans over now, he can see him—Klute, pacing in the space between the warehouses—talking on the phone.

"Yeah," he hears Klute say. "I'm taking care of them right now." Silence as he listens to whoever is on the other end. "Yeah, where we agreed. I will. I'll confirm before I leave."

Klute hangs up and disappears again from view. A moment later, there is the distinct smell of smoke. And then Klute is there again, making his way calmly back to the van. The driver never even opens the door. Jasper ducks into the woods and out of sight as the van heads back his way.

By the time the van has driven past and out of sight, the burning smell is much stronger. It brings back thoughts of Cassie, which make Jasper feel sick and guilty as he makes his way quickly to see what's on fire.

As soon as he steps past the first building, there's the actual fire; the size for sure of that cardboard box. And when Jasper is close enough, he can definitely see that's exactly what's burning. The box is already mostly just a pile of smoking black ash. What the hell was Klute burning, and why? If it was taken from Wylie's house, it can't be good, none of it. This Jasper really does need to tell Wylie—right now.

Before Jasper turns to leave, he peeks into the windows of the back warehouse. It has a long center hallway, with dozens of little rooms off to either side. Like half office, half prison. If somebody is going to work there, it's going to suck. But nothing in that warehouse tells Jasper why the hell Klute drove all the way out here. Or what he was burning.

But note or no note, Jasper needs to tell Wylie. As soon as he can find her.

JASPER GOES BACK past Wylie's, but there's no sign of her. By the time he gets to campus, he's so fixated on thinking about that agent and the box—and how to tell Wylie—that he doesn't even notice that he's carried Lethe's fixed bike all the way up the stairs instead of locking it outside to the rack next to his dorm.

"Damn it," he mutters at the top of the steps. He's still looking down at the bike in his hand when he steps through the stairway door and almost collides with Chance.

"Dude," Chance says, jumping to the side just before getting nailed in the shins by Lethe's bike. He turns back at the top of the steps, narrows his eyes at Jasper. "Man, you look like ass. You okay?"

No, Jasper's not okay. And he'd like to tell Chance all about it. But where to start? He hasn't even told Chance anything about Wylie. He didn't want to have to explain the detention facility, and not because he was ashamed—that's the last thing he would ever feel. But because it's no one's business but Wylie's.

"Yeah, I'm cool," Jasper says.

"You just missed some girl." Chance is halfway down the steps. He pauses, looks back. "She came by looking for you."

"What girl?" Jasper asks.

"Cute, wild eyes. She didn't tell me her name. I told her I might not see you—I've got a hot date." He winks. "I'm not planning on being home anytime soon. Anyway, she left you a note, and cookies. You're lucky I was on my way out when she got here, otherwise they'd be gone. Save some for me. You still owe me."

Inside his dorm room, Jasper puts Lethe's bike down. Sure enough, there is a paper plate on his desk piled high with chocolate chip cookies and wrapped tight in cellophane. Even as he's staring down at the note taped to the top (not in Wylie's handwriting), he's still stupidly hoping the cookies might be from her.

Dear Japer,

Thanks so much for getting my bike fixed.

Sorry I was a bitch before. Bad day.

xo,

Lethe

Nope, definitely not from Wylie. It was nice of Lethe, though. And for just a split second, he finds himself thinking: maybe she's . . . But he pulls himself up short. He's just considering Lethe because she's there. Available. That actually isn't a reason to like someone.

Jasper takes a deep breath, opens the plastic, and picks up one of the cookies from the plate. He takes a huge bite and drops himself down hard onto his desk chair.

Whatever. At least he knows he's got problems, right? And it's not like he's rushing off to find Lethe right now just because she made him feel good for a second. It's slow progress, maybe. But it's still progress.

Jasper pops the rest of the cookie into his mouth and closes his eyes. He's tired as hell now; all that running away from the truth has beaten the crap out of him. It's only five thirty p.m., but maybe he'll just go to sleep, be extra rested for early morning practice. He'll have to kick ass for sure at the next one. And the one after that. Make Coach forget that he's pissed at him. And everything else might look different in the morning anyway.

Jasper gets up to head over to his bed, but too fast. He's sent off balance by a head rush. The room begins to spin. He feels like he might throw up, too. Jasper puts his hands out to steady himself, but just grabs a fistful of air. The ground shifts to the side. And all he sees is the ceiling. In motion.

TOP SECRET AND CONFIDENTIAL

To: Senator David Russo, Senate Armed Services Committee
From: Department of Military Intelligence, Buildings Department
Re: Lease Extension
May 5

Your extension of lease arrangement for use of Properties 2642 in Massachusetts, 1754 in Arizona, and 1619 in Washington, DC, has been approved. Please provide all budgeting details and a Request for Proposal for the interior construction of each site as soon as possible.

The project has been given Level 1 Security Clearance, and associated confidentiality rules will apply. This will be the final communication regarding this matter. All further records regarding the use of these properties shall be maintained by your office alone.

WYLIE

IT'S FIVE THIRTY P.M. WHEN WE ARE FINALLY DRIVING OUT OF BOSTON, following Elizabeth's maps toward Framingham. Detective Oshiro stays close behind. We've agreed to ditch Gideon's phone as soon as we are outside Boston proper. It's hard to think of cutting ourselves off completely. My mom's emails haven't told us much so far. But who's to say Rachel might not send more? And the next one might finally matter. Still, it's too much of a risk to keep the phone. It would be one thing for somebody to have been following us around Newton. We can't have them following us now.

Oshiro asked for us to wait until the end of the endless day before going to Framingham. He was expected at work, he said. Not being there could raise suspicions. But I think, more important, he hoped to dig up something about where our dad was that would make it so we didn't have to go at all. Apparently, he'd struck out. We would have spent the day digging around ourselves, but Oshiro made it a condition of him helping that we didn't.

So instead, Gideon and I had just done our best to make it through the long day. That had meant heading downtown to the movies—a double feature of old martial arts movies. Gideon's pick, not that there was a lot on offer.

"Pull over there." I point at a gas station off a short exit along the busy stretch of highway.

Gideon obliges, checking to be sure that Oshiro has time to follow. I'm already leaning out the car door, about to quickly toss the phone, when I notice a text from Rachel.

Where is Wylie? She better not have left Newton. It's a violation of the terms of her bail.

She hasn't. I swear, I type back. There's some relief in pretending for a moment to be somebody other than me.

Come home, Gideon. NOW. Your mom will be here soon. She is going to need Wylie's help when she gets home. She sent another email, too.

There is an attachment, which I quickly tap open and read:

> **To: Wylie**
> **From: SwimTeacher**
> **Re: July 2**
>
> **Dear Wylie,**
>
> **On my way back from California. I can't wait to see you. Dr.**

Oduwole says that she told Dad that the Outliers might have just become visible now because of our relatively recent reliance on technology. She believes that it has changed the structure of our brains, shrunk our gray matter, specifically.

But there's something else, Wylie. She told Dad all this. He knew. But she says that Dad wanted to keep it a secret. It's really weird. Dr. Oduwole said she wasn't comfortable with that. She and Dad had a big argument about it. She thought maybe he was working with someone on the side, was selling the research.

I'm not saying that Dad did anything wrong, but Dr. Oduwole was worried. And so am I.

I love you always,

Mom

I feel a wave of anger, followed by a guilty twist in my gut. Is she seriously accusing my *dad* of something? All because some random doctor said so? I don't care whether Dr. Oduwole worked with our dad or not. We don't even know her. My mom shouldn't be out there chasing answers in the first place. Of course, as I sit there in that deserted gas station with Gideon, on my way into who knows what, I'm not exactly one to talk.

Okay. Be there soon, I type in response to Rachel.

GIDEON, I MEAN IT!! RIGHT NOW!

I turn off the phone.

"Rachel?" Gideon asks. I nod. "She must be pissed."

"Yup," I say, feeling weirdly glad she's mad. Like a two-year-old, I just want to piss someone off.

I use a safety pin to dig the SIM card out of his phone, a trick

I learned from Riel. When I finally have it out, I open the door and toss the phone. It thuds loudly to the bottom of the empty garbage can. Terrible regret comes with the sound. Like I am totally and completely wrong about something. I'm just not sure yet what.

GIDEON AND I ride for another thirty minutes until we finally reach the dot on the map Elizabeth gave us: the American Legion Hall, Framingham, Massachusetts. The place that last cell phone call was made from. It's a small brick building with a white pitched roof stuck onto the front, which makes the whole place seem off-kilter. Or maybe that's just how I feel. I'm trying hard not to let myself feel much of anything. Because we have no choice but to see this through.

Gideon pulls into a parking spot near the front door. Oshiro pulls into one much farther back and in the shadows. We agreed before we left that Oshiro would wait outside and out of sight. He will still be close enough to know if we've run into trouble, or to notice when we don't come back out. We have fifteen minutes before he comes in after us.

"Are you sure you still want to do this?" Gideon asks as I reach for the car door. I can feel his dread. No, it's worse than dread. It's fear.

I force a smile. "Define 'want.'"

"I'm serious," Gideon says, motioning to the half-filled, very dark parking lot. "There are obviously people in there. Like a decent number. We have no idea who or why. We could be walking into anything."

"I know. And I know the person who called me might not even know anything about Dad. This might all be about her getting money from us or something. But it's the only lead we've got," I say, looking over at the Legion Hall again. And I don't feel a twinge of doubt about going inside. "This Legion Hall is us heading in the right direction. And I think we need to keep on going to find Dad. He needs saving." I turn back to Gideon. "But those are all just 'feelings.' They're not like bits of data or something. You should know that before you come."

As Gideon stares at me, I feel the exact moment he calms, a little. The instant he chooses to believe in me.

"Okay, then," he says, opening his car door. "That's good enough for me."

WE MAKE OUR way inside the Legion Hall's deserted lobby. The walls are dark stone, the floor polished brick, and there is a long row of flags along one wall. It is cool inside and slightly damp, like a basement. There are some tables piled high with random pamphlets: bereavement support, veterans' services, computer tutoring for the elderly, lawn services, and dog-walking—there's not much rhyme or reason to any of it.

On the wall opposite the tables is a set of closed doors. A handwritten sign reads: *Meeting 6 p.m.* We can hear voices, laughter, clips of conversation on the other side. Gideon nods as I pull open the door, bracing myself for military men—it is a Legion Hall, after all. Cunning like Kendall, or huge like Agent Klute. But when my eyes fix on the scene—old people, young people, middle-aged, round and thin, short and tall—it has the warm, chaotic hum of a community meeting about to start. No, maybe an AA meeting. AA makes me think of Cassie's dad. And my mind sticks hard. It had been so awful seeing Vince at Cassie's funeral. He'd been heartbroken about Cassie, and so angry *at* me. But can I really blame him? After what happened to Cassie, I still kind of blame myself.

And, of course, thinking of Cassie just makes me miss Jasper all over again. That stupid note.

I look around again at the assorted faces, smiling, chatting, greeting one another in small clusters; none of them seem to have even noticed that we came in. They are ordinary, small-town people, friendly-looking, welcoming. Chairs are lined up facing an empty podium at the front; a few people are already seated. At the side of the room, there is a table with a sad collection of store-bought cookies on a paper plate next to some Styrofoam cups and two containers of orange juice.

"Let's sit down," Gideon says through gritted teeth. "Whatever it is, it's about to start."

He's right. People have started moving toward the chairs. When the room finally quiets all the way and we are seated, I feel my attention pulled left. There are two teenage girls sitting over there—cute tops, strappy flat sandals. Pretty, but not noticeably so. Except they stand out for me. Because when I look at them, I feel like I'm missing something important. The most important thing.

"Hello, everyone," a man calls from the front of the room. He has well-coiffed grayish hair, a fashionable white linen shirt, and an expensive watch. Much more sophisticated than most of the audience. "As always, we're so glad you're here. As most of you know, I'm Brother John. And no, I am not back for good. I'm just filling in again tonight. Hopefully, I will be able to continue carrying the torch for a few days more. I know how popular the meetings here have become since I took my leave a few months ago. But I won't take that personally, not to worry."

He looks around the room, beaming. Real joy, that's what he feels. Despite all the people in the room and how far away he is, it glows from him like a spotlight. I brace myself as his eyes pass our way. I wait for them to catch when he doesn't recognize us. But they just move on, calmly, serenely. Welcoming.

"Tonight, I'd like to start with something from Sir Isaac Newton: 'Gravity explains the motions of the planets, but it cannot explain who set the planets in motion.' I think this quote is particularly relevant to our mission. Because there is, of course, space for science and spirituality not just to peacefully coexist, but to enhance each other. That has always been our goal."

He keeps talking. About faith and proof, belief and facts. And he's a good talker, with a nice, soothing voice. Everyone is *really* listening, too. For sure the meeting is spiritual-ish, but not an official religion. At least not a traditional one. But a kind one, for sure. The kindness in the room grows stronger the more he talks. I've never read people in a room like that: all committed to a single, positive emotion. It's overwhelming, but in the best possible way.

Soon, I'm floating on it, suspended in a warm pool. Weightless and free as the room drops away. For one long minute, then two.

I am jerked awake then. When I look around, everyone has their heads bowed, eyes closed. Silence.

"Toward the light," Brother John says.

"Toward the light," everyone repeats.

Just like that, the spell is broken. People's random emotions flood in—kids, stress, work, *I'm hungry, I'm cold.* Brother John motions with his arms outstretched like an angel, beckoning. People begin to rise. Soon they are dispersing slowly across the room.

"Is that it?" I whisper. "It's over already?"

"'Already'?" Gideon asks. "I felt like it was never going to end."

"Oh, I guess I got distracted."

"There's juice, though," Gideon says. He raises his eyebrows when I look confused. "That's what he said: 'We're finished, but please feel free to have juice.' Nothing about the cookies, just the juice, which if you ask me, just makes the whole thing even more sketchy. I mean, he might as well have said, 'Drink the Kool-Aid.'"

I stand because everyone else already has. "Do you want some juice?" I ask.

"Um, no, I don't want some juice," Gideon says like I've definitely lost it. "I'm not interested in getting roofied."

"Roofied?" I ask. I just can't follow him. I feel so clouded.

"Wylie, what's wrong? You seem so out of it."

"How long was he talking exactly?"

"A half hour maybe," Gideon says. "Circling around and around the same idea, this whole science-and-religion-together idea. Which, I've got to be honest, started to sound like he mostly wants to ignore the whole science part. But, whatever, to each his own. Everybody else seemed super into it."

"Crowds usually make it so I can't read anything," I say. "But this was like a single roar. It was"—my voice catches—"huge."

"Are you sure you haven't already had some of the juice?" Gideon narrows his eyes at me. It's a joke, sort of. "Listen, I want to get out of here, and we are already way over our limit with Oshiro. So much for him checking on us. You want to see if we can find out anything about Dad's phone before he does come in?"

Gideon is right. I need to focus. "We should talk to those girls over there first," I say, pointing to the two who drew my attention before.

"Okay, lead the way," Gideon says, relieved. All he really wants is to get the hell out of here.

THE GIRLS ARE sitting side by side, hovering over a phone when we get to the other side of the room. One has waist-length, pin-straight blond hair and very white skin, the other short, light brown curls and freckles. They seem to be debating somebody's half-naked selfie on Snapchat.

"She could have Photoshopped it, though," the blonde says. "All I'm saying is that it could have happened."

"I don't think so," the girl with the curls responds. "No one's that good at Photoshop."

Up close, I can feel these girls have none of the dreamy purity of the rest of the group. They are harder on the outside and raw and hot underneath. Like rock over a core of molten lava. Definitely not true believers.

"Oh," the curly-haired girl says finally, blinking up at me.

It's not a hello—definitely not—but it signals my turn to talk.

"Hi," I begin, but then no more words will come. The stakes suddenly feel too high. These girls have something so important to tell us. Too important to mess this up. And so all I can do is stare.

"Hey," Gideon says finally, stepping forward to fill the void. He holds up a hand and smiles. "I'm, um, Gideon."

The girls smile slyly and bend their long bodies like two preening birds. And just like that, for the first time *ever*, I notice how good-looking Gideon is.

"I'm Grace," the girl with the blond hair says, hunching forward like she is trying to make herself petite.

"Jennifer," the other one says, and then the two girls glance at each other. I can feel them giggling on the inside. *He's so cute.*

"Can you tell us what this is?" Gideon motions to the room, doing a decent job of seeming curious and maybe a little confused, but not judgmental.

"Is it an AA meeting?" I ask. My voice sounds so sharp. I wish I hadn't said anything.

"An AA meeting?" Jennifer makes a face like I'm an idiot.

"The random people, the juice," I say, though now my evidence on this AA thing feels thin.

"An AA meeting would be *way* more interesting," Grace says

wistfully, looking out over the crowd still milling around. No one looks in any rush to leave.

"Seriously," Jennifer agrees, then looks up at me, more forcefully. Like an accusation. "Why would you come to some meeting if you don't even know what it's for?"

"Somebody called us from here," I say.

At least my voice is starting to even out. And I didn't mention that the call was from the missing, maybe stolen phone of our also missing dad on purpose because it would seem like we're looking for somebody who has committed a serious crime. It might give them incentive to lie.

"No one makes calls during meetings," Grace says seriously. "It's a rule. So . . ."

"It was a few days ago," I say. "It might not even have been during an actual meeting. I don't remember the exact time."

"Well, lots of people meet here. This is like a place where people meet, you know?" Jennifer rolls her eyes. "The Girl Scouts and their moms meet here." I feel a quick pop of jealousy from Jennifer about the Girl Scouts specifically. Like she wishes she'd had the chance to be one herself, once upon a time.

"Oh," I say. My throat is pinching shut.

I realize now as we hurtle toward a dead end, I've had too many hopes pinned on this.

"Do you have a name?" Grace asks.

"A name?" I ask, not wanting to tell them who I am.

Jennifer and Grace eyeball each other. "Um, of the person who *called you*?" Grace asks.

"Oh, no," I say. "I can't remember."

"Listen, just some friendly advice," Jennifer says. "I wouldn't seem so out of it around here if I was you. If these people decide you need 'help,' they'll make you take it. You're lucky the regular guy's not here. He's, like, relentless. They're not bad people, most of them. Actually, they're pretty good, on the scale of people. But they are not big on boundaries."

"Who's the regular guy?" Gideon asks.

"Like Brother John, but on steroids," Jennifer says, with a wave of her hand. "Sometimes you get the feeling that the people here don't believe half the shit that gets said. They just like the community and all that. But the new guy? He's *all in*."

"It's true," Grace says seriously. "Once he gets started, he just doesn't stop with the 'I can save you' crap. It can get kind of creepy. Not, like, sex creepy. Just *creepy* creepy. Which honestly makes it weirder. But, whatever, some of the girls we know like him. I have no idea why."

"What girls like him?" Jennifer asks Grace.

"I don't know, Sophie-Ann," Grace says, nervous suddenly. "Girl, I guess. One girl. But she was, like, hanging out with him."

Jennifer shoots Grace a look. There is something about this Sophie-Ann. There's no doubt about that. I need to double down on her, ever though it's not the name the girl gave me on the phone. I can't imagine she would have used her real one.

"Well, it was a girl who called us. Maybe it was Sophie-Ann," I say. "Whoever it is actually has our dad's phone, too." I can only leave that out for so long.

"Your dad's phone?" Grace asks, intrigued. Jennifer, though, looks like she's about to get up and leave. "She stole it?"

"Technically, she said she found the phone," I say. "But we still really need to find her. Because we need my dad's phone. He's missing. And we're definitely not saying Sophie-Ann or whoever has it had anything to do with that. We just want the phone, that's all. It might help us find him."

"Well, like *we* said, lots of girls come here." Jennifer's voice, her feel, is ice-cold.

I consider for a second—the voice was distinctive. It's still ringing in my head.

"Wait, she had a hard-core Boston accent," I offer, so relieved that I have anything useful to add. Amazed that it actually didn't occur to me until now. "Like 'remembah?' She talked like that."

Grace claps her hands together excitedly. "That's so Sophie-Ann!" She turns to Jennifer. "Right? That sounds just like her!"

Jennifer stares at Grace in disbelief. "Jesus, Grace." She shakes her head. "Let's go before you say more shit you definitely shouldn't."

Grace looks confused, then ashamed as she gets to her feet and quickly goes to stand behind Jennifer. She may not understand why, but she's ready to accept she's in the wrong.

"Where can we find Sophie-Ann?" I ask. "Do you know?"

"Nope," Jennifer says instantly. A lie. Or sort of. Because, weirdly, it seems both true and untrue. "Grace, come on. *Now.*"

Jennifer steps away, tugging on Grace's arm.

"Sorry," Grace says, following her obediently. "But Mrs. Porter, our foster mom, says we're not allowed to talk about her. I can give you her address—"

"Gr—"

"We live at three nineteen Culver Side Drive."

"—ace!" Jennifer has hung her head and closed her eyes. "This is on you, Grace," she says quietly as she heads on for the door. "All you."

"Come on, Jennifer!" Grace calls as she rushes after her and out the door. "You're not really mad, are you?"

IT ISN'T UNTIL we're back out in the lobby that I realize we should have asked Grace and Jennifer for the name of the group. Grace gave us the right address for Mrs. Porter's, I think, but there is always the chance that we'll have to backtrack.

Luckily, there's a janitor sweeping the lobby. He is young—twenties maybe—pushing a broom. I head over to him.

"Excuse me, do you know the name of the group meeting here tonight?"

But the janitor just continues on with his work. It isn't until I ask a second time that I realize he has earbuds in. He startles when I wave a hand in front of his face, then smiles up at me brightly.

"Sorry," he laughs, pointing at the headphones. "I was just listening to the podcast. You know, the new guy? These days everyone needs a podcast, right?" When he shakes his head and smiles this time, I can feel how trusting he is. Like an unlocked door. "At first, it was a little out there for me, but I've been listening for an hour, and damn if it isn't starting to make a whole lot of sense. My girlfriend would say that's how this kind of stuff is supposed to work. Wear you down. She's the suspicious type."

"What do you mean 'this kind of stuff'?" I ask. "What is this?"

And in the moment before he answers, I can feel a train hurtling toward me. No time to leap clear.

"It's The Collective. But the podcast is called EndOfDays," he says as he puts his earbuds back in. "And come to think of it, it still does kind of seem out there, I guess. Don't tell my girlfriend she's right."

GIDEON AND I rush out of the American Legion Hall, headed toward Oshiro's car, now partially out of view behind a white van. The hair on the back of my neck is standing on end. *EndOfDays. The Collective. EndOfDays. The Collective.* I did feel some of it coming, didn't I? They have my dad's phone. They have my dad. I did feel some of it. Just not assembled in this particular way. Also, I still don't know who "they" are. Quentin? That doesn't feel like the key, just like one more turn of the knob.

I expect to feel better as we get closer to Oshiro's car, but I only feel worse. I have to believe Oshiro will have some idea what we should do now, though. Because I can't see how anyone could claim that my dad would have gone somewhere "voluntarily" with someone tied to a group who were at least partly responsible for Cassie being dead and almost killing me. That's true no matter how little anyone has been interested in getting to the bottom of any of it. So far the camp has been left as just another unsolved tragedy. Contained, though, not likely to repeat.

"Holy shit." Gideon freezes as we come around the van. Through the back window of Oshiro's car, we can see him leaning to the side. "No wonder he didn't care how long we took. He's fucking asleep. So much for protecting us."

No, I think, unable to move. *He is not asleep.* But I can't get myself to say a word.

The rest is so terribly slow. Gideon moves ahead of me to the driver's side window. "Oh my God," he says.

When I get close enough, I can see the shattered window, bits of glass hanging around the edges. And inside the jagged hole is Detective Oshiro, motionless and bleeding.

TOP SECRET AND CONFIDENTIAL

To: Senator David Russo

From: The Architect

Re: Bracelet Identification Registration and Enforcement

May 11

Though the research threat has unfortunately not been contained, as of yet, we anticipate a solution is imminent. We recommend proceeding nonetheless.

As discussed, our model predicts that the principal obstacle to the successful implementation of a program to identify and track the targeted subgroup population "Outliers" will be compliance. If a member is determined to be noncompliant, our model suggests that the following penalties will be most effective.

First offense: Subject will be placed on house arrest for a period of no less than three days.
Second offense: Subject will serve a jail term of no less than three days.
Third offense: Subject will serve a jail term of no less than three months.

Fourth offense: Our models predict that fewer than 1 percent of the targeted subgroup will commit a fourth offense. We recommend a prison term of no less than two years.

Though penalties may meet with initial civil rights objections, we believe that a continuous, strategic public relations campaign focused on safety and security will result in gradual support of these measures.

For maximum benefit, we believe this approach should be outlined early in the campaign, as soon as the target population is publicly identified.

RIEL

TURNS OUT, DAVID ROSENFELD LIVES IN BEACON HILL, NOT THAT FAR FROM Trident Booksellers & Café, which is maybe the reason that Riel was drawn there in the first place. It's early evening when she heads out following the map Brian printed for her, finally finding Rosenfeld's converted carriage house tucked down an alley. The sun hasn't yet set, but down there it is already pretty dark.

There's good reason to think that *this* David Rosenfeld is the Rosenfeld whose name is written on the envelope. But his name might have been there because he is the main guy to avoid. That's the real reason Riel insisted on going herself despite the risk that someone will see her. After everything Marly has done, Riel can't put her in harm's way like that.

At least Riel knows Leo's still okay. According to Level99, there has been regular activity on Leo's credit card, suggesting that he's been going on with his life. At least for now.

Riel takes one last deep breath, rings Rosenfeld's doorbell. And then she waits. And waits. And waits. But Rosenfeld is home. Riel can feel him inside, watching. Waiting for her to go.

Riel rings the bell again, tries to feel her way forward. If Rosenfeld is afraid—and Riel can feel he is, which is a relief, given the alternatives—she has to make it more dangerous for him to leave her standing outside than to let her in.

"I just wanted to thank you!" Riel shouts as loud as she can, hating that getting in means drawing attention to herself, too. She just hopes it works quickly. "For all that information! I think we have enough now!"

Sure enough, the door snaps right open and Riel is yanked in so forcefully that her head jerks back. Inside, she bangs hard into something.

"Fuck!" she shouts, grabbing at her throbbing shin as the door slams shut behind her, locking her in. "What the hell!"

"You're asking *me* what the hell?!" Rosenfeld yells. And, wow, is he pissed behind his square black glasses when Riel's eyes stop watering enough to make him out clearly. Like pissed enough to consider for a second what it would take to kill her with his bare hands. He is leaning heavily on a cane, but she is sure this would not slow him down. Actually, he might have whacked Riel with it already. She takes a step back so he can't do it again.

"I have some pictures with your name on them," she says. "I just wanted to ask you about them. Oh, and I read your book. It's really good." She throws in that last part in a lame attempt to win him over with flattery, which she senses works a lot of the time with him. Or would if he weren't so pissed.

"My book?" Sure enough, Rosenfeld feels a split-second tug toward softening. But he swallows it away. He shakes his head as he reaches for the door to open it again. "Nope, no thanks. Get out. You have questions, call Hope Lang."

"Hope Lang is dead," Riel says.

Rosenfeld freezes, closes his eyes. His hand is still on the door. "Oh, for fuck's sake."

Without another word, Rosenfeld turns and makes his way down the hall. He doesn't invite Riel to follow. But she does anyway. She has no choice. Despite her sense that Rosenfeld would still happily do her harm.

THE BACK OF Rosenfeld's house opens up into a beautiful, newly remodeled kitchen and open living room, complete with fireplace and skylight above, all of it much nicer than the house looked from the outside. It's completely free of clutter, too, apart from a perfectly organized, color-coded bookshelf and dozens of folders lined up like soldiers in expandable metal racks along the opposite wall. Riel stares hard at them. The files matter. Whatever they are.

"You didn't know Hope was dead?" Riel asks.

"Listen, I'm lucky to be alive myself. I've made it my business not to know anything about anyone anymore." Rosenfeld uses his cane to point toward a back door. "Now, out, that way. It's safer than the front."

"But I'm—"

Rosenfeld holds up a hand. "Nope," he says. "Not another

word. I don't want to know anything more. Out."

"No," Riel says, crossing her arms and sitting down defiantly on the couch. "I'm not going anywhere."

Rosenfeld steps closer, more pissed, gripping the top of his cane harder. Yup, he definitely whacked her with it before. And he'll definitely do it again. "Maybe you misunderstood. I'm not asking. Get out."

"If you touch me again, I will scream my head off. *And* I still won't leave." Riel reaches into her bag and pulls out the pictures. "Now, look, your name is right here on this envelope of pictures."

"And that is probably what almost got me killed," he says, gesturing to his leg.

"What do you mean?"

"All Hope Lang did was tell me *about* those pictures. On the phone. I didn't know her. I'd been an expert for some reporter friend of hers. Anyway, I never even saw the pictures. Just the one quick call. And then boom!" He smacks his palms together loudly. "I was taken out in a crosswalk. I flatlined in the ER. Massive internal bleeding." He shakes his head, but Riel feels a tremor of doubt. He isn't sure anymore about throwing her out. He's even a tiny bit curious. "Doctors say it's a miracle I survived. And I'd like to keep it that way."

The folders. Riel feels a tug toward them again, probably because Rosenfeld is worried about her looking in them. There is something there. She motions toward the folders.

"But you researched it already," she says. It's a guess. A Hail Mary pass. "You must have figured something out."

Rosenfeld narrows his eyes. Wary of what she already seems

to know, but also kind of wanting somebody to ask. He doesn't want to be the only person who knows. He makes his way closer to the folders and looks down. He exhales, and with his breath out goes his anger.

"You know, I've devoted my entire career to exposing all the messed-up shit our government does in the name of winning wars. Or just winning, period. But I accept now that they will win. Always. And I'd really like not to die for it."

"If you don't help me, other people might die, though. Innocent people. Teenagers. They haven't even had the chance to live their lives yet. They haven't done anything wrong," Riel says. Suddenly there it is: a crack in Rosenfeld's rock-hard shell. And he is oozing out fast all over the place. She just needs to keep pressing. "Please, we really need your help. What is the place in the pictures? Why does my grandfather care so much about it?"

"Your grandfather?"

"Senator David Russo," she says. "And if it makes you feel any better, I think he tried to kill me, too. I'm pretty sure he's going to keep on trying."

"Senator Russo is your grandfather?"

"Yep."

"All right, fine. I'll look at the pictures, but only because Russo for a grandfather is definitely a shitty deal."

RIEL SITS IN silence as Rosenfeld flips through the stack of photos several times, studying them.

"See this?" he says finally, pointing to a small route sign in the distance behind what looks like it could be a guardhouse. "I wasn't sure from what Lang said, but now I am: these pictures are of the WSRF."

"What's the WSRF?"

"The Watuck Soldier Research Facility," he says, then motions to his folders. "Based on what Lang told me when she called, I had it narrowed down to there and one other place. She said she was going to send the pictures, but then there was my accident. And, not that I wanted to after that, but I never heard from her again. Anyway, that route is near the WSRF."

"But I don't understand. If Hope Lang took these pictures, wouldn't she know where she was when she took them? Why did she need you to tell her?"

"I never said she took these pictures," Rosenfeld says. "Maybe she was tight-lipped, but I got the sense that she really didn't know what she had."

"Oh," Riel says, feeling like she knows less and less somehow the more she learns. "And *what* exactly is the WSRF?"

"It's a research facility that was officially shuttered a few years ago. Meaning only that it's up and running and in private hands. Compass Industries—this shit is all they do. They create whole shell corporations for the express purpose of running a facility like that when they want to do real fucked-up studies. Then when they're done with their fucked-up studies, the shell folds up and disappears. It's like none of it ever happened. Definitely nowhere to lodge a complaint, no one to stop, no one to sue."

"What kind of fucked-up studies?"

"All kinds." Rosenfeld holds her stare. "That's why they want it away from the official government dime. No accountability, no oversight from those other pesky aboveboard government agencies. Like remember those tests they did in the sixties with LSD?"

"LSD?" Riel asks.

Rosenfeld shakes his head, disgusted. "See, like it never happened. The army wanted to see if they could use LSD on enemy soldiers in combat," he says. "But to do that, they needed live human subjects to test because it's hard to extrapolate a totally internal psychological experience from, you know, rats. So the army research division rounded up a bunch of people they thought wouldn't be missed, wouldn't be listened to. People died, others had psychotic breaks, permanent ones. And they got caught. Upper-level military went to jail, and strict oversight of *military* testing was put into place. *Military* testing. A private company, on the other hand? Especially if they keep it all off the books? They've got a hell of a lot more leeway, so if you want to be left alone—"

"You outsource it."

Rosenfeld smiles, genuinely pleased. "Now you're catching on," he says. "Companies like North Point . . ."

"North Point?"

"It's one of those Compass Industries shells I was talking about," he says, ticking his head in the direction of the folders. "North Point did some messed-up shit trying to figure out how to use PTSD as a weapon. Which, you know, means that you've got to *give* people PTSD first." Rosenfeld goes back to studying the pictures, pauses on one, and puts his face in close. "But North

Point is gone now. Like it never was. See, look at this. This is a telltale sign of something suspect." He's holding a finger to the grainy image of the construction buckets.

"Plaster or something, right?" Riel asks. "Construction is a telltale sign?"

"Plaster? No, no, it's a close-up." He peers at it again. "They're drug vials. I guarantee you the WSRF never had FDA authorization for a study using them. They'd never met the standards. So they just do it and pretend they aren't. If your results are never meant to be public anyway, you can do that."

Riel has the most awful feeling now that this is why she was so intent on coming here herself, despite the risk. That she needed to hear this.

"What kind of drugs?" Riel asks. Her voice is small as she braces herself.

Rosenfeld squints at the pictures again. "It's hard to make out the name on the vials," he says. "But I'm pretty sure it's a kind of morphine."

"DO YOU KNOW how she died yet?" Riel's aunt had asked in the hospital. The doctor was nice and young, with a nervous smile and a tentative way about him that seemed to draw the ire of Riel's aunt.

"A drug overdose," he said. He was standing right in front of Riel, but she heard him as though he was very far away. "Sorry, I thought someone told you."

"We know *that*," her aunt said. "What *kind* of drugs?" Because for her aunt, there were good drugs and there were bad, shameful drugs. She wanted to know if she should be mentioning this unpleasantness with her niece to her friends and coworkers. Or if she should be keeping this whole thing to herself.

"An opiate, we believe," he said uneasily.

"An opiate?" Her aunt's words were shellacked in judgment. "Could you be more specific?"

"We need the report to be sure," the doctor said. "But it seems likely it was morphine."

Riel's aunt had turned to face Riel. "Morphine?" As if she had been the one to take it and not Kelsey. "God, what was wrong with her?"

"YOU OKAY?" ROSENFELD asks. How long has he been talking? Riel hasn't been listening. "I could be wrong, too. All of this is mostly a guess. I mean, I'm not usually wrong, but you never . . . Does all this mean something to you? Because you got really pale all of a sudden, and I really can't have you passing out in here, so . . ."

"Yeah, it means something." Riel nods. "Something terrible."

May 15

This is not the way it was supposed to turn out. It's not at all what I planned. I lie awake at night now, trying not to let my faith be shaken. I try to rededicate myself to the cause. My own loss has changed nothing. But it is not easy to bear. Rage and sadness are confusing twins.

But I know what I must do now, more than ever: finish what I started. That is the way to make something out of this loss. To not let it be in vain.

I still hold the gift I was given. I must honor that by keeping my own promises. Making sure that the guilty pay. An eternity in fire.

WYLIE

WE SPRINT BACK TOWARD THE AMERICAN LEGION HALL. OSHIRO NEEDS HELP, now. There was blood on the side of his chest—but he was still breathing. He is still alive.

When we pound back inside the lobby, the janitor is still there, headphones still on. He doesn't hear us come in, and jumps when I rush over and grab him with both hands.

"Call the police! And an ambulance!" I shout. "Someone's been hurt!"

"What?" He looks around, confused. "What do you mean? Where?"

"A man was shot in his car. In the parking lot!" I shout again. "Call an ambulance. Right now! I think he might be dying!" My breath catches on that word: "dying." Oshiro could end up dead because he was trying to help me.

"Oh, jeez." The janitor finally startles to life, digging in his pocket for a flip phone. He peers through the glass doors to the parking lot. "Which car is it?"

"The red one," I say. "Parked right next to that white van."

"What van?" he asks. "I don't see any van."

And he's right. When I look, the van is gone.

ONCE WE'RE SURE the ambulance is on its way, Gideon and I slip out and rush back to our car. By that time, the lobby is filled with worried members of The Collective. I hear the janitor call out after us, "Hey, where are you going?"

But we don't turn back, don't slow down. We can't stay. If the police find me here—outside of Newton in violation of my bail conditions—I will be sent back to jail. Not to mention that whoever shot Oshiro must also be after us. But if that's true, why didn't they shoot us when we were standing out there in the open next to the car? And did they find us because of Gideon's phone? Or were they following us from the start? Because I have no doubt Oshiro was shot because of us. Because of me. And he was so worried about helping in the first place. I bend over as I open the car door, afraid I might be sick right there in the parking lot.

"Come on," Gideon says. "We have to go."

We pull out of the Legion Hall parking lot and park in an out-of-sight spot down the street. We can see the emergency vehicles arrive from here, but are far enough away that no one will see us. Soon there are lights flashing, people rushing everywhere. Then they are working on Oshiro so frantically. At least when they finally move him, it's more calmly, toward the ambulance. Like they have things under control. Oshiro is stable, hopefully. And, hopefully, he will stay that way.

"Do you think Oshiro will be okay?" I ask Gideon. Because I have no clear instinct about whether he will survive.

Gideon turns to look at me. "The truth?" he asks.

"I guess," I say, though I am not sure I am ready.

"No," he says. "I don't think any of this is going to be okay."

MRS. PORTER'S HOME is a fifteen-minute drive from the Legion Hall, in a much more run-down part of Framingham. We debated going back home, but as bad as I feel about what happened to Oshiro, our dad still needs us to find him. Now more than ever. Which means we need to find Sophie-Ann. I feel more sure than ever that she's the person who called.

As we head down the twisty roads, the houses get closer together and more beat-up. Still, I keep hoping that things will start feeling better. That *I* will start feeling better. And I do sense that we are headed in the right direction, literally and figuratively. But right, of course, is not the same as comfortable. Or safe.

EndOfDays and The Collective are working with Quentin somehow still? Or maybe Quentin *is* EndOfDays? This is not the first time the possibility has occurred to me. But it still doesn't feel exactly right. I wish now I had asked what the "regular guy" looked like. For all I know he *is* Quentin. I just have to hope that we will find Sophie-Ann at Mrs. Porter's and that she will have my dad's phone, along with some real answers to go with it.

More than once, I feel Gideon consider saying something the closer we get to Mrs. Porter's. And more than once, he decides against it. He doesn't speak until we have almost arrived.

"That EndOfDays blog is . . ." Gideon hesitates. "I've read it, you know. And it's just, whoever wrote it, it's really bad."

I close my eyes and take a breath. I don't want the details. They will just make this harder. But Gideon needs to tell me. I can feel that he does. "Bad how exactly?"

"At first, the guy was all like, 'shepherds of the peace' and whatever. He didn't love scientific research like Dad's, and he did mention Dad specifically. But then after the camp happened, it was like he snapped. Started calling what he was doing 'the reckoning.' He went from a little out there to full-on homicidal. The 'shepherds of the peace' were gone, replaced by 'soldiers of God.'"

"Soldiers?" I ask. "That doesn't sound very spiritual."

"I don't think it is," Gideon says. "Whatever this guy really cares about, I don't think it has anything to do with God."

MRS. PORTER'S MAILBOX is rusted and pitched way to the side. Not exactly welcoming as Gideon and I pull into the driveway. Still, I am relieved to finally arrive. Maybe it will stop my gut churning—I have been trying to convince myself that how bad I feel doesn't necessarily reflect the severity of Oshiro's condition. But living in denial isn't all that easy when you're an Outlier.

Mrs. Porter's driveway comes to a stop some distance short of the house—no garage, no clear place to park. To the left is a miniature windmill plunked there, like it was stolen from a miniature golf course. In between, in the middle of the yard, is a large pile of discarded mattresses, furniture, clothes, and a few broken-down bed frames, stacked high in a bonfire of despair. Mrs. Porter's is not a happy place. I can read that much loud and clear.

"Should we have a signal or something?" Gideon asks. "You know, if one of us thinks that something is off once we're inside? I guess you, mostly. You would definitely know before me."

I turn and look at him. "Something is off," I say. "That's pretty obvious already."

Gideon takes a deep breath and looks back up at the house. "Yeah, but a sign would make me feel better. How about 'pancakes'?"

"'Pancakes'?" I ask. Gideon is obviously new to this world of subtlety and intrigue. "How about 'It's hot in here' or 'I feel really hot,' something like that?"

Gideon nods, relieved. "Hot. Got it. Sounds good."

ON MRS. PORTER'S sloped front steps, we stand under the small circle of light cast down by a single bulb. It feels weirdly cold there in that spot, like one of those suspect patches in the ocean that hints at a threat—a shark, a riptide. I'd swim the other way if I had a choice. But Mrs. Porter is our only link to Sophie-Ann. And Sophie-Ann is our only link to our dad's phone. And that phone is still our only link to him.

He needs us more with each passing minute, too. I can feel it.

I ring the doorbell and am surprised when it actually chimes.

A second later, there is the dead bolt thudding open, a chain inside dropping. When the door finally cracks open, it sounds like it's being broken into pieces. Mrs. Porter won't be happy to see us there. I know nothing about her, and yet I feel completely sure of this fact.

Sure enough: "Get off my steps!" comes an angry voice before a face has even come into view. "Whichever girl you're here to see, you aren't seeing her! It's late, so shoo!"

Mrs. Porter is late middle age, in high-waisted pale blue jeans that highlight a spectacular paunch, stiff blond hair cut like a helmet. And this barking is her go-to tactic—strike first, ask questions later. And it works for her most of the time. Mrs. Porter is a bully—a big, scared bully. I've got to come out hard and strong, knock her off balance.

"Let us in, or we'll report you," I say calmly, staring her right in the eye. I don't need to know exactly what she's done to feel sure she's done plenty.

Her lip curls. "What do you want?"

Notably not: *Report me for what?* Because even she's got something in mind.

"We need to find Sophie-Ann," I say. "She has something that belongs to us."

"Ha," she says, but with a weird flatness, and then without another word, Mrs. Porter turns and walks toward the back of the house. She doesn't tell us to follow. But she did leave the door hanging open, which is probably as much of an invitation as we're going to get.

•••

INSIDE, THE HOUSE smells so strongly of body odor that I have to breathe through my mouth not to gag. We follow in the direction Mrs. Porter disappeared. Walking tentatively, keeping an eye out. Because Mrs. Porter isn't the only threat in this house. I feel sure of that. The only question is whether she is leading us to them.

We finally catch up to Mrs. Porter in the kitchen, grease-stained, with yellowish-beige wallpaper, unwashed dishes in the sink, and open packages of food everywhere. Mice and insects probably also. I make a point of not looking too closely. Mrs. Porter is at the stove, an ancient, rusted appliance, lighting a gas burner with a match. She sets a pot of water on top of it.

"So, Sophie-Ann . . . ," I begin.

Mrs. Porter turns back from the stove and crosses her arms. "She's not here," she says. *Already* this is a lie. No, not a lie—just absurdly incomplete.

"I don't believe you," I say. "And like I said, if you don't tell us the truth, we'll report you."

"Yeah, report me for what?" Mrs. Porter snaps. Crap, I knew that making the same threat twice could be pushing my luck.

"You make the girls you foster go to religious meetings," I blurt out. It's the first thing that comes to mind. Comes to mind and then right out of my mouth. Before I've fully considered the consequences.

"Oh please." She laughs, and, like, for real she finds this funny. She's relieved, too, which means that whatever she's really done is much, much worse. "I don't even go to church. Never have."

"Um, The Collective?" Gideon says.

"Who told you about that?" She glares from Gideon to me and back again. "You just came from there? Jennifer and Grace are over there tonight, aren't they?"

Damn it. I don't want to get Jennifer and Grace in trouble. I wasn't thinking.

"We were there this morning," I say, praying that I sound convincing. "It was the new guy who leads the meetings who told us. He told us that Sophie-Ann lived here."

"Him. He's not right, that one. Not right at all." She huffs in disgust. "Anyway, that's not a religion. It's a group of like-minded people."

"Call it what you want. We can let social services sort it out," I say. "Or tell us where Sophie-Ann is. Our dad is missing, and we think that Sophie-Ann has his phone."

Mrs. Porter smirks viciously. "Well then, I'd say you're screwed." She looks over to see if her water has boiled yet. When she turns back, she is much calmer, more composed, almost like she's enjoying this now. "Sophie-Ann is dead."

I feel nauseous, my heart pounding so hard it feels like it might burst. *No, no, no. She was all we had.*

"What happened?" Gideon asks.

"She was hit by a car over in Watuck," Mrs. Porter says. She flicks off the stove like she's changed her mind about whatever she was making.

Not an accident. Not an accident. Not an accident.

"When?" I ask. "Where?"

"Couple days ago," she says, then points a crooked finger my way. She's more defiant now that the cat is out of the bag. "And before you get any ideas, I reported all this, just like I was supposed to. My guess is Sophie-Ann got wasted at some party, couldn't see straight, and stumbled into the road. These aren't some sweet schoolgirls, you know. They're like stray dogs. They come, they eat some food, sleep, then they go. All of 'em, Sophie-Ann, Lethe, Teresa, they're—"

"Teresa?" I ask, feeling light-headed. "Kind of small with really big glasses?"

"Could be," Mrs. Porter says. "Now you're looking for her, too?"

"I want to see her, yes. Teresa lives here?"

"She not here anymore either." She screws up her face. "But I told child services when she ran off just like I was supposed to. And that was weeks ago." Mrs. Porter shakes her head. "I swear they still call about her. Least Teresa could have done was go down to the office and get herself officially emancipated like Lethe did. One of her last days here, Lethe had some other girl up here, got her high as a kite. That's my point: these girls breed badness. Little bacteria."

"You're a terrible person," Gideon says. And like he didn't even intend to. The words just popped out.

"Maybe," Mrs. Porter says. "But I am a terrible person with a shift to go to. My son got me a good new job at the facility up the street, and I am not going to lose it on account of you two assholes."

There's a noise behind us then, the floorboards creaking. A person. The terrible someone I felt was in the house. Right behind us now. The hair on my arms has lifted.

"Oh, there's Freddy now. That's my cue. Like I said, I ain't gonna be late."

As I turn slowly in the direction of Mrs. Porter's son, the world stutters to a stop. *Breathe,* I tell myself. But it is no use. There he is, right there, only inches away. The Wolf. The guard from the hospital who wanted me dead. Now, he'll finally have his chance.

"It's hot in here, Gideon," I manage in a whisper. "So, so hot."

TOP SECRET AND CONFIDENTIAL

To: Senator David Russo, Armed Services Committee, Research Chair
From: WSRF, Special Projects
Re: Protocol X/Utilization of Special Population
May 22

Per the findings at Watuck Soldier Research Facility, we propose additional research into how these abilities may be affected by stress, hunger, pain, and other forms of discomfort. However, blocking seems most fruitful avenue for further research. We believe we have already developed several crucial alternatives that should prove almost impossible to detect.

JASPER

IT'S DARK WHEN JASPER OPENS HIS EYES. PITCH-BLACK. HE'S ALMOST CONVINCED his eyes are still closed until he blinks a few times. Where the hell is he? And what the hell happened?

Jasper tries to move but his arms are pinned behind his back. He wriggles left and right but can't get them free. His wrists and shoulders have begun to throb.

He thinks back: Chance, then the bike, and then in his room. He was so dizzy on his way to the bed. He must have passed out? And now this.

Jasper uses his shoulders and body to rock back and forth, the bed or cot he's laid out on creaking loudly underneath. When he's finally pushed himself up to sitting, his head throbs. And the harder he stares into the darkness, the blacker it becomes. He keeps waiting for his eyes to adjust, but they've got nothing to get a foothold on. Finally, Jasper pushes himself to stand.

The claustrophobia sets in fast, not from the smallness of the space—that Jasper doesn't know—but from the pressure of the unknown.

He needs to stay calm, though. To keep it together. He can figure this out. He will. But his head feels so cloudy, like he's coming off something. Like he's been drugged.

"Hello?" Jasper calls out. Not frantic or loud. Just a normal voice. He hopes it'll make him freak out less to sound calm. His voice is hoarse, though, and his throat burns, like he's been out much longer than he knows.

When no one answers, Jasper shuffles slowly forward, turning to the side, hoping his shoulder will make contact with whatever is in front of him first. He needs to know the contours of the space he's in. Finally, he hits a wall. One that he can put his back up to. One direction at least no one can sneak up on him from.

The walls are cool and rough, cinder block, maybe, except for one side, which feels like wire fencing. The air feels damp, too. A basement. That would explain the darkness. It isn't until the very last wall that Jasper finally feels a door. He turns to feel for the knob with his bound hands. But when he finally gets his hands on it, it won't budge.

"Hello?!" Jasper shouts this time, kicking at the door.

Silence.

"Somebody?!"

Silence.

"What the hell is this?!"

More silence.

"Fuck you!"

He rams his shoulder against the door. And it feels so good he does it again. And then again, thinking each time how much he wants to kill whoever put him in here. But pounding his shoulder against the door goes fast from feeling good to feeling really, really bad. And soon his shoulder is throbbing so bad that Jasper worries he's seriously messed it up.

Wylie. This must have to do with her and the Outliers or her dad, right? All roads that start with being grabbed or locked up seem to end there. But that's it. That's all Jasper can guess.

Eventually, he sits back down, and then a while after that, when there is nothing else to do, he lies down. And focuses on the in-and-out of his breath. Tries not to feel choked by the silence and the dark.

IT'S A NOISE that wakes him, the door opening. And so much light flooding the room it takes a second for his eyes to adjust to the brightness. Quickly, Jasper takes in the room—small, square, concrete walls, wire fencing on one side, metal shelves along the wall beyond with file boxes stacked high.

And then there she is, walking in the door.

Lethe. Jasper feels a stupid split-second jolt of relief—like, *oh my God, Lethe is here, now everything will be fine.* But that's ridiculous. Lethe isn't tied up. She looks different now, too, older, wiser. More satisfied. She'd had a bit of an edge before when they met. Now that edge is a blade.

The cookies. Of course. That's what made him pass out.

Jasper doesn't bother to ask himself how he could have fallen for Lethe's act. He wanted to buy it—that's how. He needed to. That's always his bottom line.

"Untie me," he says. "Now."

"Yeah, sorry, but no," Lethe says. "I'd like for my limbs to stay intact. You've got some serious rage issues, my friend. I say that, and I have spent time with some pretty terrible people."

"What is this?"

"A house," she says, motioning above her. "The basement of a house. Don't worry, we didn't take you far. And thank you for leaving the door to your room unlocked. Could have caused all sorts of problems if we'd had to break in."

"Who are you?"

"You should have led with that: like, 'Oh, wow, who are you, really?' Surprised but, you know, curious," she says. "Starting with all that anger is so off-putting."

"Who are you?" Jasper asks again. "Why did you bring me here?"

"Honestly, in a way, you ended up here because you are so obsessed with Wylie," she says.

"What the hell are you talking about?"

"I was going to get close to you, get you to tell me where Wylie is casually. Keep you out of it," Lethe says. "But you're so obsessed with her, I couldn't even get you to pay attention to me for more than five seconds. So we had to move to plan B. Brute goddamn force."

"I'm not obsessed," Jasper says, even though he knows that's hardly the point.

"You may believe that's true, Jasper. But the thing about being an Outlier," Lethe goes on, turning to look straight at him, "I can read *all* your feelings, even the ones you don't know you have. Trust me: you're obsessed with Wylie."

"So you're an Outlier," Jasper says. He wishes now that he had listened more to Wylie when she told him about blocking. But he'll try what he does remember. He's supposed to picture a box. . . .

"Don't bother," Lethe says, kind of exasperated. "You won't be able to block me. I can feel you trying. I'm too good and you have no idea what you're doing."

"What time is it?" Jasper asks. "How long have I been here?"

"Only a couple hours," Lethe says. "It's about eight p.m., I think. I was sure you'd be out for much longer with how much shit I packed into those cookies."

"Why do you want Wylie?" Jasper asks, trying again to pull his arms apart. Even with them tied, he could knock Lethe out of the way and run past her.

"I'm not alone, by the way," she says. "Before you start thinking escape. He's just outside, and he's way more nervous than me. Even took a kitchen knife from upstairs. Between you and me, he is kind of useless, but with your hands tied . . ." She shudders. "Anyway, all we want is to get something Wylie has in her possession. We won't lay a hand on her. We just need to find her."

"Go to hell," Jasper says. "I would never help you."

Lethe looks mystified and kind of pissed. "Wow, you really can't stop protecting her, can you? That's not love, you know. It's stupidity."

"I have no idea where Wylie is anyway. She broke up with me." Jasper tries to swallow back his hurt before Lethe has time to enjoy it. "I haven't seen her."

Could Jasper rack his brain for some possibilities about where Wylie could have gone? Maybe. But he won't even let his mind go there. Lethe will follow.

"Jasper, seriously, I can feel you again trying not to think things. It's sweet, but so totally goddamn obvious." Lethe shakes her head. "If you don't care about keeping yourself from getting hurt, maybe we should hurt somebody you care about instead? Like your mom, maybe?"

"My mom?" Jasper asks. "Are you serious?"

"Yeah, Jasper. I am," Lethe says. "Unfortunately, this is *that* important. All we need are some pictures Wylie had. As far as I'm concerned, Wylie gives us the pictures and you and she can go ride off into the sunset together. She's a nice girl, and bygones or whatever. I just want to go on living. And I need those pictures for insurance. Otherwise, I'm the next head on the chopping block."

It isn't until then that Jasper sees the infinity tattoo on Lethe's wrist. It had been covered by a leather cuff both times Jasper saw her before. He hears in his head Wylie's voice in that alley behind Delaney's. *She's got this tattoo on her wrist.* That's who Lethe is, the "fake Kelsey" Wylie talked about from the hospital. The third original Outlier. God, he really is a dumb-ass.

"I saw some pictures once, before Wylie was arrested. But I have no idea where they are now," Jasper says, scrambling to think of things he can say that are true. That could make it seem like he's cooperating without risking Wylie. "We had them at one point, but then we had to swim somewhere, so Wylie left them. She must have. She didn't swim with them."

"Left them where?" Lethe asks. She is suspicious. But at least Jasper really is telling the truth. She must feel that. "Where did she have them?"

"At some house on Cape Cod," Jasper says, and it seems safe enough to tell her that much. "Senator Russo, that was the guy's name."

"Shit," Lethe says.

The door to the room opens then for a second time. When Jasper turns, there is someone he recognizes in the doorway, but his brain refuses to see. And then a wave moves through him. Fear, fueled by rage.

Quentin. He's right there. Only inches away. The person who killed Cassie, who would have killed Wylie. Jasper is going to kill Quentin. Right now. He feels a sick rush just thinking about it. It's hard to breathe.

"Did he just say Russo already has the pictures?" Quentin asks. "Now what the hell are we going to do?"

Quentin looks shrunken, like somebody's let all his air out. Easy to take out. Or easier. Jasper's fists clench as he imagines Quentin's neck beneath them. Jasper is going to kill him, for sure. He just needs to stay calm enough to get the chance.

"What are you doing, you idiot?" Lethe shouts at Quentin. Then she turns back to Jasper. "And whoa with the rage, big guy. Remember the part about him having a knife? I wasn't making that up. None of us want anyone to get hurt here. Not when we still need you."

"You're not dead," Jasper says to Quentin.

"Wylie didn't tell you? She knew. I saw her in jail." Quentin smiles dickishly, then shakes his head. "That girl and her secrets."

Jasper feels stupidly hurt and he can't even bother to try keeping it from Lethe. Why wouldn't Wylie have told him Quentin was alive? Luckily, Lethe doesn't poke at Jasper's hurt feelings; she's too busy glaring at Quentin.

"I've only been in here for like three fucking minutes," Lethe snaps, arms crossed. "And we *were* making progress before you barged in and made this all about you."

"What progress?" Quentin says. "You heard him: Wylie doesn't even have the pictures. This whole thing has been a useless waste of time."

"You know, half the time I can't remember why the hell I decided to let you glom on to me."

"Glom on?" Quentin snaps. "We need each other, remember."

Lethe's nostrils flare as she looks down at the floor, considering. She calmly holds out a hand to Quentin. "Give me the knife. We'll get rid of him and figure something else out."

"Seriously?" Jasper shouts. He doesn't want to be panicking, but he is. "You're going to *kill* me? They will figure out it was you."

Though really Jasper's not sure how.

"Nothing to figure out. Not if they find you here in Wylie's basement," she says. "With her track record of bumping people off, they'll think it was her."

Wylie's basement. Jasper looks over at the rack on the far wall and reads one of the labels: *HEP Run September 10.* Dr. Ben Lang's files. Lethe isn't wrong that they'd suspect Wylie. They already do.

Quentin pulls a short kitchen knife out of his pocket and looks down at it before reluctantly handing it over to Lethe. The knife is so short, too. It would require so much stabbing to kill anyone. Lethe grips it in her hand and steps closer. Jasper has to think of some reason they still need him. And fast.

"Wait, wait!" Jasper shouts. "I do know something, maybe."

"What?" Lethe asks, skeptical.

"I saw some guy take a file box from here to these warehouses in the middle of nowhere," Jasper says. And it might be something. For sure it could be. "He's some kind of government agent or something. Klute, I think his name is. It could have been the pictures. I don't know. She might have gotten them back."

"What warehouses?" Quentin asks.

"I have no idea," Jasper says. And, luckily, that's the truth. "But Klute took the box there and set it on fire. I don't know exactly the road names or whatever. I was following him, and it was out in the middle of nowhere. But I think I could show you the way."

Lethe narrows her eyes, reading him. Thank God Jasper is telling the truth.

"Fine," Lethe says finally. "You show us where it is. And if the pictures are there—and not totally destroyed—we'll let you go." She steps closer then, the tip of the knife pressed against his nose. "And if you are fucking with us, we'll end you out there instead. In the middle of nowhere. Where no one will ever find you."

EndOfDays Blog

June 12

I'm just one man. But lit up by righteousness, one man can stop a mighty darkness.

IT'S AN ABOMINATION, A STAIN ON THE HUMAN RACE TO RUN TESTS ON YOUNG GIRLS. IT MUST BE STOPPED ONCE AND FOR ALL. THEY MUST BE STOPPED. WHATEVER THE COST. I WILL STAY THE COURSE AND STOP IT. I MUST.

Go in peace, everyone. To the light.

RIEL

MARLY IS WAITING EAGERLY WHEN RIEL GETS BACK TO HER ROOM. RAMONA AND Elise are waiting, too, sitting on the edge of the bed like little kids waiting for a circus to start. Riel tries not to get pissed they're so giddy. They have no way of knowing why her head is spinning.

The drug they'd been using at the WSRF to test on girls was morphine. Morphine was what they'd been ordering to use on the girls in the hospital. Riel had unearthed that email with Wylie saying as much. Kelsey had OD'd: on morphine. It's all way too much of a coincidence.

Riel may not believe that her grandfather literally stuck a needle in Kelsey's arm. But she has no doubt he is to blame for her death.

"What's wrong?" Marly asks Riel, because it's obvious something is.

But Riel just shakes her head. *Not now,* she means. Marly seems to get it. Meanwhile, Ramona has crossed the room to the phone sitting in the middle of Marly's desk. She holds it up, triumphant. "This should cheer you up!"

"What's that?" Riel asks Marly and not Ramona.

Riel doesn't trust Ramona, that's the bottom line. And, yeah, it's because Ramona betrayed Wylie. It's one thing to talk about a clean slate. It's not always easy delivering one.

"Your grandfather's phone," Ramona jumps in before Marly can respond, grinning with delight. "With enough shit on here probably to put his whole motherfucking plan on the nightly news."

"To be clear, we don't know for sure yet what's on it," Marly says. "And it's locked. But it is his actual personal phone. My guess is there is *a lot* on there."

"How did you . . . ?" Riel stares at the phone in disbelief.

"Because we are awesome," Ramona says.

"And we got lucky," Elise adds. "We left here and went straight to the Russo campaign headquarters to volunteer like you said, and then, all of a sudden, your grandfather just showed up at the headquarters like an hour after we got there, to 'talk to the troops.' They said he was in town for meetings."

"Meetings," Riel scoffs. Her grandfather is not even bothering to hide. "I guess that's one way to put it."

"Do people really buy his bullshit?" Ramona sticks her finger down her throat. "Because it is so gross."

"Buy it? People love it," Riel says, and sharply. And it is important that they know this. That none of them ever forgets.

"A lot of people, actually. It might feel like such obvious bullshit to you because you're Outliers. But it's easy for people to believe what they want."

"Lucky for them," Elise says. "It might be easier not to see through everything."

"Easier in the short term," Marly says. "In the end, you're always left with the truth."

"Anyway," Ramona goes on, desperate to get back to the part of the story where she is awesome. "They brought a bunch of us into this one room in a big crowd, and your grandfather—"

"Just call him Russo, for Christ's sake," Riel says. "He's nothing to me. He never was."

"*Russo* was making his way around the room," Ramona goes on. "He had his phone out because he was taking selfies with volunteers. Or trying to. It was mostly just for show. Trying to be funny or whatever."

"And he was making all these bad dad jokes about how hip he was." Elise shudders.

"Except most of the other volunteers did kind of eat it up." Ramona rolls her eyes. "Anyway, Russo got distracted by some dude telling him he was awesome and put his phone down for a second and . . ." Ramona looks at Elise, who has an eyebrow raised. "Okay, technically, Elise grabbed it. But I distracted his security people so she could jet out the door with it. They were still crawling around on the floor looking for his stupid phone when I ducked out myself—no one even asked where I was going."

There's a loud knock at Marly's door then, startling all of them.

"Did you take his SIM card out?" Riel asks.

"Yes, of course," Marly says, and she puts a hand on Riel's shoulder. "It's Level99. I asked them to come get the phone. Seemed safer than bringing it to them."

MARLY OPENS THE door and Brian steps inside, bristling already. He didn't like being Riel's errand boy to begin with. He likes it even less now that he has been reduced to following the instructions of her friends. But maybe that's not even what his bad, wound-up energy is about. Honestly, Brian has so many mixed-up, bad feelings Riel isn't sure. And she doesn't like not being sure. But the phone is worth nothing without Brian's help.

Marly hands Brian the phone and the SIM card. "We need anything incriminating or potentially incriminating off here."

Brian looks down at the phone in his hand, then tucks the SIM card in his pocket. "Incriminating? You got anything more specific?"

When he looks over at Riel, she feels only smug condescension. Brian can't even keep it in check temporarily. He must know Riel will read it. Maybe Brian wants her to. Riel is on her feet before she realizes it.

"Don't be an asshole," she growls at Brian. "'If you don't know what incriminating looks like after all this time, then I can find someone else who does."

Brian's eyes drop and his cheeks flush. Behind him, Riel can feel Marly, Ramona, and Elise silently cheering. But he's actually more pissed than embarrassed. Also, he still feels pretty smug.

"Nope, it's fine," Brian says through gritted teeth, turning the phone in his hand. "I'm on it."

For a split second, Riel considers taking her grandfather's phone back from Brian. But again she thinks: without Level99's help, the phone is worth nothing.

"Oh, yeah, we found Kendall, too," Brian adds, turning back on his way to the door. "Or the guy who was pretending to be him."

Riel's heart speeds up. "Really?" She was sure they never would. "Where?"

Brian's eyes flick down. "Well, I mean, I guess technically Kendall found me," he says. "Dude was waiting at my house when I got home. My mom let him in. It was freaky."

"You still live with your mom?" Ramona chirps. "Aren't you, like, twenty-five?"

Riel shoots Ramona a look, and she holds up her hands, mouths "sorry."

"Twenty-three," Brian snaps back. "And not all of us were born to privilege."

"What did Kendall say?" Riel asks.

"He asked me to give this to you." Brian hands her a small folded note. "That was it. I tried to ask him who he was, but he wouldn't answer me. I didn't read it."

A lie definitely. She eyeballs Brian.

"Okay, fine," Brian says. "I did look at it. But just to be sure it wasn't something totally messed up."

When Riel opens the note, there is a time—eight thirty p.m.—and directions for driving, followed by walking, to a location. Then a warning: *Come alone.*

• • •

RIEL DRIVES MARLY'S car away from Boston, south toward Connecticut, already knowing she'll be late. It isn't long before the directions take her off the brightly lit highway and onto a more local route, then for a while longer on a seriously narrow two-lane, twisty road plunging deep into the woods. It's already coming up fast on eight, almost dark.

As the miles click by Riel feels less and less sure that she is going to get any of the answers she is hoping for. Still, she has no doubt about going to meet Kendall, even alone. Riel thought Wylie was a stupid asshole for trusting Kendall. But from the second he put his hands on Riel in that crowd, Riel has known what Wylie did: Kendall's intentions are good.

It's another ten minutes of winding through trees and more trees before Riel finally spots the turnoff the note describes: the third on her left, a dead end, no street sign. She pulls slowly down the street and parks on the side of the cul-de-sac. From there, she is supposed to find a path cut in the trees and follow it into the woods. Then, in a quarter of a mile, the path will open up to a clearing. Hopefully, at least.

Riel stays in the car until she spots the opening in the trees. The path. Hard to believe she is actually going to follow it alone and in the dark. But she is. Definitely. So much dread has crept into her chest, though, she could choke on it. But curled up right next to that dread? Certainty.

ONCE SHE'S OUT of the car, Riel moves quickly down the narrow path, flashlight in hand, branches clawing at her arms and legs. She tries not to think about what lies ahead, or who might be following behind. It isn't long before she finally sees something up ahead. Two long buildings set in a small clearing. Riel stops and stares. Just ordinary warehouses, but there seems nothing good about seeing them out there in the middle of nowhere. And Kendall didn't pick this spot to meet by accident.

Riel takes one last deep breath before stepping toward the warehouses and—

A hand has clamped down over her mouth. Riel screams loud and raw and animal. But the sound is muffled under the set of strong fingers. She tries to wriggle away, too, but the hand is too tight. She can't even move her head.

"Shhh!" A whispered growl in her ear. Something hard pointed into her back. A gun? Is that possible? "Stop screaming!"

And so Riel does as she is told. The hand is still on her, that something that could be a gun still jammed against her spine. As she is shoved forward toward the back warehouse, she tries reading the person behind her. Kendall, it must be. She hopes. Whoever it is, he's not feeling anything she can read, though, except focus on the task at hand.

"Open it," he says when they reach the warehouse door. "Go in."

INSIDE, RIEL IS pushed forward so hard she stumbles. When she finally regains her footing and turns, there is Kendall behind her, near the door, scanning the darkness outside the windows. The strong lines of his set face are outlined in the moonlight, his taut arms defined beneath his snug shirt. He certainly looks like someone who could have killed all those people up at that camp without giving it a second thought. He could easily kill Riel now, and probably still wouldn't feel a thing. But this is bullshit. Riel has done what he wanted.

"What the fuck?" she shouts.

"I needed to make sure you weren't followed." Kendall's eyes are still locked on the trees outside.

"I'm not stupid. I was careful," Riel says as she looks around the warehouse, trying to get her bearings. There is an empty room at the front, with a dusty concrete floor. A wall of windows at either end, none on the side. A long hall in between with lots of doors. "What the hell is this place?"

"There is no such thing as careful enough," Kendall says, without making eye contact. He heads on, checking the interior of the building. Like a machine—quick, methodical. This is not an act and does not take effort. It's reflex.

"What is this place?" Riel asks again.

Kendall doesn't answer. Instead, he heads down the hall, clearing the other end. He opens each of the doors on the long hall on his way back, checking inside.

"Who the hell *are* you?" Riel asks when Kendall still does not say a word. She tries again to read him. But Kendall's only real emotion still is concentration—he doesn't seem to feel anything else. "I mean, who are you *for real*?"

Finally, Kendall stops his checking and stands feet square, arms at his side, staring at Riel. Sure enough, there is an actual gun in his hand, the one he must have had pointed into Riel's back.

"I'm no one," Kendall says, and he means this. Simply and completely. "They've spent years making me that way."

"You work for my grandfather?"

"Not specifically."

"Then who?"

"Military intelligence. That's who I report back to. But they'd deny my existence." He isn't torn up about confessing this. It's like he already knows it doesn't matter. That *he* doesn't matter. "They function as a go-between. I go where they tell me. I'm not usually privy to the why. Only the what. But this, this I looked into. And yeah, it goes back to your grandfather. All of it."

Finally, a flicker like a trapdoor has flashed open for a second. Regret. Way deep down, Kendall is drowning in it. Somewhere in there is an actual person.

"You shot all those people at the camp," Riel says quietly.

Kendall shakes his head. "I was supposed to, but the first target I ran into was some old lady. Said something about being a nurse, asked if I was wounded and needed help. I think she thought we were in Vietnam or something," he says, haunted by the memory. "After all these years, after all I've done—she was my line in the sand. She had no idea what the hell was going on. I tried to take out the other agent there with me so he couldn't finish the job. Klute was his name. Biggest regret of my life is never getting a clear shot at him."

"So, let's assume for a second that I believe you—what do you want now?" Riel asks. "Why did you bring me here?"

"There were girls up at that facility. Young girls. I saw them there."

"You mean Boston Hospital?"

He makes a confused, annoyed face. "No, before the hospital. The WSRF," he says. "I was there long before I got sent up to the camp in Maine."

"The WSRF," Riel repeats. Her whole body is tensed, bracing for a truth she'll never be ready to know. *Morphine. Morphine. Morphine.*

"Yeah, it's a testing facility," he says. "Where the doctors talked way more in front of us than they should have. I guess they thought we were too stupid to understand. At first they were trying to see if they could use some kind of hallucinogenic state to mimic this whole Outliers thing. That's not what they called it, but that's what it was. Then they were using stressors—pain, sleep deprivation—to see if it could somehow be learned. When none of that worked, it was all about blocking."

"Where did they get the girls to test?" Riel asks, thinking of Kelsey, of course.

He shrugs. "Paid them. They needed a lot of girls to come up with a single Outlier. Most of them weren't. These were girls without a lot of options. Ones who wouldn't be missed if the tests turned south. Which they did all the time. They had some of them high out of their minds. They lost a lot of girls."

Riel takes a deep breath, tries to swallow. She doesn't have it all connected yet, but this is how Kelsey died. It had something to do with the WSRF. The last thing Riel wants is to cry in front of Kendall, but it's too late.

"How long was this going on?" Riel asks, trying to ignore her ragged voice. "When did it start?"

Kendall shrugs. "Few years ago. Three. Four."

Riel feels a nauseous sense of vertigo. Like she's been on a train she thought was moving. But it's been the train next to her this whole time.

"Years?" Riel repeats. "But Ben Lang only found—"

"Ben Lang wasn't the beginning of this," Kendall says, waving a finger in the air. "He was the end. The end of Russo being able to keep it a secret. He was the first person to call them Outliers, but that's it. I hoped Lang's wife, the reporter, would do something with those pictures I sent her. But she didn't even know what she had before they tried to kill her, too."

Riel has gotten so many details wrong. Her grandfather started this, not Dr. Lang. They were Kendall's pictures, not Hope's. That explains why Hope didn't know where the WSRF was.

"They *did* kill her," Riel says.

"No, no," Kendall says. Like Riel is the one who's lost it now. "She's still alive. But only alive because the Architect wants her that way."

"The Architect?"

Kendall shrugs. "Whoever the Architect is, he's behind most of what Russo does. The strategy." He motions to the warehouse. "This included. He sees to it that the dirty work gets done so Russo can keep his hands clean. You got to give it to them—it's working. Russo was a nobody senator, and now he's running for president. Looks like he could even win."

"Are you sure the Architect is still alive?" she asks, thinking of Quentin. But she's already got her doubts.

"I think so. But since the camp, I'm not sure of anything," he says. "I've been mostly off the grid. They don't like it when we don't follow orders."

"But you put the note under Leo's door, didn't you?" Riel says.

"You went into the hospital to see Wylie."

Kendall shrugs. "I was trying to warn both of you. Seemed like the least I could do."

"And so what is this place?" Riel asks.

Kendall takes a breath and looks around as he backs up to lean against the windows. "They'll have dozens of these built before anyone realizes it. They rely on that, being a couple steps ahead. Hard to kill a weed once it's got its roots established. Easier to defend something that's already done. But they do cleanup first—the camp, Wylie, her dad. You. They won't leave a single loose end."

This is the truth as Kendall knows it. And Riel has a terrible feeling he is very close to exactly right.

"I still don't understand what this place is."

"The next phase," Kendall says. "It'll be—"

There's been a small pop. Kendall is frozen. Riel glances down, worried she's somehow stepped on a piece of glass. Crushed it beneath her shoe. There's a dull, heavy thud.

Kendall has collapsed facedown on the ground.

"Oh, shit." She rushes over. "Kendall, are you—"

Another pop. And then another. Riel hits the ground. Shit. Holy shit. Bullets. There are bullets cracking holes in the glass.

And the first one hit Kendall square in the base of the head.

WYLIE

I'M STILL TREMBLING BY THE TIME WE FINALLY MAKE IT TO THE WATUCK PUBLIC Library. Inside, it's almost completely empty. Not surprising for 8:40 p.m. Even so, it's a pretty cheerful and charming place—brand-new, but made to look old so that it fits in with the rest of the picture-perfect downtown. There's only one other customer, an old man reading a newspaper, and three young, attractive librarians—two women, one man—behind the desk, talking. *They were all in here first,* I remind myself. *They had no way of knowing we were coming here. They did not follow us.*

I don't think the Wolf is coming after us, either. He would have by now. Still, I can't shake the feeling of being blindsided by seeing him, standing right there in Mrs. Porter's kitchen. Terror. That's what I felt. So much I was choking on it.

As soon as I said the word "hot," Gideon bolted for Mrs.

Porter's door. He was so jacked up and nervous to begin with that he was ready the second I said the word. I wasn't far behind. And I didn't look back until we were safely locked in the car.

The Wolf followed only as far as the front steps of the house. Then he loomed there in the doorway, blinking at me. He looked so much weaker out of his security officer's uniform, under the light of that bare bulb. It made the fact that anyone had put him in charge of the girls at the hospital all the more frightening.

Even if the Wolf isn't behind us, I still feel hunted. Being in the town where Sophie-Ann died isn't helping. But the Watuck Public Library was the best choice to dig up whatever we could find on Sophie-Ann's accident. Especially in case we had to resort to asking the librarians; they might have firsthand knowledge. And while being online isn't the safest thing right now, we need answers about Sophie-Ann. But we don't have much time. The library closes at nine p.m.

As Gideon and I head toward the computers, I try to get a better read on the room. Nothing stands out, except the two female librarians definitely flirting with each other. And the old guy, it turns out, is asleep. Whoever shot Oshiro could be waiting outside to shoot us, too. Definitely. But at least they aren't inside the library. At least, not yet. We'll just have to hope that whatever terrible reason they had for letting us leave that parking lot where they shot Oshiro still stands.

They. The Wolf being connected has only complicated my assumptions about who "they" might be. I've been so focused on Quentin as the link between the camp, and The Collective, and Sophie-Ann, and where my dad is. But the hospital, too? Unlikely.

That was an official operation with genuine support. Something someone like Senator Russo could make happen. Russo is the kind of somebody who could also make a DC missing-person case disappear.

"Let's check in with Elizabeth first," I say. "I want to make sure Oshiro is okay."

"Are you sure that's a good idea?" Gideon asks. "What if he's not?"

He's right that I haven't really let myself absorb that possibility. I'm hoping that's because I know it's not true, but I can't be sure.

"Either way I need to know. And I want to tell her that I'm sorry."

Gideon's fingers move quickly over the keyboard, opening the Gmail account he set up at Elizabeth's house. Two new messages from LizzyBusy123, but sandwiched between them is a third, which I instantly don't like the look of—the sender's email is just a series of numbers and the subject is blank. Spam, maybe. But the awful spinning in my gut seems to already have rejected that possibility.

Gideon starts with the message from Elizabeth that was sent before Oshiro was shot. He's protecting me, in case Elizabeth's most recent email is bad news.

EndOfDays was started years ago in Germany. It was abandoned for two years before it was reclaimed nine months ago by a totally different ISP in Massachusetts. (That happens with abandoned blogs all the time.) It stayed quiet, though, until posts started up in Florida

six months ago. Then two months ago, it jumps from Florida back to all around Massachusetts. Including Framingham and Watuck. Even Newton: a couple were posted from 412 Juniper Street.

Hope that helps. If he posts again, I'll let you know right away so you know where he is.

xx Elizabeth

My eyes stay fixed on *412 Juniper.* I keep hoping I'm imagining it—but no, it's definitely right there.

"What's wrong?" Gideon asks.

"That's Jasper's address."

Jasper, who appeared in the hospital right before that baby showed up. And not long before Teresa died. Jasper, who has somehow been everywhere anything important has happened throughout this entire thing. But no. No. That doesn't mean he's involved. That is just what someone wants me to think.

"Jasper?" Gideon asks, in true disbelief himself. "He's End-OfDays?"

"He's not," I say as I search myself for doubt. But there is none, not a trace. It's a setup to make Jasper look guilty.

"Could it be somebody he lives with?"

"Jasper's brother is pretty out of it. And his mom—I don't think she even has a computer."

"But doesn't that just leave Jasper?" Gideon feels sorry for me. So, so sorry. Like he did before, outside Delaney's. Except this is worse.

"It's not Jasper," I say sharply, then lock eyes with Gideon. "That's not wishful thinking, either. I know he didn't post them.

And no, I don't have another explanation. Maybe we should just—let's look at her other email."

The second message from Elizabeth was written only an hour ago, after we found Oshiro:

> **Evan is going to be okay. Don't feel bad. He wanted to be there, helping you. But you should come home. Right now. It's not safe out there. He wanted me to tell you that, too.**
>
> **xx Elizabeth**

I let go of the breath I've been holding, making a sound loud enough that the librarians look our way. I keep my eyes on the computer.

"That's good news about Oshiro," Gideon says.

"Definitely."

"She's right about going home," Gideon says.

"Can you open the last message?" I ask, ignoring him. "The one in the middle."

Still, I have that terrible feeling about it, even before Gideon clicks on it. And then there it is, up on the screen:

> **Hurry. Your dad is running out of time. The EndOfDays is nigh.**

My heart is beating so hard it rocks my body as Gideon and I stare silently at the screen. But no matter how long we stare, that's the whole message. No explanation, no introduction. Nothing to take the threat away.

"Hurry where?" Gideon asks quietly.

"I don't know," I say, though the email definitely does feel like a trap.

"How can it tell us to hurry and then not tell us where to go?" Gideon asks, like this is the one and only injustice of this entire situation.

"Write back," I say. "Ask where."

"Five minutes until closing!" one of the librarians calls as Gideon types.

"Now, look up Sophie-Ann quickly," I say. "We can't leave here without that."

"Yeah, yeah," Gideon says, trying to focus as he types the reply, then opens up a new search. "Okay."

Within seconds, a list of articles about the accident pop up: "Sophie-Ann Payne, a resident of neighboring Framingham, was struck and killed on the edge of a nearby highway while walking late at night." There is a judgmental tone, though, somehow. A question hovering between the lines: What was Sophie-Ann doing out there at that time of night? And a girl like her? What did she think was going to happen? In some of the articles, it's more text than subtext. One of them even cites a "confidential source" who apparently said Sophie-Ann's partying was what probably made her "stumble into traffic," a source that sounds a whole lot like Mrs. Porter.

Then comes the toxicology report. It's in the most recent article, from only that morning. The headline: "Is Sunset Highway Teen Another Victim of Rising Opioid Epidemic?" And the subhead: "Framingham Teen Had Morphine in Her System."

My eyes stick on the word "morphine."

Just like they were going to use on the girls in the hospital. On me, too, I suppose. This is not a coincidence. I know it's not.

According to the article, Sophie-Ann—high to the point of confusion—had indeed wandered into the road and was struck and killed. No excuse for the driver leaving the scene, of course. But Sophie-Ann—a troubled foster child with a history of behavior problems, so high that she could barely see straight—was also at fault.

But there's one line of the article that really jumps out: "She died on a lonely stretch of Sunset Highway, past mile marker seven, near what was once the Watuck Soldier Research Facility."

"The facility," I say, putting my finger on the screen, before sending the article to print. "That's probably what Mrs. Porter was talking about: the facility where they work. Watuck Soldier Research Facility. Google that."

I half expect to find no mention of the place. But within moments, we've found out quite a lot. Once a government facility where cutting-edge research on everything from treatments for PTSD, to cyberwarfare to psychological interrogation techniques was conducted, the WSRF was taken over by a private contractor called Compass Industries three years ago, then closed shortly after. The WSRF sounds untraditional by military standards, a place where research about the Outliers would fit right in.

"So that's where they work," Gideon says, with a heavy sigh. "A place that is supposedly closed. Well, that's not suspicious or anything."

"Search for Quentin and the WSRF," I say, the burn of disappointment already at the back of my throat.

Gideon tries several variations of Quentin's name and the Watuck Soldier Research Facility but comes up empty. He then tries just *Dr. Quentin Caton* and gets a couple mentions—all quotes by or related to our dad, mentioning Quentin as his excellent research assistant. Because Quentin Caton did not exist before he met our dad, not by that name. I already knew that. But seeing all those articles with my dad praising Quentin still makes me feel sick.

"How about WSRF and Senator Russo?" I say, glancing over at the librarians, who are already switching off lights at the far end.

The search yields just the one link—an article from three years earlier, with only a single reference to research approved by the Armed Services Committee relating to PTSD. Senator Russo is quoted as saying, "Research is absolutely central to the health of our soldiers, and to the safety of our country. With the help of cutting-edge facilities like the WSRF, the military is constantly innovating." And at the end there is another name listed among the doctors on staff at the WSRF: Dr. Cornelia.

I lean over and Google Russo and Cornelia together, to save Gideon the discomfort of even having to type Cornelia's name.

A beat later there it is: a repurposed photo from a Compass Industries retreat twelve years earlier, apparently before Riel's grandfather even was a senator. The article is about Dr. Cornelia, related to a book published in the late nineties. Beneath it is a caption: *Compass Industries Board Members David Russo and Dr. Peter Cornelia.*

WE DRIVE FAST on Sunset Highway toward the WSRF, hoping to find the spot where Sophie-Ann was killed. It feels with each passing moment like we're running out of time. I did consider insisting that we head straight to the WSRF to look around—but even I know that's too dangerous to head straight where we know the Wolf will be.

I pull out the copy of the article I printed out at the library and read aloud: "'She died on a lonely stretch of Sunset Highway, past mile marker seven, near what once was the Watuck Soldier Research Facility.'"

Sure enough, up ahead, there is mile marker six, clear as day. "Wait, slow down." I point to a spot where the shoulder curves into a dirt oval. "Pull off over there."

Gideon pulls the car onto the gravel and looks nervously in the rearview, but says nothing. He feels some version of *I don't think this is a good idea*, though. I know that he does. And it makes me wonder again whether any of this is really fair.

"To be clear, I don't *know* what I'm looking for here. Just that I should look," I say. And that is the truth—it's no simpler or more complicated than that. I look over at Gideon, bracing myself for objections or concerns or questions, but all I feel is understanding and compassion and love, so much it takes my breath away.

"That's okay." Gideon nods as he reaches into the glove compartment for a flashlight. He smiles grimly as he looks around at the dark. "Because our best-case scenario is that you're wrong and there's nothing to find."

WE WALK IN silence toward mile marker seven. The night air is eerie—warm and heavy. The mist so thick it clouds the light from a nearby streetlamp. There is hardly any shoulder, so we walk single file on the edge of the road. Because it does feel like a car could come out of nowhere at any moment, like maybe there's one somewhere waiting to do just that. I am relieved when up ahead there is a cluster of three trees, and beyond them, mile marker seven.

"That's it," I say, making a beeline for the trees. "This is the spot where it happened."

Fear. I feel it even before we reach the spot. But there is no sign of an accident, except a few tiny fragments of glass on the edge of the road, which could be from anything.

"Come on," I say. "We should keep going."

We walk on again in silence until eventually I find myself drifting off the road and through a different break in the trees. Back there, with the streetlights eclipsed by trees, it's suddenly very, very dark.

"Here, I'll shine the light," Gideon says, pointing the flashlight in front of me. "You lead the way."

We search on, walking deeper and deeper into the woods, through some fields and into trees again. Gideon is behind me the whole time, moving the beam of light back and forth. I pick up a long stick at one point, brushing the ground with it, hoping to hit—I don't even know what. But all I find is dirt and rocks and leaves. Every once in a while, I look over my shoulder back the way we came, to make sure we haven't yet lost our way.

About five more minutes later, the light in front of me suddenly disappears, and I am plunged into darkness.

"Wylie," Gideon says, his voice weird and strangled behind me.

When I turn, I can see he has the flashlight pointed to the side. The light is glowing over some tall grass to our right, where the field gradually blends into marsh. Pools of water stretch between the grass. But I can tell by the way Gideon is frozen that he is looking at something specific. And I can feel that he is scared. Completely and totally terrified.

"Gideon, what is it?" I ask, heart thumping, hands trembling. "I don't see anything."

Wordlessly, Gideon moves the flashlight around like he is highlighting something. "There," he whispers, stepping closer behind me to point the light more precisely at three different spots in the grassy water. Three specific places he wants me to look. "And there. And there. Something in the water."

I squint harder. And then, finally, I see it. Or rather, I see them: hands. Three hands. So far apart that none could possibly be attached to the same body. Three hands for three different people.

No, not people. Girls. Three different girls. Outliers. Already I feel so completely sure of that most awful fact. The bodies of girls sunk into the marsh. Girls who were killed. Outliers left for dead.

JASPER

JASPER KEEPS HIS EYES CLOSED. TRYING TO STAY CALM. IT'S NOT EASY IN THE dark with his body vibrating. And with the noise. It's so damn loud in there.

Lethe and Quentin shoved Jasper in the trunk after he told them the general location of the warehouses. The plan is to get Jasper out once they're close, so that he can show them the rest of the way. Jasper tried to get them to untie him first, but it was no use. Lethe can read too clearly how much Jasper wants to kill them both.

At some point, with all that vibrating and his eyes closed, Jasper falls asleep. He wakes to the sound of car doors slamming. They are nearing the end. Soon Quentin and Lethe will know that even if there were pictures in that file box, there's nothing left now but ash. Jasper has been careful not to think about that, so Lethe won't know. And getting to the warehouses was at least a way to get out of the basement, a temporary solution. Jasper doesn't have the rest worked out. He's been hoping some great idea will come to him, some great escape. But nothing has.

The trunk finally cracks open and the light inside goes on, plunging the figures outside into darkness. "We're close," Quentin says. "Get into the passenger seat and show us the rest of the way."

"I don't know if I'm going to be able to find it," Jasper stalls after Quentin and Lethe haul him out.

"You'd better," Quentin says. "Or this won't end well."

"Dude, it's not going to end well either way," Jasper says. "Am I right?"

"Maybe not for you." Quentin shrugs. "But I'll walk away from this. I always do. And then, who knows, maybe I will even track Wylie down again." It's a threat.

Jasper shoots a look at Quentin. "Stay the hell away from her," he says through clenched teeth. *Kill Quentin. Kill Quentin.* It's like a taste in Jasper's mouth.

Quentin smiles. "I'll stay away from her," he says. "As long as you get us to the warehouses and help us find those photos."

IN THE END, Jasper remembers the way to the warehouses pretty easily. But as they get closer and closer, he prays for some way out, that something is going to jump in and call a stop to all this crazy shit. Nothing does.

"They're down there." Jasper motions to the driveway. "I think."

"You think?" Lethe asks as she makes the turn.

"I'm sure," Jasper adds, and he is. He's also sure this is his last chance to head this situation off at the pass. "Why don't you just help Wylie, work together to, like, protect the other Outliers or something? Aren't you on the same side?" Jasper asks as the warehouses finally come into view. "Together you could . . ." He's not even sure what he's trying to say. He can't imagine Wylie wanting to do anything with Lethe. "You could do something good with this whole Outlier thing."

"I tried talking to Wylie in the hospital about working together," Lethe says. "She wanted no part of it."

"No part of what?" Jasper asks. "Maybe she didn't understand."

"Oh, she understood," Lethe says. "Think of an Outlier used as a jury consultant, or as a dealer at a casino. Or better yet, with a seat at a corporate negotiating table. We could make people money, a lot of money. And we're even more valuable if we're rare. If there are fewer of us." Lethe shrugs. "But all Wylie cared about was 'saving' everybody. She won't accept that the world isn't going to let that happen."

"That's because of people like him." Jasper jerks his head toward Quentin in the backseat. He's hoping he can cause friction between them. That he can slip out in the space wedged between. "Maybe Wylie would feel differently if you hadn't hunted down her best friend just to get to her."

"What?" Quentin laughs, and for real it sounds like. "No, no, no, Cassie brought *me* into this, not the other way around."

"That doesn't make sense," Jasper says. "At all."

"It may not make sense, my friend, but it's definitely true," Quentin says. "Cassie was a part of The Collective way before I ever met them. She came and found me at the lab. And she already had a plan to bring down Lang. She used my 'enhanced résumé' to encourage me to play along, said she would out me to Lang if I didn't. Said she could make me an actual famous scientist if I did. But that was all bullshit."

"But I was there. You were the one—"

"Listen, I'm not going to say I didn't get carried away at the camp. Didn't like the idea of actually being who I was pretending to. It was fun being like the main guy," Quentin says. "But the whole plan to grab Wylie to get to Lang, *that* started with Cassie. Obviously, now it wasn't just her. Not all of this. But I was only doing what she told me to do."

Quentin says some other things, but Jasper can't hear over the sound of *Cassie, Cassie, Cassie.* He felt so guilty for what happened to her because he said all those hurtful things right before she died. About what a terrible person she was and how everything was her fault. And now, here it was, the truth: Cassie was involved from the start.

"Come on, enough of the walk down memory lane," Lethe says, as she pulls to a stop in front of the warehouses. "Let's get this over with. Show us where he took the box. And who knows? Maybe you can be on your way."

"You are not going to let me go, no matter what you find," Jasper says.

"There's a chance," Lethe says. "And that's a hell of a lot more than you had when you were locked in the basement."

• • •

OUTSIDE THE CAR, Quentin uses his phone to light their way, the pale bluish light reminding Jasper of how Wylie lit their way as they ran through the woods away from the diner. But this time, Jasper is pretty sure there will be no escape.

When they finally round the corner between the buildings, he can see right away that things have been moved, cleaned up. Reorganized. The box is gone, and so are the ashes, which means he can pretend to look around for them. Hope something comes to him.

"Where is it?" Quentin asks.

"Man, it was right here, I swear," Jasper says. His confusion is genuine at least, Lethe should feel that. "Right here, out in the open. He didn't even stick around until it had burned all the way. And there was other junk back here, too. Someone has been here, cleaned things up."

"What other stuff?" Lethe asks, and she sounds different than she has. More nervous.

"Garbage, some wooden pallets stacked over there, and there were some cans and stuff, too." Jasper looks around, trying to remember what he saw exactly. "And maybe some, like, flattened empty boxes and newspapers tied together. Over there." With his arms still tied, Jasper has to jerk in the direction with his shoulder. It's when he turns that he sees something move inside the back warehouse, the one farther from the road. A shadowy figure. Too tall for any kind of animal. "What was that?" he asks, ducking down to look.

"What was what?" Quentin steps toward the back warehouse.

"I don't know," Jasper says, squinting closer. "I think I saw somebody in there at the far end."

Quentin turns to Lethe. "Don't look at me," she says. "You go check it out."

"It was locked before," Jasper says.

"Yep," Quentin says, checking the knob. "Still is."

"Why don't you go around and check the far end, see if there's another way in?" Lethe asks. "I'll stay here and stand watch."

"What, are you scared now?" Quentin sneers. "You need the men to go take care of things?"

"Not scared," Lethe says icily. "Just smart. Now go. Get your ass back there and check it out."

EndOfDays Blog

July 3

The End of Days is upon us. Will we meet our end with grace and the utmost faith? Will we, in our final moments, be able to accept the plan for us even if's not what we want for ourselves? Will we be strong enough to carry the weak, the sick, the broken, the deluded, and the unbelievers with us toward our final destinations?

I realize now that I have been wrong about many things. That I risked too much that wasn't mine to give. But I have to believe that this is not how my story ends. That I can find grace in this failure. And salvation. That I can honor the sacrifice of those I love.

It is faith that gives us strength to reach out as we are carried into the flames.

Go in peace, everyone. To the light.

WYLIE

WE SPEED AWAY FROM THE MARSHES, HEADED BACK TOWARD NEWTON. AWAY from those hands reaching toward the sky. Eventually we spotted six of them. Six hands. Maybe or maybe not attached to something.

We stop at the first gas station we can find, three miles down the road. Large and new, with brightly lit pumps and a huge, sparkling mini-mart, it reminds me of the Freshmart where Jasper and I met Doug and Lexi and the Cape Cod market where we later bought dry T-shirts, except much nicer than both.

Thinking of Jasper, I am swamped again with regret. That letter was such a risk. Why did I think it would be so easy just to take back? Even now, I am much more worried about that than some blog post somehow coming from his house.

"Can I use your phone?" I ask the clerk once we are inside.

He has limp blond hair and an empty face, half-asleep behind the gleaming counter with its vast selection of the newest candies.

This time, I am calling the police even if I don't entirely trust them. Even if I don't trust anyone anymore.

"Phone?" the clerk asks, like he's never heard of such a thing.

I point to the landline behind the counter. "Yeah, your phone. My cell is dead, and it's an emergency."

I have no intention of telling him what kind of emergency, or mentioning that we don't have cell phones because we've tossed them to avoid being followed. Anything remotely suspicious will make this guy refuse to help; two seconds in that store and I am *sure* of that. I need to stay vague. Pressure him enough to get what we want, but not enough to make him freak out.

"Fine, whatever," the clerk says finally, handing me the receiver. "I've got to dial for you, though." He pushes his slack hair back behind his ears. "No customers behind the register."

"Nine-one-one, please," I say, trying to sound casual.

"Seriously?" The clerk makes a face. But he dials when all I do is stare right back at him.

"Nine-one-one, what's your emergency?" the operator answers.

"We found a body," I say, trying to talk fast before anybody can stop me. "At mile marker seven off Sunset Highway."

"What is she talking about?" the clerk squeaks at Gideon. I avoid looking at the clerk as Gideon shrugs and rolls his eyes, like he's got no idea.

"A body?" the operator asks, sounding not particularly surprised or interested.

"Yes, a dead body," I press on, willing my voice to sound trustworthy. "Back in the woods, where the marsh starts. Actually, I think there might be more than one."

"More than one?" Now I have her attention.

"Yes," I say. "It was dark, but it looked like maybe."

"And you just happened to spot this. In the woods alongside a highway. At this time of night?"

Luckily, I'm ready for this question. "I had to pee. We pulled off. Um, sorry."

"Oh, well," she says, "are you still there now?"

"No, we left to find a phone," I say. "Mine was dead."

"Okay, I see where you are here on my system." And I am kind of alarmed by just how fast they can trace the call. It makes me think again of whoever might be following us. "Stay put. I'll send an officer right out to you. I'll send another to the mile marker location."

"Thank you," I say. When I hang up, I turn to Gideon. "We have to go, now."

"Hey!" the clerk calls after us when we're almost at the door. "Is that true about dead bodies?" He looks toward the darkness, more intrigued than scared. He likes a good conspiracy, and also, maybe the idea of dead bodies. "Around here?"

I turn back. "Yeah, it is true. Tell as many people as possible, too. Before somebody makes them disappear."

GIDEON AND I are quiet on the drive back toward Newton. Or the BC campus, specifically. With Sophie-Ann dead, Jasper—of all people—is now the only possible link to our dad. Jasper didn't post those EndOfDays blogs from his house. I know that he did not. But the reality is, someone did.

"So, what do you think happened to them?" Gideon asks. "Those . . . girls. Outliers, probably, right?"

He is hoping that I know something more than him. That I have a feeling. And maybe I even do.

"Probably all girls. Outliers, maybe. Some of them, at least. I think somebody killed them because they became a problem or were no longer useful. The WSRF must be doing some kind of testing either about Outliers or on Outliers. Or they were."

"And then they killed them?" Gideon asks.

"Or they died accidentally," I say. "Mrs. Porter's son, the Wolf—that's what I called him when I was in the hospital—is probably giving them a steady stream of foster girls. I think he was responsible for at least some of them being in the hospital, too. Maybe he's even helping dump them."

"But he's not the criminal mastermind behind the whole thing."

"I don't think so," I say.

"Any chance you know who is?"

"Not yet," I say, turning to look at him. "But I think I will."

IT DOESN'T TAKE long to find the dorm on campus where the preseason hockey players are staying. Then Gideon and I wait outside Hamilton Hall, with its white columns and tall stairs, until someone in a BC hockey shirt comes out, a nice, totally oblivious kid with a Southern accent and huge hands, who has absolutely no issue with letting us inside when we say we are there for Jasper. He even tells us where Jasper's room is, even though it's almost ten p.m. and we don't even say who we are.

As we head down the hall toward Jasper's room on the third floor, I think about what to say. I do have to ask him about the EndOfDays posts. I have no choice. But after my letter, who knows what Jasper is feeling or what he might say? He might claim that he's EndOfDays just so he can hurt me back.

An attractive blond boy answers Jasper's door. He is sleepy but welcoming.

"What's up?" he asks, like maybe we've met already. He's not sure, but he likes to give people the benefit of the doubt.

"We're looking for Jasper," I say, both comforted and troubled by his ease.

"You and everybody else, man," he says with a shake of his head.

"What do you mean?" I put a hand on Jasper's door frame, afraid his roommate might try to close the door before he explains.

He scrubs at his sandy hair with a hand. "Jasper, um, is missing, I guess, technically. I mean, not for long. Like a few hours. I personally wouldn't even say that's missing, but his mom is freaking."

"Missing?" My heart picks up speed. I lean closer. "What are you talking about?"

"His mom thinks maybe he took off, with someone who I guess is bad news," he says. And I know that person would be me. "Supposedly, he wasn't so sure he wanted to be here to begin with. I mean, I never noticed that. But that's what his mom said.

And, man, is she pissed. I thought there was a chance she was going to pop *me* when she was here before. Like *I'm* the one who told him to take off. If that's even what happened. But I said something to her about this girl who was here earlier and—"

"What girl?" I ask, and too harshly. Gideon eyeballs me in disbelief: *Seriously? Jealousy, now?*

Jasper's roommate holds up his hands, worried he's back in the hornet's nest. "Listen, maybe they were just friends, I don't know. She came by to see Jasper this afternoon. He wasn't here, so she left some cookies and said she'd come back. That's all I know."

Cookies?

"What did she look like?" I ask, and guiltily. These are facts we need, but maybe that's not the only reason I'm asking.

"Long curly hair, big greenish-yellow eyes," he says. "She was pretty. Oh, and she had this tattoo, on the inside of her wrist. Some kind of symbol."

My heart stops. Kelsey from the hospital? Jasper would have had no way of knowing it was her, either. Unless. Unless Jasper *did* know it was the fake Kelsey. Between the EndOfDays posts and now Jasper being with the fake Kelsey, I'd be an idiot not to consider the possibility.

Still, it doesn't feel right. There's some betrayal somewhere. But not that. Not Jasper.

"What was her name?" Gideon asks. Such an ordinary question, one that I hadn't even thought to ask.

"Lethe," Jasper's roommate says. "For real. I asked her twice."

• • •

"WYLIE, SLOW DOWN," Gideon calls after me as I run down the dorm steps in front of him.

Lethe. Lethe. Lethe. The fake Kelsey is named Lethe, and Lethe is one of the girls Mrs. Porter mentioned, her name wedged between Teresa and Sophie-Ann. I don't stop running until I am all the way outside, standing in the darkness. I lean over, trying to catch my breath. Hoping my heart will slow.

So Lethe and Teresa actually knew each other before the hospital. And they both knew the Wolf the whole time. Ramona said something about the fake Kelsey talking to the guards, the Wolf, surely. Is it possible Lethe let Jasper in? And that the two of them together . . . No. No, I don't think so. I really don't.

"Wylie, what's wrong?" Gideon asks, finally catching up to me. He's panting.

And I realize then how much he doesn't know—I never even told him about the fake Kelsey. There'd been no reason to.

"Either Jasper did something really, really bad, or he is in serious bad trouble." I look around the campus, like the answer lies somewhere out there in the darkness.

"Okay," Gideon says, doing his best to sound like the levelheaded one. "Which do you think it is?"

"I believe in Jasper," I say, because that's how I've felt the whole time. "And I think he's in trouble now. Really, really terrible trouble."

WHEN WE FINALLY arrive home, there's a woman standing at our door in the dark. She has brown skin, chin-length hair, and high cheekbones highlighted in the glow from the streetlight. And from her crossed arms and the way she keeps looking over her shoulder back at the house, she seems like she's been waiting for some time.

"Who's that?" Gideon asks as we pull up to the curb.

"I have no idea," I say. But already I'm sure that this woman knows something that we need to. "Come on, let's go find out."

"Are you sure?" Gideon asks. "We could keep driving. She wouldn't even know we live here. I mean, at this point, we should be careful, shouldn't we?"

"Yes," I say. "But I think careful right now *is* talking to her."

THE WOMAN STARTLES and turns in our direction as our car doors slam closed. "Hello?" she calls, squinting in our direction. She sounds and looks more hesitant now.

"Can we help you?" I call, trying to move quickly into the light so she can at least see that it's Gideon and me coming—two teenagers—and not someone like Agent Klute.

"I'm Dr. Oduwole," she says, once we are coming up the steps. And the way she says her name, it's like that alone should explain everything. "I'm looking for Hope Lang or Dr. Ben Lang. Though I don't think he's here, is he? Are you Wylie and Gideon?"

Finally, I place the name. Dr. Oduwole was one of the people my mom went out to see in California, the neuroscientist from UCLA my dad was working with. Dr. Oduwole was helping my dad discover why the Outliers existed. She was to be part of the study he was trying to get funding for.

"Our mom went out to see you," I say. And I feel sure that

this woman is telling the truth about who she is. More importantly, I can feel that her intentions are genuine. "She just sent me an email saying she'd met with you."

"Met with me already?" she asks, stepping closer. Dr. Oduwole has gone in a flash from tentatively concerned to full-on worried. "Several weeks ago, your mother and I exchanged emails that said she would be coming. She asked me not to say anything to anyone about having heard from her. That it would put you in terrible danger. But then she never showed up, and I became worried that something had happened to her." And now Dr. Oduwole looks past us for an actual incoming threat. "When was the last time you spoke to her?"

Gideon looks at me: *Should we tell her? Should we trust her?* I nod at him before turning back to the doctor.

"I saw her a couple weeks ago. But I was, it was—we really didn't talk," I say. "And our dad has been missing for almost three weeks."

"Yes, I am so sorry. Your mother did tell me," she says. And with real regret. She genuinely cares about our dad, that much is for sure. "Your mother said he had gone missing while trying to secure funding for our study. I thought maybe—"

"When was the last time you talked to her again?" I ask, already with a terrible churning in my gut.

"About three weeks ago," she says. "That's why I'm here. I got concerned when we lost touch."

"She said that you and my dad had a big fight about him wanting to keep some things secret about why Outliers were just being discovered now." But already I'm skeptical. Hearing it out loud, it just doesn't sound right.

"An argument with me?" Dr. Oduwole asks, eyes wide. "Your father and I were always in complete agreement. And he was never at all interested in secrecy. The opposite, in fact."

"Then why would my mom tell me that?" I ask, though I already feel like an idiot. The "SwimTeacher" email name, her little secret message between the two of us. It made me believe it was her. But it could have been anybody.

"I'm not sure."

Dr. Oduwole looks past us again and into the darkness warily. "But someone has just published a study. Exactly like the one your father and I were working on. It definitively establishes the existence of the Outliers. The race to try to make our findings public—" She hesitates. "Well, I guess it's not much of a race once someone else has won."

"That's a good thing, right?" I ask, because wasn't going public supposed to be the Outliers' best protection, *my* best protection. But I can already feel that Dr. Oduwole doesn't see it that way.

"I am troubled by where this research came from. Frankly, it looks very much like ours," Dr. Oduwole says. "It's hard to believe they came up with it on their own. There are very few corners of the scientific community that would be capable of working in such secrecy. In fact, I can think of only one."

"What's that?" I ask.

"The US military."

RIEL

IT TAKES MORE THAN AN HOUR FOR RIEL TO GET FROM THE WAREHOUSE TO HER parents' closed-up house in East Boston, perched high on the top of Eagle Hill. It's past ten p.m. when she arrives, and the house—big, old, Victorian—is dark when she pulls up, as it should be. As it has been for months now. No one has lived there since Kelsey died.

Riel told her aunt she would keep an eye on the place, that she'd just be staying with a friend for a little bit. And then she'd come back. Not that it mattered. After Kelsey died, no one cared anymore what Riel did. No one, it turned out, except for her grandfather. Apparently, he never took his eyes off her. And yet, he's kept her alive. She's afraid to find out why.

IT WAS TEN minutes, twenty maybe, that Riel had lain, cheek pressed against that cold warehouse floor. She was afraid to move. Afraid whoever shot Kendall would shoot her, too, afraid to go near where Kendall was lying lifeless on the floor.

For a long time, Riel had hoped he'd wake up. Alive and well because he was wearing a bulletproof vest or something or because he was just . . . him. But once the blood started to pool under his head like the petals of some terrible flower, Riel knew it was really over, that Kendall was dead.

And if she didn't get out of there, she knew she might be next.

Riel stayed low as she crawled past Kendall toward the door. It was then that she spotted the handgun, tucked at his side under his arm. She turned her head away as she reached in to pull it out.

"Thank you," she whispered to Kendall even though it felt so shallow. "For everything."

RIEL FINDS THE spare house key still where it always is, under the biggest rock alongside the steps up to her old front door. The key is a little rusty. Maybe it always has been. She can't remember. Looking down at it in her hand now, she is too overwhelmed by sadness. So little that she has left. So few people. It's right that it ends this way then, with her doing whatever it takes to get rid of her grandfather. She's willing to pay the price, too, no matter how high. Or how permanent. She owes that to the Outliers. And to Kelsey.

Inside, the house smells musty, and there's a big pile of unopened mail spread out under the slot in the door. But otherwise it is exactly as Riel remembers it.

She turns on a few lights on her way up the stairs, holding Kendall's gun down awkwardly at her side. She fired the gun once, out in the woods. Just to be sure she could. And it was in all ways different than she thought it would be—the gun was heavier, harder to aim, more painful when it kicked back. Her hand still feels like it's vibrating. But she's ready now. Next time she fires it, at least she won't be surprised.

Upstairs, Riel pauses in the hall outside Kelsey's closed door, presses her palm flat against it. She can't bear the thought of opening it, not even now to take one last look. Especially not now, maybe. Because all she can think is how she should have fucking known. Should have seen her grandfather coming. Should have been able to keep her sister alive.

She continues on to her own dusty bedroom. Riel finds her old phone and the SIM card exactly where she left them, separate and tucked between her mattress and box spring. She'd been right to leave them behind all those months ago. Though at the time, she definitely hadn't pictured needing them for this: to draw her grandfather to her. He had Kendall shot right in front of her but left her alive. Because he wants her for something himself. If he isn't already on his way because he followed her from the warehouse, she expects they'll still be on the lookout for her phone, no matter how long it's been since she used it.

Riel reassembles her phone and finds the cord to charge it, then makes her way back downstairs. To wait. In a place with her back against the wall.

IN THE LIVING room, Riel watches the front windows, waiting for thirty minutes, the gun tucked behind her back in the seat cushions. Her grandfather won't be alone, she already knows that. But she has a plan. Or maybe "plan" is too strong a word.

This has only one step: shoot first.

Finally, there is a flash of headlights across the room. Riel sucks in some air, exhales hard as she stands. She *can* do this. She will. She has to. She's made so many mistakes, missed so many things. But right now, she knows her grandfather has to be stopped. And she may be the only one able to do it.

Riel heads over and tucks herself behind the front door, gun out. Ready to go. She hears the footsteps a moment later and then there is the knob turning slowly, the door opening quietly. Her heart is racing.

Agent Klute steps inside first, followed by her grandfather. As soon as they are through, and Riel can confirm that Klute's gun is not yet drawn, she steps forward and kicks closed the door.

"Don't move," she says, voice steady and strong, the gun pointed at her grandfather.

Agent Klute looks over his shoulder, eyebrows raised. "Do you even know how to—"

Riel fires a shot at the ground over in the corner. The bullet ricochets and shatters one of the windows.

"What the hell are you doing?" Klute shouts, ducking slightly.

"Answering your question. I do know how to use it," Riel says calmly, eyes locked on her grandfather still. She does feel better now. This is the right plan—however it ends up. "Now get the fuck out. I want to talk to my grandfather alone."

"Thank you, Agent Klute. I can take it from here," Riel's grandfather says, going to sit calmly on the couch. Beyond him, out the window, the lights of downtown Boston shimmer in the distance.

Agent Klute doesn't look like he plans on going anywhere. "I don't think that's a good—"

"Thank you, Agent Klute," her grandfather repeats, more firmly. "That will be all."

Once Klute has backed reluctantly out the door, Riel can sense that her grandfather is actually a little more nervous about the gun than he seemed at first. For a man who is sickly overconfident, gunpoint is apparently his limit. Good.

"I'm sorry that all the loss in your life—first your parents and then Kelsey—has made you so angry, Riel," he begins, his voice syrupy and condescending. "Honestly, I have nothing but sympathy for you."

"Did you kill them, too?" she asks. It's something she has been wondering.

He laughs, like he actually thinks it's goddamn hilarious. Riel can feel him relax slightly. "Kill who?"

"My parents, you asshole," Riel says, readjusting the gun,

fighting back the urge to pull the trigger. She will. But she needs some answers first. "Because I know for sure that you killed Kelsey."

Her grandfather tilts his head to the side, wrinkles his brow. "Your parents were killed in a flash flood. You know that. Their problem was that they tried to 'help people' in all the wrong ways. When you try to rescue people from the natural consequences of their own actions, they never learn to save themselves. And good, hardworking people like your parents pay the price."

"Is that what you were trying to do with Kelsey?" Riel asks. "Teach her to save herself?"

"I'm not responsible for what happened to your sister."

"She overdosed on *your* drugs, from *your* test, at *your* facility." And, yeah, Riel is fishing. Some of this is a guess. But it feels pretty damn close to the truth. The party that last night was at some abandoned research facility. "Did you get her high so you could run tests? Or did you just hope she would kill herself by accident?"

"What happened to Kelsey is a very good example of precisely what we need to protect you from—other Outliers. Has it not occurred to you that you're *more* valuable if there are fewer of you? Because it's definitely occurred to at least one of the other Outliers. The girl with the infinity tattoo? I believe you've spoken to her," her grandfather says, and so goddamn pleased with himself. "We were taken in by her ourselves at first. Once we realized how skilled Lethe was, we sent her to take Ben Lang's test to see if she could find out more. But she only cared how being an Outlier would benefit *her*. I will admit that it was my mistake to tell her about you and Kelsey. I was merely trying to establish a rapport with her. I can only guess she planned to use the two of you against me." He shakes his head, feels genuinely disappointed. "Lethe claims all she did was leave Kelsey alone in a room with access to those drugs. Possible, but doubtful. I do think she intentionally killed another girl at the hospital, Teresa. Wylie being blamed was, I expect, her intent. To be honest, it's an issue she was able to be in there in the first place undetected. Regardless, you see how dangerous Lethe is. She is proof enough of why you need us: to save you from yourselves."

"Go to hell," Riel says, raising the gun again. "We don't need you for anything."

Her grandfather presses his lips together. But he is still so calm, too calm. He knows something Riel doesn't.

"Pointing that gun like that is extremely dangerous, Gabrielle," he says. "You don't want to do something you'll regret."

"Where is Wylie?"

"Yes, Wylie is another excellent example. At such risk. There are genuinely unstable people in the world. People confuse their own desires with some higher power. One of those people is about to wipe out Wylie and Jasper, and Wylie's entire family. Because he blames them for something that isn't their fault. These are the people who you need to be protected from, Riel. And we can do that. We can keep you all safe."

Kendall was right: her grandfather is tying up loose ends. Wylie is not dead yet, though. Riel can feel her grandfather is still a little worried about Wylie causing him trouble. Which means that Riel can still save her, if she moves quickly.

"Join me," her grandfather says then, looking at Riel like she is some precious key to something. It makes her feel sick. "Join me and I'll make sure you are safe."

"What?" Riel asks, recoiling. "I'm not doing shit with you. I'm going to shoot you."

"If you do that, who knows what will become of the Outliers? I want to be sure that the Outliers are protected and respected. I want to make it so that we can all peacefully coexist. That's all I have ever wanted—systems in place that will work for everyone."

Riel doesn't believe a word he is saying, of course. But she can't shoot him without knowing first what he's talking about.

"What kinds of systems?" she asks, trying to keep the scorn from her voice.

"ID cards," her grandfather says. "That way everyone's privacy can be protected: Outliers and non-Outliers. Nothing more complicated than a driver's license."

"But let me guess, only the Outliers have the IDs?"

"Come now, we're not talking about some kind of branding. Honestly, the intake centers will be just like the DMV."

The warehouses. That was why Kendall brought Riel there: an intake center, almost completed. The next phase.

"And what if the Outliers refuse?" Riel asks.

Her grandfather tries to swallow back his irritation, but it stays stuck behind his teeth. "See, this is exactly why you need to join me, Riel. You can be the voice for the Outliers. Having you with me on the campaign trail—as family, no less—would make clear that my intentions are good. And I'd be happy to listen to any suggestion you might have. You could work for me *on behalf of* the Outliers."

The hairs on the back of Riel's neck rise.

"Over. My. Dead. Body." Riel's voice trembles with rage. She can do this. She will.

"I wouldn't do that," he says. "Your boyfriend is in the car with Agent Klute."

"What?" Riel asks, glancing toward the window. "What do you mean, my boyfriend?"

"Leo. Under the circumstances, I'm sure Klute will be bringing him inside any moment." They wait a beat, staring at the door. Sure enough, it opens and Klute drags Leo inside, a gun already to his head.

Riel is careful to keep the gun on her grandfather, but her hand has started to shake. "Leo, are you okay?" she calls over to him.

"I'm okay," Leo says, though he does not at all sound or feel like he is.

"Now that we have the situation clarified, I will give you a chance to reconsider my offer," her grandfather says. "Also, I will need those pictures."

"What pictures?" Riel asks.

"Come now, Riel," her grandfather says. "A bit late for games, isn't it? The pictures you went to see Rosenfeld about."

Riel hesitates, but only for a second. When she looks over at Leo, she can feel him willing her to hand them over. And they still have her grandfather's phone. They have other evidence. They can still make him pay for what happened to Kelsey, for what he plans to do with the Outliers.

"Okay," Riel says finally. Her eyes are still on Leo's as she lowers the gun. "The pictures are in the car, under the mat."

"Good," her grandfather says as Klute comes over and takes Riel's gun. Her grandfather stands. "There's been so much heartache already surrounding the Outliers, I'd hate for there to be more. The offer to join me on the campaign trail stands, Riel," he says. "For now. You should reconsider."

And with that, her grandfather reaches in his pocket and pulls out his phone. Holds it in the air.

"Ask your friend Brian. He's a smart boy. He learned the benefits of cooperation a long time ago."

WYLIE

AS WE CLIMB THE STEPS TO RACHEL'S DOOR, I CAN'T STOP THINKING OF JASPER. I am more worried about him with each passing minute.

And hasn't every bad thing that has happened to Jasper been traced right back to me? His mother was right: he would have been so much better off without me.

"We should pick up the pace," Gideon says, moving around me and heading up the last of Rachel's steps.

He has his laptop gripped under his arm so we can check to see if EndOfDays has responded to our "where are we supposed to hurry" question. Gideon and I have agreed that going wherever EndOfDays says would be stupid. It's obviously a trap, which is why we're hoping Elizabeth has figured out where EndOfDays is posting from so we might at least have the element of surprise.

When Gideon rings Rachel's door, it swings open almost immediately. "What's wrong?" she asks, waving us inside as she scans the sidewalk behind us. It's a relief not to have to talk her into being on high alert. She already is. Too alert, maybe. "Come in, come in."

I feel a lightning bolt of her feeling: there, gone.

"Dr. Oduwole showed up at our house," I say.

"Really?" Rachel asks. But weirdly calm—no, weirdly, nothing. "What did she say?"

"That our mom never came to see her. And my mom's email said that she *already* had. It doesn't make sense."

"You're right. It definitely doesn't make sense." Rachel's brow creases as she looks down, crosses her arms tightly. But still no flash, crackle, gone. Nothing. When she finally looks up, she shrugs. "Well, if your mom lied—if she misrepresented exactly where she was—you and I both know she must have had a good reason."

"Lied?" Gideon asks. And I am glad I'm not the only one who thinks that's absurd.

"We don't think she lied. We think she's in trouble," I say, swamped by the terrible sensation of something hurtling toward me in the dark. Now I am the one who crosses my arms. "When was the last time you actually talked to her on the phone?" I realize now that I've been assuming there were live conversations between Rachel and our mom. But she never said that. "You actually heard *her* voice, right? I mean after I saw her in the detention facility."

I feel Rachel twitch. Nervous. Flash. Crackle. Gone. She

hasn't heard my mom's voice, not for a while. Is that the awfulness coming at me from the dark? That Rachel screwed up? Her eyes are down again.

"Your mom hasn't wanted to talk on the phone. But your mom has been right to be careful. When she showed up the night of the accident, totally out of the blue—"

"Not 'totally' out of the blue." I cut her off sharply. Rachel being loose on details has already gotten us into trouble once. "You saw each other before that night."

Gideon steps forward with his laptop and sets it on the coffee table. "I'm just going to check something," he says.

"Yeah, sure," Rachel says to him, then turns back to me. "What were you saying?"

And suddenly there is an alarm going off in my head.

Rachel lives nowhere near us. Why would she have been randomly at my mom's old-lady yoga class all the way across town?

"Hey," Gideon calls to me. "Nothing new from our reply to that 'hurry' message, but there is a new one from Elizabeth." He turns his computer toward me so I can read the message myself:

That car is registered to Senator David Russo's office.

That explains why they wanted those pictures so badly: they connect Russo to the WSRF and all those dead girls.

"What does that second one say?" I ask, pointing to another new message from Elizabeth that has just appeared above

"Oh, that must be brand-new. I didn't see it."

New post from EndOfDays just went up. This is where he is. Evan told me to tell you not to go.

It's followed by an address.

Gideon looks up at me. "What do we do?"

"We go," I say, then turn back to Rachel. I focus hard on her, but it's hard to muster the outrage I felt a minute earlier. I'm too focused now on my dad. "You ran into my mom before the accident in a yoga class in our neighborhood."

I wait for Rachel to say "no" or "what are you talking about?" Or to at least look confused. Instead her face stays frozen for an endless moment.

Then Rachel smiles at me. Hatefully. And it's like a door has snapped open and bitter air has blown through. When my eyes go wide, Rachel starts shaking her head, silently. And just like that all of her hate disappears. And I can't feel anything.

On and off, like a light switch. Just like Kelsey in the hospital.

"What the hell is going on, Wylie?" Gideon whispers in my ear. He's standing at my side now. "We should go, to the address. . . ."

"You're blocking," I say to Rachel. "You've been blocking this whole time."

And then Rachel starts clapping. Loud. And slow.

"That damn note. Your mom said she needed something from the house, so I brought her by." She shakes her head. "That was a mistake, obviously.

"And yes, blocking. We might never figure out how to turn somebody into an Outlier. But if we learn how to block, what difference does it make? And we're nearly there."

Rachel is involved. But then, didn't I always feel something bad about her? It was my mom showing up and telling me to trust her—Rachel saved her life.

"Are my parents dead?" I ask. My voice is trembling, making my chest rattle.

"I don't think so. But then people like EndOfDays can be so unpredictable," she says with put-on regret. "As an architect, all you can do is build the house: you can't control how people live in it."

"An architect?" I ask quietly.

And Rachel is so sickly proud of the label. It's against her better judgment to say more, but she just can't help herself. I wish she'd block me again. I'm not sure I want to feel any more.

"Houses, political campaigns, they all need a person with a plan. I headed off your mom's accident—that was Klute, that idiot. He decided that it would be better to scare your dad by getting rid of your mom. But it was far too early. He has no sense of timing. The baby dolls were me, too. In the end, they were what freaked your mom out the most. *Her babies.* That's what she kept saying when she came for my help. She thought the babies were meant as a threat to you. Her love for you made her easy to manipulate. And once you save someone's life, it's amazing how they'll *never* consider that you could be slowly killing them by other means."

"You're a monster," I say, feeling short of breath.

"Evil is in the eye of the beholder." Rachel shakes her head. "I know you all think this Outlier thing is going be some great advance for women. You know what I think? I think I've worked my ass off to get where I am. No one cut any corners for me. I think this Outlier thing is a bunch of bullshit, no matter what the science says. Your dad should have known when to leave well enough alone. You were *all* warned. But you people just wouldn't stop. This nonsense with the pictures, for instance—I go to the trouble to get them from your house—"

"You were the one who broke into our house?" I say, feeling momentary relief at having the mystery solved.

"Of course I did," Rachel says, mocking, vicious. And now her feelings are even colder and uglier. "And really, shouldn't you have known that? I mean, you are an Outlier."

Gideon's hand is on my arm. It's because I've stepped closer to Rachel. And my hands are balled into fists. "Come on," he says. "We need to go now, while we can."

He is tugging me toward the door.

"Gideon is right," Rachel says. "You should go. I may have given EndOfDays a little direction. A couple key allies to reach out to at the start, like your dad's assistant, and your friend Riel. But he's off on his own now. And there's no telling when he'll finally jump the tracks."

I keep on glaring at Rachel as Gideon manages to get me to the door.

"This isn't over," I say through gritted teeth.

"No," she says, and with such terrible, icy certainty. "But almost. Almost."

JASPER

AFTER LOTS OF BACK-AND-FORTH AND A BEGRUDGING AND UNSUCCESSFUL LOOP around the back warehouse, trying all the locked doors and windows and without another glimpse of the figure, Quentin is back standing between the warehouses with Lethe and Jasper. A light suddenly goes on in the front warehouse.

"What the hell was that?" Quentin asks as he steps over to try the door of that warehouse. Unlike the door to the back warehouse, this one pops right open.

Lethe, Quentin, and Jasper step hesitantly inside the front warehouse, peering toward the light, still glowing eerily from the back. They inch slowly forward, until Jasper can see that the first hallway breaks off into two smaller ones on either side, like two sides of a barbecue prong. The light is coming from all the way at the back on the left side.

"Nope," Lethe says, pulling to a stop. "You assholes do what you want. I am sure as hell not going down there."

Quentin looks at Lethe, then back at Jasper. "And I am sure as hell not going down there alone."

"Untie me. I'll go," Jasper offers, turning his bound wrists toward Quentin. He sounds too amped. He can't help it. It's the first real leverage he's had: putting himself in harm's way. "Dude, you can even stay here. Or come behind me, whatever. There's definitely somebody in here. Or there was. That light wasn't there before. I'll go check it out, but not with my hands tied up. I won't have any way to defend myself."

"I'm not untying you," Quentin says flatly. Like the idea is so stupid it's boring.

"I'm telling you, I'll go," Jasper says, trying to keep himself checked—it isn't easy. "Just untie me." Then he'll have to figure out how to get Quentin to follow. Or Lethe. Either one, just not together. First step, though, is to get untied. "Hurry up, before whoever it is comes out of nowhere. Face it. You need my help."

And then suddenly there is a tug from behind and the rope around Jasper's wrists pops open, falls to the ground.

"Try anything, and I will cut you," Lethe says. She reached around to cut the ropes and is now pointing the knife toward Jasper's face. "Go with him, Quentin."

"No way," Quentin says.

Lethe points the knife at Quentin. "Go," she says. "You goddamn coward. Or I will cut you, too."

"Fine, but he goes first." Quentin shoves Jasper forward. "Move!"

Jasper starts toward the light, thinking, *Come on, come closer.*

He wants Quentin right behind him. Quentin, who is unarmed. This is his chance, while Lethe and Quentin are separated. When it's not two against one. When the knife is back with Lethe and not with Quentin.

"Hurry up," Quentin barks. "Go on, see what it is."

But the more Quentin hustles Jasper ahead, the farther he lags behind. On purpose, probably, to keep himself clear in case there is someone there. By the time they are halfway down the hall, there is so much space between Jasper and Quentin that Jasper would have to turn around and sprint back to get his hands on Quentin. It'll never work. Jasper can finally see what it is at the end, though, the source of the light. It's a laptop on a small table, open and glowing, something moving back and forth across the screen.

"Hey, you okay back there?" Quentin calls out to Lethe in a pointless whisper, loud as a shout. They are out of her line of sight now—all the way down at the end of the hall. The timing couldn't be more perfect. Or would be if Jasper was the one behind.

But then, as Jasper is moving closer to the computer, he spots a pile of short metal pipes along the wall. Sitting there like an answer. He can already feel the sick, wet pop of Quentin's skull being crushed in.

"What is that?" Quentin asks, suddenly walking past Jasper and right up to the computer. The pipes lie behind Quentin's turned back now. And in front of Jasper.

On the computer screen, shadowy images of moths gather in a larger and larger cluster and then disappear suddenly, the screen going black, as if drawn to a suddenly extinguished flame. Quentin is watching the screen, mesmerized, as Jasper bends quickly down, grabs a short stretch of pipe, and tucks it in the back of his waistband.

"Shit!" Lethe shouts angrily from the front of the building, just as Jasper is pulling his shirt over the pipe. Quentin whips around and rushes back. Jasper follows, heart pounding, the pipe digging into his back.

WHEN THEY GET back to the front of the warehouse, Lethe is twisting the locked doorknob and rattling the door. "We are fucking locked in here!" she screams, then starts kicking wildly at the door, the sound echoing in the warehouse.

"Move, let me try it," Quentin says, giving a go at the knob. But he can't get it to budge, either. "Shit."

Lethe whips around and charges at Jasper. "What the hell did you do?" she screams so viciously that he leans back, the pipe scraping painfully against his flesh. He forces himself not to flinch.

"Me?" he asks. "I was down there. I didn't lock the door. And there's a goddamn computer in here with *moths* flying around a *flame.* Get it? Somebody wanted us in here."

"Well, now they have us! Thanks to you!" Lethe screams. "Fucking fantastic. I am going to die in here because of you two idiots."

"Calm down, Lethe, no one's going to die," Quentin says, sharp and condescending. "I know that you're an Outlier and all, but try not to get overemotional."

"What the fuck did you just say?" Lethe asks, the knife gripped tighter at her side. She takes a couple steps closer to Quentin. They are only inches apart now.

"I said"—Quentin leans in closer—"don't get so emo—" Lethe swings the knife over her head, but Quentin has grabbed for her wrist. "Lethe, what the fuck are you—"

Run, Jasper thinks as they struggle over the knife. But where? The door is still locked. He's looking around for another way out, when there's a small, sharp noise. A yelp, like a little dog. And then silence. When Jasper turns, Lethe and Quentin are frozen. Lethe is up on her toes. Finally, Quentin takes a step back, pulling his arm away. And the knife out of Lethe's side. She collapses to the floor.

FOR A LONG time, Jasper and Quentin stand facing each other, leaning against opposite walls, staring down at Lethe's body. Quentin looks stunned, even confused. There is blood all over his hands and his shirt. Lethe is dead, no doubt. There is way too much blood for it to be otherwise.

"This is all Cassie's fault, you know," Quentin says, motioning to the blood on his shirt.

"What the hell does you killing Lethe have to do with Cassie?" Jasper asks, though he's not even sure he wants to know.

"Everything was fine until she came along." He shakes his head. "Yeah, I lied on my résumé. I'd been about to get my PhD when I got expelled from UMass. I neeeded a job. Who the fuck cares? I was a good research assistant and then Cassie had to show up."

"Yeah, you started to say this before. And I still don't believe you."

"Believe me or not, asshole. It's true," Quentin says. "Listen, I was just there working with Dr. Lang, minding my own business, and then Cassie was there saying how much more I could be if only I helped her. How I had all this potential and so many better ideas. That I should be in charge. She was the one who sent me to that hacker chick. None of us knew then that she was Russo's granddaughter, though."

"If Cassie was involved from the start, why did she—why would she have done what she did? She's dead."

Quentin shakes his head. "Don't look at me," he says. "I didn't know she was going to do that. And I have no idea why she did. But it sure as hell wasn't to save all of you from me."

WYLIE

THERE'S NO QUESTION WE'RE GOING TO THE ADDRESS ENDOFDAYS LAST POSTED from. A place that we know is a trap. That Rachel all but suggested we go. Still, we must go. Carefully. And with our eyes wide open. We call the police on the way, but it's not easy to explain our situation to the 911 dispatcher. Pretty soon it feels more like an argument than a request for help.

"No, I don't know for sure that our dad's there, and what difference does it make if my dad's an official missing person?" I say to the 911 operator. "We think someone is holding him at this address. We're going there right now. And we're just two teenagers. If we get killed, it will be on you."

I didn't mention our mom. How much is one 911 operator expected to believe?

"Well done," Gideon says when I hang up. And not even sarcastically.

"I don't know if it'll work," I say.

Gideon shrugs. "It was worth a try."

What we don't talk about is Rachel. What is there to say? She betrayed all of us. This person I did not like from the start, but whom I decided to trust despite my initial gut reaction. I trusted her because the facts told me to, because my mom had told me to. She had saved our mom's life. And so I decided to go with the facts instead of my instincts. And now that may have cost us—and our parents—everything.

WHEN WE FINALLY get to the address Elizabeth gave us, an hour outside Newton, the car lurches hard over the dirt driveway as we make our way slowly through the trees. It's dark back there. Really, really dark. And foreboding. Still, we are doing the right thing going there. I feel sure we are.

Our dad needs us, and he is there, somewhere, waiting. Alive for now, at least I think so, and our mom, too. I hope. I haven't let myself consider what it will mean if they're not together. But I feel sure that something terrible is about to happen. There is nothing good about the fact that Rachel let us leave. She didn't do that because she feels bad, or because deep down she is a good person. She let us go because it was all a part of her plan. Still, knowing that doesn't change the fact that going to that address is our only possible chance.

Outlier Rule #8: Knowing you should run the other way doesn't mean that you can.

Gideon pulls the car to a stop between the two long cream-colored warehouses. The buildings, dark inside, look new. It's a surprisingly bright night, a nearly full moon shining down on us. It reminds me of when Jasper and I first arrived at the camp in Maine, the moonlit lawn between the cabins lit up like dawn. Jasper and I had been so right to be scared then. I have no doubt that I am right to be scared now.

Because as we sit in the car, staring at those strange and terrible warehouses, my instincts are saying, *Go inside. You must. You have no choice.* And at the same time, my instincts screaming *danger, danger, danger.*

Outlier Rule #9: Knowing the right choice doesn't mean it is a good one.

"We need that flashlight," Gideon says, reaching forward and digging around his glove compartment like his life depends on it. "And we should stick together."

"Yeah." I nod, though I can already feel it won't make a difference. Maybe that email was right. *The EndOfDays is nigh.* Something definitely is.

THERE'S ONLY THE quiet when we get out of the car. No wind, no rustling. Like the world is holding its breath. In silence, side by side, we move closer to the back warehouse. I brace myself for something or someone to jump out and stop us. But no one does. And soon we are peering through the windows of the back warehouse and into more darkness.

"It doesn't look like it's being used," Gideon says, face pressed against the glass. Above Gideon's head there are a few strange small holes, perfectly round. Like they were put there for ventilation.

Through the window I can see the warehouse interior has been set up as an office or business, long hall down the center, doors on either side. But there's not much else. A few step stools at the front, some cleaning supplies on the windowsill next to a hammer. A handful of chairs, and a small rug off-center covering a weirdly small portion of the broad floor. No other signs of life. Not of my parents, either. *Hurry. The EndOfDays is nigh.* This is definitely the place, though. I'm sure.

"Do you think this was bullshit?" Gideon asks.

Before I can answer, there's a flash of light inside at the back of that warehouse. Like a shooting star. There and then gone.

"Did you see that?" Gideon asks, hope and dread colliding inside him. He wants me to have seen it. But also wants it to have been his imagination.

"Yeah, I saw it," I say, and I want so badly to feel relieved. But I do not. Not at all.

I put a hand on the doorknob, bracing for it to be locked, but the door pops open with a delicate click. An invitation, but a terrible one.

The light flashes again once we step inside. And now we can see where it's coming from: a bulb flickering at the back of the warehouse like it's about to go out.

"Should we turn on more lights?" Gideon asks, motioning to a panel on the wall. "There's electricity."

When Gideon hits the nearby switches, I'm still surprised that the lights overhead sputter to life. Such a simple thing. So obvious. The warehouse is brighter now, but the light yellow and unpleasant. Still it's better than darkness. Anything is.

With the light on, the front of the warehouse looks like a waiting room in the making: the chairs along the wall, a large cutout rectangle to the left like a window a receptionist would sit behind. Except the glass hasn't yet been installed. The chairs are way premature, too, compared to the state of the rest of the space. It's built out—the walls constructed, drywall in place. But there are no switch plates or other finishes, the floor is still concrete, and all the interior windows—there are several, not just the one at the reception desk—are waiting for glass. But weirdly, there is a small metal box in the corner, like for blood samples, ready for lab pickup.

"What is this place?" I ask, though Gideon doesn't know the answer.

"Come on," he says, waving me on.

We head tentatively down the hall, lined with so many doors. The light at the back has gone out again. "There's something off about these, isn't there?" Gideon says, motioning to the doors. "They're so narrow and close together or something."

I turn to the nearest one, expecting again for it to be locked. But it opens, too. Inside, the room is a tiny box, enough space for a couple chairs maybe but not even a desk. It's way too small to be an office, for sure. And no window, though it feels like there should be one. There's a mirror on the wall instead, which makes the room feel a tiny bit less cramped, but also creepy. Why a mirror? I come out of the first room and enter the next and then the next. But they are all exactly the same.

There were definitely windows along the outside of the warehouse that should logically back up to the rooms. Which means there must be some kind of narrow void behind them. To observe the rooms through the mirrors? To observe what? Who? The floor feels like it's rocking beneath me suddenly.

There's a loud noise then, a scraping sound at the far back of the warehouse. Gideon and I race out of the small rooms we'd been inspecting and stare down toward the end of the hall. Only darkness back there, like a brick wall. But then the sound comes again, shorter but louder. Like metal fingers being drawn against a chalkboard. Gideon and I look at each other.

"We should be careful," I whisper, though just being here is putting us in danger.

Gideon and I continue down the hall, staying close to the wall. We haven't gotten far when suddenly the light goes back on.

But this time, in the center of that distant ring of light, there is something. Someone. Gagged, and tied to a chair.

My dad.

Gideon and I sprint toward him. And the closer we get, the more frantically my dad struggles against the ties that bind him. His moving around was scraping the chair against the ground, making that terrible shrieking sound. But not because he was trying to get us to come. He wants us to turn around, to get out, to run for our lives. He doesn't want us risking ourselves to save him. I can feel that so clearly. If it weren't for that gag in his mouth, he'd be screaming at us to run.

"We're not leaving without you," I say once we have reached him. I work to loosen the knot behind his neck, so at least we can get the gag out and he can speak. Gideon tries to untie his hands. It's slow going for both of us.

"Let me try," Gideon says, turning to help me, once he has gotten our dad's hands untied. With Gideon and I taking turns, the gag finally falls away.

"Dad, are you okay?" I ask as soon as he is able to respond.

"Run. Now," he breathes, his voice hoarse. "You need to get out of here, right now."

"We will," I say as I start work on his ankles, kneeling on the cold concrete next to him. "But with you."

Someone is in there with us, of course. Our dad didn't just magically appear under that light when he wasn't there before. I can feel them, too, looming nearby in the darkness. My dad shakes his head sadly, reaching for both Gideon and me. He wraps his arms tight around us. He's not bothering anymore to tell us to run. "I'm so sorry," he says. "About all of this. If it wasn't for my work— I'm so, so sorry."

Finally, Gideon has my dad's ankles free and I want him to jump to his feet. To race toward the door, shouting, *Let's go, guys. Follow me!* But he still doesn't move.

"Dad, come on." Gideon tugs his arm. "Let's go."

But our dad still doesn't move. And he doesn't tell us to run again. Instead, his eyes focus past us on the darkness, on whoever is there. Waiting.

He shakes his head a little and frowns, as his eyes shine sadly in the darkness. "It's too late now. But it's going to be okay." By this he means: because we are together, no matter how terrible the end. His voice is quaking, too. You don't need to be an Outlier to know that he is terrified. "We need to stay calm, no matter what. That's the most important thing. Trust me, I have been with him for a while now."

"Him, who, Dad?" I ask.

There's a different sound behind us then—feet on the concrete floor, shuffling. Someone coming toward us. But it's the rifle that emerges first from the darkness. The muzzle pointed up and to the side, not right at us at least. I close my eyes. *Breathe,* I tell myself. *Breathe.*

I also think: *This is the beginning of the end.* The EndOfDays is nigh.

"Why don't all of you sit down?" A voice.

A familiar one, but my mind is racing too fast to place it. And the man is still out of view, swallowed by the shadows. Finally, there are more footsteps, and there he is. Long salt-and-pepper hair held back in a messy ponytail, arms sinewy. He has on a faded yellow T-shirt with the outline of a palm tree and some loose-fitting cargo shorts hanging off his hips. He was always a smallish man, but the huge gun makes him look tiny.

Cassie's dad, Vince, is EndOfDays?

It is at once impossible to believe and the only thing that makes sense. I feel a hand on my arm. When I look down, my dad is staring up at me.

"We're going to be okay," he says. "All of us."

And when I turn back, I see finally who Vince has his shotgun pointed at.

Our mom. She's standing there on the edge of the darkness next to him. Exhausted and so afraid. Terrified. But still alive.

RIEL

ALREADY RIEL IS DREADING WHERE THE THREE OF THEM ARE HEADED. BUT THEY have no choice. Or at least Riel has no choice. As she, Leo, and Marly drive on deeper into the darkness, she tries bracing herself. But it doesn't help. All she can think about is how much she doesn't want to go back to that warehouse, not now, not ever.

As it is, she'll never forget the way Kendall's voice cut out when he was shot, the way his body fell to the floor. But Riel has no choice. Wylie needs her help. She knows that because of what her grandfather said. She can feel it in her bones.

RIEL HAD RACED inside as soon as Marly opened the door to her room. "I need your computer, right now."

"Leo?" Marly called out when she saw him in her doorway behind Riel. She reached forward to hug him. "It's so good to see you."

"The computer, Marly," Riel pressed. She and Leo had driven so fast from her house to Marly's, she was surprised they were in one piece. "Please, right fucking now. They have Wylie somewhere. We need to try to find her. I think my grandfather is going to kill her, and her family. Wipe out everyone who knows anything. And like right now. He's trying to make it like none of this ever happened. Cleaning house. I think this has been his plan all along."

Marly looked ashen as she pointed Riel toward her computer on a side table. "But isn't it dangerous for us to be online looking for her from here?" Marly asked. "They'll find you."

"It doesn't matter. They already have," Riel said as she took a seat in front of the computer. "I'm still here because my grandfather is hoping I'll change my mind and help him."

"Help him what?" Marly asked.

Riel hooked her fingers in air quotes. "'Protect the Outliers.'"

"Seriously?" Marly sounded disgusted.

Riel shrugged. "Yep."

"How are you going to find Wylie?" Leo asked, coming to stand next to Riel.

"That one picture you gave to her." Riel took a breath.

"Any chance you remember part of the license plate of the car?"

Leo had told Riel about the one remaining picture as soon as they were safely back in the car. He'd thought he'd put it back in the envelope that night Marly had seen him looking at the photos. It wasn't until the fire department let him back into his room to get some clothes after the fire that he spotted the picture, found by the firefighter under a soaked carpet.

Leo stepped forward and pulled out his phone, tapping through screens. When he handed it to Riel, it was open to a photo of a photo of the car, the license plate fully visible. Riel looked up at him, gratitude washing over her. "Come on," he said. "I have been listening."

"Thank you." She kissed him hard, then turned back to her computer.

It didn't take long for Riel to hack into the DMV, to figure out that the car is registered to the federal government. It was a little longer until she tracked that registration directly to the office of Senator David Russo. She wondered if her grandfather had realized yet that the one picture he doesn't have is the most important one, the one that ties him to the WSRF.

"Now what?" Marly asked. "How does knowing that car belongs to your grandfather help us find Wylie?"

"We look for somebody else searching up this license plate," Riel said. "I'm sure that's what Wylie has been doing, too. Or having someone do for her. One way or another, this license plate will lead us back to her."

Within minutes, Riel had figured out who'd been poking around looking for that license plate: one Detective Evan Oshiro. She had to admire Wylie's resourcefulness; a cop running a license plate would never raise a red flag, but hacking into the DMV could. But once Riel had Oshiro singled out, all she had to do was follow his trail—Oshiro's cell phone pings to his home around the same time two brand-new Gmail accounts were created. There were only a couple exchanges between the emails, but they seemed to be directed at Wylie. The last message had an address. The same one Riel followed Kendall to.

"I have to go," Riel said, already headed for the door. Marly and Leo were right behind her. She turned back to stop them. "No. No way. I don't want— This is definitely dangerous. My grandfather is going to try to kill Wylie and her entire family to save himself. He basically told me that. He'll kill me if he has to. He'll definitely kill both of you."

"All the more reason you need us," Marly said firmly.

"Yeah," Leo said. "And there is no way we are letting you go alone."

THEY HADN'T EITHER. And so now the three of them drive on through the twisty darkness. Whatever terrible things lie at the end of this drive, at least Riel won't have to face them alone.

WYLIE

MY MOM RAISES HER HAND TO ME, EYES WIDE AND GLASSY. RAGE. FEAR. LOVE. They thunder inside of her.

But relief, that's all I feel. "Mom," I say.

"Hi," she whispers, blinking back tears.

"Sit, please," Vince says, moving the gun so that it is more obviously pointed at my mom's head. But he looks strangely pained for being the one with the gun. And he is holding it awkwardly, like he's surprised to find it in his hands. Which actually might make it more likely he'll accidentally fire it. "I don't want things to get uncomfortable."

Vince doesn't seem at all like the guy I remember. It's like his face has changed. His eyes are completely empty.

"I think we are way past uncomfortable," Gideon whispers.

"Listen to Vince," my dad says, then looks over at us, eyes wide. "Sit, guys. Now."

And I can feel just how afraid my dad is. Not for himself, though. He'd already made his peace. It's us he's worried about, and our mom. He's afraid of Vince accidentally shooting her.

"How did you even find me?" my dad asks quietly.

"He sent us a message: *the EndOfDays is nigh,*" I say. "And then he posted again on that EndOfDays blog. From *here.* We had someone trace it." I turn to glare at Vince, even though antagonizing him is kind of the opposite of what my dad just told me to do. "*You* brought us here."

"Something posted to my blog from *here*?" Vince asks, his face suddenly alive, eyes sharp. Like he's been woken from a trance. For a moment, he even looks like the old Vince. "That's not possible. I also didn't send any email."

"Yes, it is. *You* sent an email." I'm wrong. I already know. I have no idea how or why exactly. But I am. "And *you* posted. It's your blog."

"My work on the blog is finished. It's been finished for several days," Vince says, still looking like he's considering. "That is strange."

And the worst part is that I know he's telling the truth. He didn't bring us here with that email, followed by the perfectly timed EndOfDays post. Which means somebody else did.

"Maybe," my mom starts, but that seems to startle Vince, who moves the gun in his hands in a reckless way.

"Hope, don't. Don't talk. Don't move," my dad cautions. "Vince is under the impression that my research has been hurting young girls," my dad says. "Apparently, he met someone at an AA meeting last fall. An architect."

"An architect?" I ask, Rachel's voice calling herself that ringing in my head.

"Yes, Vince isn't sure it's her real name," he says. "But she told him all about this supposed research of mine. Ever since, Vince has been working to stop it, to stop me—I mean, it isn't me. But that's what he thought."

"Since last fall?" I ask.

This hasn't been about people chasing after my dad's research, this has been about them wanting to keep my dad off their trail.

"Yes, from way before what happened with the camp."

Rachel. That was her at the AA meeting: the Architect, "redirecting" Vince's energy. It had to be. That was her building her house. Being the "architect" for Vince, but more important, for Russo. I feel sure of that, though Rachel was smart enough not to say that outright, even now. "There is research into the Outliers that *is* hurting girls, but it's at some soldier research facility in Watuck," I say, looking from my dad to Vince and back again. "It has nothing to do with you."

"Yes, I've told Vince that I would never hurt anyone. That my research was just questions and answers," my dad says calmly but pointedly. "And your mom and I have been in Karen's house with Vince for the past couple weeks. We've had lots of time to talk. But I don't think I've persuaded Vince. After what happened to Cassie, I guess it's easy to understand why he might want proof."

And now I realize why I had been drawn to Cassie's house: my dad and mom were there. Rachel must have somehow gotten my mom into the detention facility, then afterward stuck her with Vince. I'll give credit to Rachel, though—it was seeing my mom, her note, that really made me trust her.

That and the fact that she had saved my mom's life. I look over at my mom again, so close to the end of Vince's gun. But she's worried about us, not herself.

"At Karen's house?" Gideon asks. "We went by there. We talked to that neighbor woman, and she said no one was there."

This was why I had sensed something around Mrs. Dominic. She was too interested. All wrong. I'd been right that something had been off, I'd just been wrong about what.

"Mrs. Dominic never did like Karen," Vince says with a shrug. "I knew she would keep it quiet that I was staying there while Karen was away."

"Let Wylie and Gideon go, Vince," my mom pleads. It's impossible not to imagine what might happen if that gun goes off. "Keep Ben and me. They didn't do anything wrong."

My dad looks hard at my mom, shakes his head again. "Vince hasn't had an easy time since Cassie died," my dad says. "He feels responsible."

"Responsible?" I ask Vince. "You weren't even there."

Cassie. EndOfDays. The Collective. The camp. They are razor-edged puzzle pieces sliding too fast into place. And I am trapped in between.

"I promised when I was called upon to help these girls that I would stay dedicated, that I would never waver no matter how I was tested," Vince says. And, wow, does he mean it. He would die for this idea. He would kill for it. It seems possible he already has. "I had promised God that I would do whatever he needed me to do, if he helped me get clean. And it worked. I got sober. I'm still sober. Protecting those girls was what I needed to do to repay my debt. When I lost Cassie, I thought maybe it would break me. But then I realized that for her death to mean something, I needed to finish what I started."

"This architect woman who told you about my dad and his research was lying," I say. "Her name was Rachel. She was at Cassie's funeral *with* us." Vince does not seem surprised by this, but then they'd interacted. Who knows what lie Rachel had made up to explain that. "She was using you for her own reasons. Bad reasons."

"And poor Cassie." Vince's voice catches on his guilt as he goes on like he hasn't even heard me. But if he can still feel guilt, that means he can still feel something. It means there is a chance. "She did everything I asked from the very start. She would have done anything to help keep me sober. Even those blog posts she helped me with. I could tell she was torn about betraying you. She couldn't even be friends with you anymore. But she did it anyway. For me."

Cassie posted from Jasper's house. About my dad. Even looking back now, I can't think of a single sign. But then memories I have of Cassie are so tinged with grief it's hard to see them clearly. Or maybe it wasn't Cassie's clothes or friends or even her drinking that made me pull away. Maybe it was some deep-down sense I had that she was already betraying me.

Just like Rachel betrayed my mom. Maybe my mom had felt that coming, too.

"You're wrong about everything, Vince," my mom says

quietly, her eyes closed now so she doesn't have to see the gun, probably. "Don't you want to finish your mission the right way? To stop the right people?"

It's a decent tactic. Logic. One that might even work if Vince was at all listening.

"We never should have gotten involved with Dr. Quentin Caton, obviously. But when she told me about the research, she also told me who he was, that his own lies would make him easy to convince. I should never have sent Cassie to speak with him." Vince shakes his head and takes a deep, exasperated breath. "But liars like Dr. Caton have their own agenda. And often it's not at all what you expect. Like Sophie-Ann. I asked for her help, but she decided there might be a way to profit from Ben's cell phone instead."

"Is that why you killed her?" I ask.

Vince looks shocked, and from what I can tell it is genuine. "Sophie-Ann is dead?"

"She was hit by a car."

"Oh." He seems actually sad, and definitely surprised. "Well, that is terrible. But I don't know about that. There is so much, I find, that I cannot explain. Like what happened to Cassie. I know that her death was my fault, no matter exactly what happened or why. But I am hoping when my architect friend gets here to learn—"

"She's coming here?" I ask.

"She told Vince to bring us here and wait for her to arrive," my dad says.

"We have to get out," I say, turning to my mom and dad. "This is a trap."

Just then there's a loud pop and a flash of light outside. All of us turn toward the windows twenty feet away, at the back of the warehouse. Even Vince looks. We are all still watching when, from the darkness, come the flames.

"Oh my God," I whisper. "They're burning the building down."

When I look back, Vince has lowered the gun as he stares, transfixed by the yellow and orange flames. My mom is inching slowly away. And Vince doesn't seem to notice. Soon the gun is resting all the way on the ground. He watches the fire, perplexed but chillingly relieved. He is ready for his end to arrive.

"Come on!" my mom shouts, jerking me up by the arm. My dad and Gideon have already started to run toward the front.

I wait for Vince to lunge forward, to snap to life and come after us. To try to block our way. But he just sits down on my dad's chair. He sets the gun all the way down, too. Rests his head back and closes his eyes.

BY THE TIME my mom and I make it to the front of the warehouse, my dad is already rattling the door.

"It's locked!" he shouts. "They locked us in."

"Come on, we need to find another way out," my mom says. She's trying to be calm, but there's terror in her voice. "Try the windows."

We race from window to window. None will open. My mom grabs a folding chair and smashes it against the glass, but all it does is splinter.

"Stop, stop. It's shatterproof," my dad says as she lifts the chair again. "We need to find another way."

Gideon presses his hands flat against the far wall. "It's already hot."

We race around the room, checking every nook and cranny for some key that might help get us out. It's only then that I find the book jammed inside that small metal sample box. When I flip through, it looks like it could be Vince's journal. And tucked at the back, torn-out pages from Cassie's like those that were sent to Jasper. Sent to Jasper by Rachel, surely. To be pinned now on Vince, along with his journal. Or what may be his journal. I only have a second to flip through it, but it seems possible it was written by someone else—Rachel, maybe—trying to make Vince look especially unstable. More proof that he would do anything to exact vengeance—including killing himself and all of us.

This is the way we are to be erased. Tied up neatly with a bow. Everything terrible that has happened will be explained by Vince and Vince alone—unstable, grief-stricken, fringe-believer Vince.

As my dad yanks at the door again, flames dance up the sides of a front window. And the temperature has definitely begun to rise. I try not to wonder what might kill us first—the smoke, the flames, the building collapsing in.

No. We still have a chance. I feel like someone is out there, not far away. And not just whoever started the fire. Someone who will help us.

And so I begin to bang.

"Help!! Help us!!" I take a breath and pound some more. "We're locked in here!!" I turn back to my family. "We need to make noise. A lot of noise. I think there is someone out there."

"Hello?! Hello?!" Gideon steps up next to me, striking even harder against the door with his large closed fist. "We're in here!"

Soon our parents are beside us, too, all of us knocking and shouting. The flames are too high now to look again toward the window.

But then, finally, there is a sound outside.

"Wait, shh, shh!" I wave for everyone to stop.

And then I hear it again, muffled but unmistakably real. A voice. "Get back from the door!"

"Okay!" my dad shouts back, waving us clear. "We're away!"

There is some loud banging, the door rattling and shaking as if from blows from a hammer. And then, finally, it pops open. Just like that. There's a moment of silence. And then disbelief. Then Riel rushing in with a large dumbbell in her hand. Leo and another girl are behind her.

"Come on, come on!" Riel shouts, waving us out. My dad, Mom, and Gideon race ahead and out the door. I hang back when she seems to be looking behind me for something. "Jasper's not here?"

"No, why?" I ask, and already I know the answer won't be a good one.

"Shit," Riel says, still looking around. "He's here somewhere." She turns toward the other building. Beyond it, smoke has also begun to rise. "Come on. We need to check the other building. And then we need to get away from here. My grandfather sent somebody to start this fire. If they are any good, they'll be somewhere nearby making sure they got the job done."

I turn to Leo and the other girl. "Please, tell my parents I'll be right behind them?"

Leo scowls. "I'm not going to—"

"Go, Leo, please," Riel says. "You too, Marly. We need you to make sure no one comes in after us. If we don't come back out, you need to—"

"I'm not leaving you!" Leo shouts.

"Please," Riel says, rushing over and putting her hands on his face. "Please, Leo."

"Okay, okay, go," Marly says, tugging Leo with her. And I'm not sure whether I should be flattered that Riel has chosen me to come along with her, or if she simply sees me as the most expendable.

OUTSIDE, RIEL AND I take turns using the weight to break off the knob on the second warehouse door. It's not easy: the weight is heavy, the knob strong. But finally it cracks to the ground.

When we push the door open, smoke billows out. It's dark inside apart from an eerie glow down at the far end of one hallway, beams of light bending through the smoke like a frozen disco ball. Behind us, in the distance, I can hear my parents screaming my name. We don't have much time. I can't have them coming inside after me.

Riel and I drop to our knees, crawling below the smoke, our faces down low. I glance back over my shoulder once to see how far we have gone, but behind us there is only haze.

"There's something, someone . . . ," I whisper, not exactly

sure how to phrase what I feel—except that we are in even worse danger than I felt before.

"It's bad," Riel says. "I know."

"But Jasper . . ."

"I know. He's here, too," she says. "Come on, we don't have much time."

We inch farther into the building. "Jasper!" I call out. "Are you in here?"

We listen as we continue forward, occasionally shouting into the darkness as we move along the wall where there seems to be less smoke.

I am just thinking that we are going to have to turn back when I am yanked up suddenly from the ground and to my feet. And then there I am: face-to-face once again with Quentin. My arm is in his one blood-covered hand. In his other, he's holding a knife. Quentin twists me around and puts the knife to my throat.

"What did you do to Jasper?" I gasp.

"Wylie!" Jasper's voice. "Let her go!"

He's alive. We found him alive. I feel so relieved that for a second I forget Quentin and his knife.

"We all need to get out. Now, Quentin!" Riel shouts. "This entire place is on fire!"

Quentin shakes his head. "*I* need to get out," he says calmly. "You aren't going anywhere."

I watch Riel glance past Quentin. It's quick, only a split second really. But I can feel it wasn't casual. Wasn't an accident. And when Riel and I meet eyes again, she is willing me to pay attention. The weight is still gripped in her hand. I'll need to be ready for whatever she has in mind.

"Russo!" Riel shouts, looking past Quentin again, as if for someone coming from behind him.

It startles Quentin for a moment. Just long enough for Riel to throw the hand weight at him as he turns to look. "What are you—" A thud as the weight bounces off Quentin and hits the ground.

"Fuck!" he shouts, bending to grab his foot.

And just like that the knife is off my throat. I race forward out of his reach.

"You fucking bitch!" Quentin shouts as he charges at Riel with the knife raised.

But Jasper is faster. He has something in his hands. And he swings it at Quentin's head. With all the force and precision of the athlete he is.

Quentin stumbles from the blow to his head but stays upright for a moment still. He lifts his hand toward his head but doesn't get all the way there.

"Uh" is the last sound Quentin makes before he crumples to the ground.

Jasper stands over Quentin's body, stunned and sickened by what he's done. He looks down at the pipe still gripped in his hand.

"Jasper, come on!" I tug him toward the door. "It's okay. We have to get out of here. There could be somebody coming. Let's go!"

WYLIE

HOURS LATER, WE ARE GATHERED BACK AT OUR HOUSE: MY DAD, MY MOM, Gideon, Marly, Leo, Jasper, and Riel. It is still a ways until dawn. Stunned and silent, we alternate between moving like zombies and startling at every tiny noise. We know, of course, that we aren't really safe at home. But then we aren't safe anywhere anymore, and we had no place to go.

My mom and dad have showered, and so has Jasper. He's now wearing some of my dad's old sweatpants, which is both comforting and totally weird. Marly and Leo help my mom put out all the snacks we have on the kitchen table—mostly crackers and some stale chips. She then starts pouring a glass of water for each of us.

"Sorry, it's not much," my mom says, motioning to the food.

"Is anyone even hungry?" Jasper asks, staring at the table like he might be sick.

We do that a lot: stare. Shell-shocked, that's probably the word for it. For how you feel when you survive, but you know you probably shouldn't have. And it's not like this is a car accident, the danger past and gone. They can't just leave us out here. Knowing what we know. Which means that we have no choice but to go after them before they come to finish the job.

"We're lucky whoever started the fire didn't just shoot all of us or something," I say though I don't feel lucky at all.

"That wouldn't fit with the story they set up," Riel said. "It would lead to too many questions. This whole fire, all of you killed at once, was supposed to be the answer to all their loose ends. They'll try again definitely. But not tonight. They're too careful."

"We need to call the police," my mom says.

"Hopefully, they're already on their way out to the warehouses," my dad says. "You guys did call them, didn't you?"

"That doesn't mean they actually sent anyone," Gideon says.

"We should call someone else then," Leo says. "We have to tell somebody about your grandfather, Riel."

"Agreed. But who?" Riel asks. "Who can we possibly trust?"

"We could call Oshiro's wife, Elizabeth," I say, mostly to Gideon. It's half a question, half an answer. "And she could ask Oshiro. He will know people we can trust."

Gideon nods and gets up to make the call. "Good idea."

"Everyone should have something to drink," my mom says. "And are we sure no one is hurt?"

She looks around at all of us until we all shake our heads: no, we aren't hurt. She is in full-on mom mode. It's the way she's always been when she's worried about a very big thing. She'll focus on the small ones, the things she can do something about. I've always found it annoying. Until now. Now, it feels like the best quality anyone has ever had.

My mom comes over when she catches me staring at her. "Can we talk for a minute?" she asks. When I nod, she links an arm through mine and guides me out to the living room couch. We haven't talked yet. About anything.

"I'M SORRY, WYLIE," she says out in the living room. She's staring out the window as I sit on the couch. Her arms are crossed. "For ever trusting Rachel. For ever making it so you would trust her. When I wrote that note I gave you in the detention facility, I didn't know yet that she was involved. After the accident, she had me totally convinced that it would be safer for you if I left. And she'd helped me stay safely out of sight for months. I stayed at her cabin. She said it would help you more if I focused instead on gathering allies, building some team. She even helped me find people to talk to, all of whom I realize now were actually helping her." She shakes her head, disgusted with herself. "Really, she just wanted to use me to get you to trust her so she could get rid of us all at once with this crazy Vince nonsense as cover."

"She lied, Mom," I say. "And she spent months, years maybe, getting good enough at it so that even I would have no idea. That's why you trusted her. That's why I trusted her."

Though I know my story is a little more complicated. That it isn't about missing out on warning signs. It's about me, still—even now—not trusting myself enough to believe my own instincts.

"I knew Rachel was a bad person, though," she says, racked by guilt as she sits down next to me. "That was why I stopped talking to her in the first place."

"You wanted to believe she changed," I say. "You wanted to give her the benefit of the doubt. Emotions aren't perfect things. Even when you can read them, sometimes it's still hard to believe. And by the way, people get facts wrong, too. All the time."

"But I'm supposed to protect you," she says, her eyes glassy as she searches mine. "That's my whole job."

"I'd say you did okay, all things considered." I motion to my body. "I *am* alive."

She smiles and wraps me in a tight hug. And all I feel is love. Simple and pure and deep. Her love. And mine. "Where did you learn to be so generous?"

"From you," I say, my voice muffled into her hair. "I learned everything from you."

Jasper appears in the living room then.

"I think I need some air," he says, gesturing to the door.

I stand. "I'll come with you."

"Just be careful out there," my mom says warily. "Stay close to the house, on the porch."

And I want for that warning to be so much more ridiculous than it is.

"We will," I say.

JASPER HAS TOLD me that he's okay at least a dozen times since we rushed away from the warehouses. But it's so obvious that he's anything but. I wait until we're sitting outside on the steps, staring at the sky above the house across the street. It's just beginning to brighten in the distance. Sunrise coming. That's something.

"I'd be dead if it wasn't for you," I say, because I am pretty sure it's the feel of that pipe in his hand that's haunting him. "You did exactly what I needed you to do in there."

"I thought about it before, though. That I wanted to. And that was before I 'needed to.'" Jasper keeps his eyes on the horizon. "If killing Quentin was the right thing, why do I feel so bad about it now?"

I shrug. "Because doing the right thing sucks a lot of the time."

Jasper smiles. "Is that all you got, seriously?"

I smile, too. "Sorry, I'm an Outlier. That doesn't mean I'm great at pep talks. Maybe you should stop looking for proof of the worst of yourself in everything you do, though. You get to decide what you do with who you are."

"See, that was much better." Jasper leans against me.

"Yeah, that's because my therapist said it first."

After that, we are quiet for a while.

"This isn't over, is it?" Jasper asks finally.

"I don't think so," I say. "I think they will keep coming, unless we shut Russo down."

"And how will we do that?" he asks.

"Somehow," I say. "Listen, I am really sorry I wrote that letter. Your mom asked me to. But I shouldn't have, no matter what she said. I knew it was a risk."

"If you hadn't written it, you might be in jail," he says. "And I'd probably be dead."

"You do know that what I wrote—it's not the way I feel," I say, not looking at him on purpose.

"No, I have absolutely no way of knowing how you really feel," Jasper says, turning to look at me so intently I have no choice but to look back. "I'm not an Outlier, remember? You have to spell it out for me."

"Okay," I say. I close my eyes and try to breathe. And I remind myself of what my mom once said: that there are all different ways of being brave. "I think, maybe, I'm starting to fall in love with you."

When I force my eyes open, Jasper is staring at me, eyebrows raised, a small smile at his lips. "'Maybe'? 'Starting to'? A lot of qualifiers, huh?" He exhales then with mock exasperation. "I guess it'll do, though." He nods. "Yeah, it'll definitely do."

It's the last thing he says before he starts kissing me.

FROM HIS HOSPITAL bed, Oshiro sends officers who we can trust. Uniformed Newton police who have no interest in anything except doing their jobs: protecting local people from imminent harm. It's dawn by the time they arrive.

We gather in the living room and try to methodically explain what happened in the warehouses by starting the only place we can: the beginning. We focus first on Vince and Quentin and my dad's research. But there is just so much to unpack. In the end, Riel is the one who gets to Russo, our final destination. She is the best equipped to explain.

"Senator Russo is definitely the person behind this whole thing," Riel says. "He's my grandfather."

"You mean the guy running for president?" one officer asks. He is round, with kind, puffy eyes and a bald head.

He turns to look at his partner, a woman who has a half-sleeve tattoo and the sharp expression of someone who has not a moment for anyone's bullshit.

"I knew that guy was an asshole," she says.

"Um, well," the round officer says. "For us to be able to do something, you got to have some proof that this senator committed an actual crime. Because ethics laws or whatever, those aren't exactly our department."

"We have proof." I turn to Riel. "Right?"

"We will," she says. "We will."

"And you'll help us once we have that?" my mom asks the officers.

"Or we'll find you someone who can," the female officer says.

I can feel how much she means this; how she believes she is going to find the right people to swoop in and save the day. But I already know that she will not. I know that we were the only people who could ever save us. Even now, we still can.

We, the Outliers. Each of us, individually, is so much more than just our ability to read people. We are strong and we are weak. We are special and we are ordinary. We are kind and we are generous and we make mistakes. We are complicated and we are human.

But together, I believe we can be invincible. That right now, we will have to be.

TRANSCRIPT OF AUGUST 15 INTERVIEW WITH *PRIME TIME NEWS*: SENATOR DAVID RUSSO

CHAD MAYER: When we last spoke, there were rumors you might run for president. Now you've officially announced your candidacy. What would be the priorities of your administration?

SENATOR RUSSO: Security and privacy. The world is a rapidly changing place, and we must adapt. Just recently, a study established that certain individuals seem to have heightened perceptive abilities. These revelations are news to much of the country, but we on the Armed Services Committee have been looking into them for quite some time.

CHAD MAYER: Are you referring to the Outliers in the news so much lately? They seem to be all anyone is talking about.

SENATOR RUSSO: Yes. Voters should be asking themselves who is best prepared to deal with complex challenges like the Outliers. We must protect the privacy of the public who are not Outliers, and we must, of course, protect the Outliers themselves. We are developing the means to protect these young girls, many of whom are very confused by this new ability. Furthermore, there's no telling how certain fringe aspects of our society will try to exploit them. We must protect them from that as well.

CHAD MAYER: Would you care to elaborate on your specific plans?

SENATOR RUSSO: To do so now would undermine our efforts. And I won't do that, no matter how advantageous it might be to my candidacy. No election is worth winning at the expense of the American people.

THE OUTLIERS

INDIANA IN THE MIDDLE OF SEPTEMBER IS EXACTLY WHAT YOU'D IMAGINE: HOT and filled with corn. We flew into Indianapolis, a city smaller than Boston, but a real city nonetheless, with tall office buildings and fancy-looking restaurants. We passed them as Chance's brother drove us to the rally. He is our local contact. He knows his way around and how to keep us out of sight. He's connected us with lots more local people who can help. Food, shelter, and the other necessities. They will also lie for us if they need to. They will lay down their lives.

There are five of us here, in addition to Chance's brother. Three Outliers and two not. United, despite our differences, to stop Russo. We picked this rally specifically because it is expected to get some national news coverage. What we are about to do needs that coverage, too.

In the end, the Newton police did their best to help us. But they were shot down pretty fast, threatened like so many others by the powers that be. We knew all along we'd have no choice but to take matters into our own hands. To fight on the front lines. And we are well-organized now. We have a game plan—not just for this day, but for the ones that follow. We have people—a lot of them—who are willing to help. People who have all sorts of skills. And some, even a little bit of power.

But for this, today, we are on our own. We wanted it that way.

We lost whatever might have been on Russo's cell phone, of course. And all the photos, except the one. But that photo was the most important one. And we have seen to it that the bodies of those dead girls—the lost ones—were tied to the WSRF, Mrs. Porter, and the Wolf. That wasn't hard, with a few well-placed calls. Russo has proven a lot harder to nail to the wall. This is our chance, though, with that photo of his car in front of the WSRF, and the other documents Elizabeth has been able to lift since. Together they tell a story that will stick this time. We believe it will.

We've had most of the evidence for a while now, but we've been waiting for the right time, the right place to expose him—too early before the election and the awfulness might be absorbed as noise. But now that Russo is *the* candidate, now that everybody is looking, everybody will know.

Most Outliers have stayed out of this entirely, to continue on if this particular plan goes south, if we are not able to finish. We do not expect to fail, though. We have planned too long and too carefully. But the road to victory, we have learned, can be much longer and rougher than you ever expected.

We can only hope that this will end with Rachel, the Architect, being taken down, too. These days she is Senator David Russo's campaign manager and right-hand woman. Word on the street is that she'll have a top post in his administration—secretary of state, attorney general—should things all go as planned. But who's to say how things will turn out for Rachel? Once a puppet has cut himself free, it can be easy to get tangled in the strings.

SENATOR RUSSO'S RALLY is on the far side of the state fair. As we drive past it, the scent of popcorn and funnel cake mix with hay in the car. It's the smell of hope and innocence.

It's even warmer now that we are farther from the city. Too warm, Chance's brother says, even for Indiana. His brother is a genuinely nice guy—totally uncomplicated, like Chance, who would be here if he didn't need to be back in Boston at hockey practice, covering for Jasper's ass.

We look over toward the tall Ferris wheel and the merry-go-round spinning, at the laughing children tugging their parents toward the gates to the fair. It seems impossible that they could be so unaware.

We can only hope it will be different when all the details are out. When they know just how bad it is. When they understand what Russo really means when he talks about "protecting the Outliers." But so many people already agree with him. He's been good at hitting his talking points. The whole idea that some out there—the Outliers—could actually see into your private feelings hardly seems right to a lot of people. Unfair, definitely. Unseemly even, and akin to witchcraft. Russo has churned up more than enough fear to do away with goodness. And with the Outliers so few in number, why should their interests override those of so many others?

In the end, the real question will be: How far will anybody really go to protect somebody who isn't just like them?

WHEN WE FINALLY arrive, we climb out of Chance's car and into the warm September sun. We head slowly toward the gates, wearing our *Russo for President, Privacy Is Power* T-shirts. We are imposters, of course, but at least none of the people at the rally will be trying to read our feelings. Even the ones who can will pretend they cannot. As we get closer to the entrance, we are swallowed by a sea of Russo supporters in the very same T-shirts. More people than we expected. More people than we hoped.

But we cannot let the fact that we are outnumbered change what we are going to do.

At the gate, we put on our VIP passes, very good imitations, courtesy of Elizabeth Oshiro. Level99 is defunct now, its members scattered to the wind. In the end, they heeded Riel's warnings more than Brian's assurances.

We have already decided which one of us will do the talking if we get caught. And we will adhere to another core principle. **Outlier Rule #10:** A lie is always better when it is very close to the truth.

Rachel knew that. She knew so much more than we ever gave her credit for.

We wave and smile at the older woman at the gate. She looks like a kind person who will be persuaded by our story. We lift our homemade VIP badges. We tell her about our special connection to Russo, how it's a family thing. Margie, an assistant to Senator Russo, said it would be okay.

There is an assistant Margie, though she's never actually heard of us.

"Oh!" the grandmotherly-looking woman exclaims. "Aren't you the sweetest!" She waves over a security guard. "Take them backstage. To Margie."

From there, we become a game of human telephone. Deliberately, of course. Who we are and why we are there becomes more unclear as we are handed off from security person to assistant to backstage hand—until eventually no one has any idea who we are. The last person we are delivered to is Margie, petite with huge blue eyes and a perfectly manicured bob.

"Oh," she says, blinking at us as she searches her memory for some possible exchange in which she would have agreed to give backstage passes to anyone, even a relative of the senator. *No,* she thinks, she'd never be stupid enough to do that. But she is too worried to trust her own instinct. "Of course" is what she says instead.

And all we really need is just to get close enough to flip one particular switch to the AV; Elizabeth has described what it should look like. Elizabeth can hijack the system then. She can be sure our broadcast will also go to the live feed and out to the rest of the world as long as we flip the switch.

Margie leads us toward where a large trailer is set up. Like the senator is some kind of movie star. Surely, it is part of why he wants this. Maybe even the biggest part. Margie checks her watch. She's stalling. She doesn't want to disturb him.

That's when we spot the panel of AV switches we need. They are right there. We are already in the perfect location.

The door to the trailer has swung open, and Senator Russo descends the steps in a sharp blue suit, his hair especially silver in the sunshine. He is distracted, speaking with someone behind him. Perhaps someone introducing him, definitely someone inflating his ego. There she is a moment later: Rachel. Glowing. At long last exactly where she wants to be. And in that moment it's hard to decide who is worse.

Russo is halfway down the steps when he spots us. We raise our hands in a wave. And there it is, the delay. The pause. Russo motions angrily to a security man. Surely he is saying some version of: *Take them away.*

It is time to go. To run and knock something over. To flip the AV switch in the commotion. And so, that is precisely what we do.

All right on schedule. And exactly as planned.

A HALF HOUR later we sit on top of the water-gun game at the very west edge of the state fair. We look out over the rally, the chimes sounding again and again beneath us, each time somebody wins. We have been waiting—through initial speaker after initial speaker—for the senator to finally take center stage. The sun is sinking quickly now, the sky beginning to pink in long, crooked streaks. The air smells of charcoal and the sunset. It is so peaceful up here near the trees, above the laughter and the crowds. Yes, this will work, we think. We can feel it this time.

Rachel comes onstage to introduce Russo, talking with such pride about all his accomplishments. We try hard not to let the words sink in. Otherwise our rage will multiply, it will swallow us whole. Instead, we have to keep believing in goodness and justice. In the end, that's all we have: hope.

We watch the small outline of Russo finally at the podium in the distance. Hands clasped, we sit side by side, faces to the setting sun. Our breath held, we pray that this is an end. And also, maybe, a beginning.

And then, finally, it is happening. The screens behind Russo scramble and catch, their images replaced by a loop of long, steady flashes. Each a document, classified and personal. Each a step in the terrible route Russo took to that stage. All the awfulness that he is already responsible for. There is the photo of his car. Riel and Kelsey as young girls. The WSRF. The fake news articles praising him from EndOfDays. The very last image is a picture of the girls. The lost ones. The Outliers maybe, their fingers reaching out desperately for someone or something to grab hold of.

There is noise and confusion then, audible gasps from the audience as people begin to make sense of it. The images are too fast to understand in one go. But the media will slow them down and parse them out. They will be obsessed with understanding what they mean. Scattered dots for now, but images that can be connected. Ones that will eventually collide.

Then everyone will see exactly what Russo has done. Exactly

the person he is and will always be: someone who cares only about power. His power.

And in that moment, we finally become what we were always meant to be. Each different in her own way, but warriors all the same. Ones who think but also feel. Warriors who will fight longer than they believed possible for the people they love and the things they believe in. For people they have never met, and will never know. For an idea about what is right. For the way the world should be.

Warriors who are strong and whole. And, finally, free.

EPILOGUE

SENATOR RUSSO WAS DEFEATED IN THE GENERAL ELECTION BY SENATOR LANA Harrison, but only by a very slim margin. Despite an extensive federal investigation, he is not expected to be charged with any crime.

President Lana Harrison has already begun a push to amend part of the Civil Rights Act of 1964, known as Title VII, to include broader rights and several additional protected classes. One of them will be the Outliers.

She has also created the Freedom Institute, dedicated to the protection of all minority groups. Still in the planning stages, the Freedom Institute already has its slogan: Knowledge Is Power.

ACKNOWLEDGMENTS

Many thanks to my dedicated editor Jennifer Klonsky for being so kind and attentive throughout this trilogy, and to the very patient and extremely diligent Catherine Wallace. Thanks also to Claudia Gabel and the rest of my terrific HarperTeen team: Gina Rizzo, Ebony LaDelle, and cover designer Sarah Kaufman.

A special thank-you to Kate Jackson, and also to Suzanne Murphy.

Thanks to the rest of the fabulous HarperTeen marketing, publicity, sales, and library teams for all your work on the entire series. And last but certainly not least, thank you to all the fantastic (and fantastically patient) people in HarperTeen managing editorial: Josh Weiss, Mark Rifkin, Bethany Reis, and copyeditor Valerie Shea.

To my beloved agent, Marly Rusoff—thank you for all the

things. There are far too many to name. Thank you, thank you to Julie Mosow for your wise advice. Thanks also to Michael Radulescu, Lizzy Kremer, Harriet Moore, and the fantastic and dedicated Shari Smiley. A huge thank-you to the incredible Katherine Faw for saving my tail on a consistent, patient, and cheerful basis. Thanks also to Laura Chasen and Deena Warner.

Thank you to the brilliant Daniel Rodriguez for yet another title. And to Victoria Cook for your ever-wise counsel and the gift of your friendship. Thank you, Megan Crane, for always being there, but especially at the eleventh hour.

As ever, I am grateful for the generous support of kind friends: Martin and Clare Prentice, Catherine and David Bohigian, Cindy, Christina, and Joey Buzzeo, Jeff Johnson, Cara Cragan and Michael Moroney, the Cragan family, the Crane family, Joe and Naomi Daniels, Larry and Suzy Daniels, Bob Daniels and Craig Leslie, Diane and Stanley Dohm, Elena and Dan Panosian, Dave Fischer, Heather and Michael Frattone, Tania Garcia, Sonya Glazer, Nicole and David Kear, Merrie Koehlert, Hallie Levin, John McCreight and Kim Healey, Brian McCreight, the Metzger family, Jason Miller, Tara and Frank Pometti, Stephen Prentice, Maria Renz and Tom Barr, Motoko Rich and Mark Topping, Jon Reinish, Bronwen Stine, the Thomatos family, Meg and Charles Yonts, Denise Young Farrell and Peter Farrell, and Christine Yu.

To Nike Arowolo: thank you for your warmth and generosity.

Emerson, Harper, and Tony: I will be forever most grateful for the three of you.